The Book of Salt

The Book of Salt

Monique Truong

W F HOWES LTD

This large print edition published in 2003 by
W F Howes Ltd
Units 6/7, Victoria Mills, Fowke Street
Rothley, Leicester LE7 7PJ

1 3 5 7 9 10 8 6 4 2

First published in the United Kingdom in 2003 by
Chatto & Windus

A CIP catalogue record for this book is available
from the British Library

ISBN 1 84197 669 5

Typeset by Palimpsest Book Production Limited,
Polmont, Stirlingshire
Printed and bound in Great Britain
by Antony Rowe Ltd, Chippenham, Wilts.

For my father, a traveler who
has finally come home

THIS BOOK WAS WRITTEN ON TWO ISLANDS, in two countries, three states, and five cities. It has been a trying, scary, but above all an amazing journey. For making the amazing parts possible, thank you to the Edward and Sally Van Lier Fellowship, Fundacion Valparaiso, Corporation of Yaddo, Hedgebrook, Lannan Foundation, Asian American Writers' Workshop, Barbara Tran, Andrea Louie, Quang Bao, Hanya Yanagihara, David L. Eng, Isabelle Thuy Pelaud, Elaine Koster, Janet Silver, Lori Glazer, Carla Gray, Jayne Yaffe Kemp, and Deborah DeLosa.

I might never have had the courage to go in the first place, if long ago I had not met the following supportive souls: Grace Yun, Russell Leong, and Dora Wang.

But in the end the metaphor of a journey is empty, utterly meaningless, without someplace and someone to come back home to. Gratitude to Damijan Saccio, without whom I would not have either.

We had certainly luck in finding good cooks, though they had their weaknesses in other ways. Gertrude Stein liked to remind me that if they did not have such faults, they would not be working for us.

—ALICE B. TOKLAS

The Book of Salt

CHAPTER 1

Of that day I have two photographs and, of course, my memories.

We had arrived at the Gare du Nord with over three hours to spare. There were, after all, a tremendous number of traveling cases and trunks. It took us two taxi rides from the apartment to the train station before all the pieces could be accounted for. A small group of photographers, who had gathered for the occasion, volunteered to watch over the first load while we returned to the rue de Fleurus for more. My Mesdames accepted their offer without hesitation. They had an almost childlike trust in photographers. Photographers, my Mesdames believed, transformed an occasion into an event. Their presence signaled that importance and fame had arrived, holding each other's hands. Their flashing cameras, like the brilliant smiles of long-lost friends, had quickly warmed my Mesdames' collective heart. More like friends too new to trust, I had thought. I had been with my Mesdames for half a decade by then. The photographers had not been there from the very beginning. But once the preparation for the

1

journey began, they swarmed to the entrance of 27 rue de Fleurus like honeybees. I could easily see why my Mesdames cultivated them. Every visit by a photographer would be inevitably followed by a letter enclosing a newspaper or magazine clipping with my Mesdames' names circled in a halo of red ink. The clippings, each carefully pressed with a heated iron, especially if a crease had thoughtlessly fallen on my Mesdames' faces, went immediately into an album with a green leather cover. "Green is the color of envy," my Mesdames told me. At this, knowing looks shot back and forth between them, conveying what can only be described as glee. My Mesdames communicated with each other in cryptic ways, but after all my years in their company I was privy to their keys. "Green" meant that they had waited desperately for this day, had tired of seeing it arriving on the doorsteps of friends and mere acquaintances; that the album had been there from the very beginning, impatient but biding its time; that they were now thrilled to fill it with family photographs of the most public kind. "Green" meant no longer their own but other people's envy.

I know that it may be difficult to believe, but it took the arrival of the photographers for me to understand that my Mesdames were not, well, really mine; that they belonged to a country larger than any that I had ever been to; that its people had a right to embrace and to reclaim them as one of their own. Of course, 27 rue de Fleurus had always been filled with visitors, but that was different. My Mesdames enjoyed receiving guests, but they also enjoyed seeing them go. Many had arrived hoping for a permanent place around my Mesdames' tea table, but I always knew that after the third pot they would have to leave. My Mesdames had to pay me to stay around. A delicious bit of irony, I had always thought. The photographers, though, marked the beginning of something new. This latest crop of admirers was extremely demanding and altogether inconsolable. They, I was stunned to see, were not satisfied with knocking at the door to 27 rue de Fleurus, politely seeking entrance to sip a cup of tea. No, the photographers wanted my Mesdames to go away with them, to leave the rue de Fleurus behind, to lock it up with a key. At the Gare du Nord that day, all I could think about were the flashes of the cameras, how they had never stopped frightening me. They were lights that feigned to illuminate but really intended to blind. Lightning before a driving storm, I had thought. But I suppose that was the sailor's apprehension in me talking. It had been eleven years since I had made a true ocean crossing. For my Mesdames, it had been over thirty. The ocean for them was only a memory, a calming blue expanse between here and there. For me it was alive and belligerent, a reminder of how distance cannot be measured by the vastness of the open seas, that that was just the beginning.

When my Mesdames first began preparing for

the journey, they had wanted to bring Basket and Pépé along with them. The SS *Champlain* gladly accommodated dogs and assorted pets, just as long as they were accompanied by a first-class owner. The problem, however, was America. No hotels or at least none on their itinerary would accept traveling companions of the four-legged kind. The discussion had been briefly tearful but above all brief. My Mesdames had in recent years become practical. Even the thought of their beloved poodle and Chihuahua languishing in Paris, whimpering, or, in the case of the Chihuahua, yapping, for many months if not years to come, even this could not postpone the journey home. There was certainly no love lost between me and those dogs, the poodle Basket especially. My Mesdames bought him in Paris at a dog show in the spring of 1929. Later that same year, I too joined the rue de Fleurus household. I have always suspected that it was the closeness of our arrivals that made this animal behave so badly toward me. Jealousy is instinctual, after all. Every morning, my Mesdames insisted on washing Basket in a solution of sulfur water. A cleaner dog could not have existed anywhere else. Visitors to the rue de Fleurus often stopped in midsentence to admire Basket's fur and its raw-veal shade of pink. At first, I thought it was the sulfur water that had altered the color of His Highness's curly white coat. But then I realized that he was simply losing his hair, that his sausage-casing skin had started to shine through, an embarrassing peep

4

show no doubt produced by his morning baths. My Mesdames soon began "dressing" Basket in little capelike outfits whenever guests were around.

I could wash and dress myself, thank you. Though, like Basket, I too had a number of admirers. Well, maybe only one or two. Pépé the Chihuahua, on the other hand, was small and loathsome. He was hardly a dog, just all eyes and a wet little nose. Pépé should have had no admirers, but he, like Basket, was a fine example of how my Mesdames' affections were occasionally misplaced. Of course, my Mesdames asked me to accompany them. Imagine them extending an invitation to Basket and Pépé and not me. Never. We, remember, had been together for over half a decade by then. I had traveled with them everywhere, though in truth that only meant from Paris to their summer house in Bilignin. My Mesdames were both in their fifties by the time I found them. They had lost their wanderlust by then. A journey for them had come to mean an uneventful shuttle from one site of comfort to another, an automobile ride through the muted colors of the French countryside.

Ocean travel changed everything. My Mesdames began preparing for it months in advance. They placed orders for new dresses, gloves, and shoes. Nothing was extravagant, but everything was luxurious: waistcoats embroidered with flowers and several kinds of birds, traveling outfits in handsome tweeds with brown velvet trims and buttons, shoes identical except for the heels and the size. The larger pair made only a slight effort at a lift. They were schoolgirlish in their elevation but mannish in their proportion. The smaller pair aspired to greater but hardly dizzying heights. Both my Mesdames, remember, were very concerned about comfort.

"We'll take a train from Paris to Le Havre, where the SS *Champlain* will be docked. From there, the Atlantic will be our host for six to seven days, and then New York City will float into view. From New York, we'll head north to Massachusetts, then south to Maryland and Virginia, then west to Ohio, Michigan, Illinois, Texas, California, all the way to the shores of the Pacific and then, maybe, back again." As my Mesdames mapped the proposed journey, the name of each city—New York, Boston, Baltimore, Cleveland, Chicago, Houston, San Francisco—was a sharp note of excitement rising from their otherwise atonal flats. Their voices especially quivered at the mention of the airplanes. They wanted to see their America from a true twentieth-century point of view, they told the photographers. Imagine, they said to each other, a flight of fancy was no longer just a figure of speech. They wondered about the cost of acquiring one for their very own, a secondhand plane of course. My Mesdames were still practical, after all.

I was somewhat superstitious. I thought that fate must have also been listening in on this reverie about travel and flight. How could I not when the letter arrived at the rue de Fleurus later on that same day? It was quite an event. My Mesdames handed me the envelope on a small silver tray. They said that they had been startled to realize that they had never seen my full name in writing before. What probably startled them more was the realization that during my years in their employment I had never received a piece of correspondence until this one. I did not have to look at the envelope to know. It was from my oldest brother. No one else back there would have known where to find me, that 27 rue de Fleurus was my home. I sniffed the envelope before opening it. It smelled of a faraway city, pungent with anticipation for rain. If my Mesdames had not been in the room, I would have tasted it with my tongue. I was certain to find the familiar sting of salt, but what I needed to know was what kind: kitchen, sweat, tears or the sea. I wanted this paper-shrouded thing to divulge itself to me, to tell me even before the words emerged why it had taken my brother almost five years to respond to my first and only letter home.

I had written to him at the end of 1929. I was drunk, sitting alone in a crowded café. That December was a terrible month to be in Paris. All my favorite establishments were either overly crowded or pathetically empty. People either sipped fine vintages in celebration or gulped intoxicants of who cares what kind, drowning themselves in a lack of moderation, raising a glass to lower inhibitions, imbibing spirits to raise their own. The expressions abounded, but that December

7

the talk everywhere was the same: "The Americans are going home." Better yet, those who had not were no longer so cocky, so overweening with pride. Money, everyone was saying, is required to keep such things alive. It was true, the Americans were going home, and that, depending on who you were, was a cause to rejoice or a cause to mourn.

The city's *le mont-de-piété*, for instance, were doing a booming business. "Mountains of mercy," indeed. So French, so snide to use such a heaping load of poetic words to refer to pawnshops, places filled with everything of value but never with poetry. The pawnshops in Paris were swamped, I had heard, with well-made American suits. At the end of October when it all began, there were seersuckers, cotton broadcloths, linens. Hardly a sacrifice at that time of the year, I thought. Paris was already too cool for such garb. I have always thought it best to pawn my lightweight suits when the weather changed. It provided protection from hungry moths and a saving on mothballs. My own hunger also played a somewhat deciding role. But by the beginning of that winter it became clear. The Americans were pawning corduroys, three-ply wools, flannel-lined tweeds. Seasonal clothing could only mean one thing. Desperation was demanding more closet space. Desperation was extending its stay. The end of 1929 also brought with it frustration, heard in and around all the cafés, about the months' worth of unpaid bar tabs, not to mention the skipped-out hotel bills or the overdue rents. "The funds from home never made it across the Atlantic," the departing Americans had claimed. The funds from home were never sent or, worse, no longer enough, everyone in Paris by then knew. Americans, not just here but in America, had lost their fortunes. An evil little wish had come true. The Parisians missed the money all right, but no one missed the Americans. Though I heard that in the beginning there had been sympathy. When the Americans first began arriving, the Parisians had even felt charitable toward them. These lost souls, after all, had taken flight from a country where a bottle of wine was of all things contraband, a flute of champagne a criminal offense. But when it became clear that the Americans had no intention of leaving and no intention of ever becoming sober, the Parisians wanted their city back. But it was already too late. The pattern of behavior had become comically clear. Americans traveled here in order to indulge in the "vices" of home. First, they had invaded the bordellos and then it was the cafés. Parisians could more than understand the whoring and the drinking, but in the end it was the hypocrisy that did not translate well.

"But there are still the Russians, Hungarians, Spaniards . . . not nearly as well endowed but in other ways so charmingly equipped." The laughter that immediately followed this observation told me that the table next to mine was commenting on more than just money. When gathered in their cafés, Parisians rarely spoke of money for very long. They exhausted the topic with one or two words. Sex, though, was an entirely different story, an epic really. I always got my gossip and my world news for that matter from the cafés. It would certainly take me awhile, but the longer I stayed the more I was able to comprehend. Alcohol, I had learned, was an eloquent if somewhat inaccurate interpreter. I had placed my trust that December night in glass after glass of it, eager not for drink but for a bit of talk. I also had that night no other place I had to be, so I sat and stared at the cigarette-stained walls of the café until my wallet was empty, my bladder was full, and until I was very drunk. Worse, the alcohol had deceived me, made me promises and then refused to follow through. In the past the little glasses had blurred the jagged seams between the French words, but that night they magnified and sharpened them. They threatened to rip and to tear. They bullied me with questions, sneering at how I could sit there stealing laughter, lifting conversations, when it was now common knowledge that "the Americans are going home." Panic then abruptly took over the line of questioning: "Would my new Mesdames go with them?" Or, maybe, the question was just a matter of "When?"

I did not remember asking the waiter for pencil and paper, but I must have, as I never carry such items in my pockets. The cafés used to give them out for free. So French to sell water and to give such luxuries away. The content of my letter was dull, crammed with details only my oldest brother would be interested in: my health, the cost of underwear and shoes, the price of a *métro* ticket, my weekly wage, the menu of my last meal, rain bouncing off the face of Notre-Dame, Paris covered by a thin sheet of snow. I had forgotten how different my language looks on paper, that its letters have so little resemblance to how they actually sound. Words, most I had not spoken for years, generously gave themselves to me. Fluency, after all, is relative. On that sheet of paper, on another side of the globe, I am fluent. The scratching of the pen, the writhing of the paper, I did not want it to stop, but I was running out of room. So I wrote it in the margin: "My Mesdames may be going home. I do not want to start all over again, scanning the help-wanteds, knocking on doors, walking away alone. I am afraid." I had meant to place a comma between "alone" and "I am afraid." But on paper, a period instead of a comma had turned a dangling token of regret into a plainly worded confession. I could have fixed it with a quick flick of lead, but then I read the sentences over again and thought, *That is true as well.*

The first line of my brother's response startled me, made me wonder whether he wrote it at all. "It is time for you to come home to Việt-Nam," he declared in a breathtaking evocation of the Old Man's voice, complete with his spine-snapping ability to stifle and to control. But the lines that followed made it clear who had held the pen: "You are my brother and that is all. I do not offer you my forgiveness because you never had to apologize to me. I think of you often, especially at the Lunar New Year. I hope to see you home for the next. A good meal and a red packet await you. So do I." The letter was dated January 27, 1934. It had taken only a month for his letter to arrive at the rue de Fleurus. He offered no explanation for his delay in writing except to say that everything at home had changed. He wrote that it would have been better for me to hear it all in person. What he meant was that paper was not strong enough to bear the weight of what he had to say but that he would have to test its strength anyway.

At the edge of that sheet of paper, on the other side of the globe, my brother signed his name. And then, as if it were an afterthought, he wrote the words "safe journey" where the end should have been.

I folded my brother's letter and kept it in the pocket of my only and, therefore, my finest cold-weather suit. I wore them both to the Gare du Nord that day. The suit was neatly pressed, if a bit worn. The letter was worse off. The oils on my fingertips, the heat of my body, had altered its physical composition. The pages had grown translucent from the repeated handling, repetitive rereading. The ink had faded to purple. It was becoming difficult to read. Though in truth, my memory had already made that act obsolete.

The first photograph of the journey was taken there at the station. It shows my Mesdames sitting side by side and looking straight ahead. They are waiting for the train to Le Havre, chitchatting with the photographers, looking wide-eyed into the lens. They wear the same expression as when they put on a new pair of shoes. They never immediately get up and walk around. They prefer to sit and let their toes slowly explore where the leather gives and where it binds. A pleasurable exercise for them, I am certain, as they always share a somewhat delinquent little smile. I am over there on the bench, behind them, on the left-hand side. I am the one with my head lowered, my eyes closed. I am not asleep, just thinking, and that for me is sometimes aided by the dark. I am a man unused to choices, so the months leading up to that day at the Gare du Nord had subjected me to an agony, sharp and new, self-inflicted and self-prolonged. I had forgotten that discretion can feel this way.

I sometimes now look at this photograph and wonder whether it was taken before or after. Pure speculation at this point, I know. Though I seem to remember that once I had made up my mind, I looked up instinctually, as if someone had called out my name. If that is true, then the photograph must have been taken during the moments before, when my heart was beating a hard, syncopated rhythm, like those of the approaching trains, and all I could hear in the darkness was a simple refrain:

I do not want to start all over again.
Scanning the help-wanteds.
Knocking on doors.
Walking away alone.
And, yes, I am afraid.

CHAPTER 2

LIVE-IN COOK
Two American ladies wish
to retain a cook—27 rue de
Fleurus. See the concierge.

Two American ladies "wish"? Sounds more
like a proclamation than a help-wanted ad.
Of course, two American ladies in Paris
these days would only "wish" because to wish
is to receive. To want, well, to want is just not
American. I congratulate myself on this rather apt
and piquant piece of social commentary. Now if
only I knew how to say "apt" and "piquant" in
French, I could stop congratulating myself and
strike up a conversation with the *beau garçon*
sitting three park benches away. The irony of
acquiring a foreign tongue is that I have amassed
just enough cheap, serviceable words to fuel my
desires and never, never enough lavish, imprudent
ones to feed them. It is true, though, that there are
some French words that I have picked up quickly,
in fact, words that I cannot remember *not* knowing.

As if I had been born with them in my mouth, as if they were the seeds of a sour fruit that someone else ate and then ungraciously stuffed its remains into my mouth.

"Ungraciously? Ungraciously? I'll tell you who is ungracious. It's you, you ungracious, disrespectful, disappearing lout! You were taught how to say *'s'il vous plaît, merci, Monsieur, Madame'* so that you could work in the Governor-General's house. Your oldest brother, he started out like you. At twelve, he was the boy who picked up after Madame's *'petit chouchou'* when that mutt did its business in every corner of the house, warping the wood floors with its shit and urine. Now your brother is thirty and a sous chef! Wears a crisp white apron and knows more French words than the neighborhood schoolteacher. Soon he'll be . . ."

I have discovered very few true and constant things in my life. One is that the Old Man's anger has no respect for geography. Mountains, rivers, oceans, and seas, these things that would have otherwise kept the average man locked onto the plot of land that he calls home, these things have never kept him from homing in on me, pinpointing my location, and making me pay my respects. While his body lies deep in the ground of Saigon, his anger sojourns with a "no-good lout" on a Paris park bench. Even here, he finds me.

"Unemployed and alone," the Old Man surmises, distilling my life into two sad, stinging words.

I try to protect myself with the usual retort: Oh, you again? I thought I was *dead* to you, Old Man?

"No son of mine leaves a good job at the Governor-General's to be a cook! A cook on some leaky boat for sailors who don't even know how to say 'please' or 'thank you' in their own language, not to mention in French. Old whores become cooks on boats, not any son of mine," you said.

Sometimes, I cannot give enough thanks to your Catholic god that you, my dear and violent "father," are now merely cobbled together from my unwavering sense of guilt and my telescopic memories of brutalities lived long ago. Because a retort like that, a challenge like that, would have extracted from you nothing less than a slap in my face and a punch in my stomach. But now you, who art up in heaven, *will* disappear in the face of my calm cool smirk. Unemployed and Alone, however, obstinately refuse to retreat and demand that I address their needs before September disappears into October in this the year of your lord 1929.

"Two American ladies . . ." Hmm, Americans. I hope their French is not as wretched as mine. What a fine household we would make, hand movements and crude drawings to supplement our mutual use of a secondhand language. Though contrary to what the Old Man would have me believe, the vocabulary of servitude is not built upon my knowledge of foreign words but rather on my

17

ability to swallow them. Not my own, of course, but Monsieur and Madame's. The first thing I learned at the Governor-General's house was that when Monsieur and Madame were consumed by their lunatic displeasure at how the floors had been waxed, how the silver had been polished, or how the *poulet* had been stewed, they would berate the household staff, all fifteen of us, in French. Not in the combination of dumbed-down French coupled with atonal attempts at Vietnamese that they would normally use with us, no, this was a pure variety, reserved for dignitaries and obtuse Indochinese servants. It was as if Monsieur and Madame were wholly incapable of expressing their finely wrought rage in any other language but their own. Of course, we would all bow our heads and act repentant, just as the Catholic priest had taught us. Of course, we would all stand there, blissful in our ignorance of the nuances, wordplay, and double-entendres of that language that was seeking so desperately to assault us. Naturally, some words would slip through, but for the most part we were all rather skilled in our refusal and rejection of all but the most necessary. Minh the Sous Chef, as the Old Man had renamed him, had told us how the French never tired of debating why the Indochinese of a certain class are never able to master the difficulties, the subtleties, the winged eloquence, of the French language. I now suspect that this is a topic of discussion for the ruling class everywhere. So enamored of their differences, language and otherwise, they have lost the instinctual ability to detect the defiance of those who serve them.

Minh the Sous Chef used to be just Anh Minh, my oldest brother and the only brother who today can make me long for home. No one would have enjoyed this park bench and the shade of these forlorn chestnut trees more than he. Anh Minh believed absolutely and passionately that the French language would save us, would welcome us into the fold, would reward us with kisses on both cheeks. His was not an abstract belief. It was grounded in the kitchen of the Governor-General's house. He insisted that after Monsieur and Madame tasted his *omelette à la bourbonnaise*, his *coupe ambassadrice*, his *crème marquise*, they would have no need to send for a French *chef de cuisine* to replace old Claude Chaboux. The Old Man, like a soothsayer, declared that soon there would be the first Vietnamese *chef de cuisine* in the Governor-General's house. So while the rest of us in the household staff stood there dumbly experiencing the balletic surges of Monsieur and Madame's tirade, Anh Minh alone stood in agony, lashed and betrayed by all those French words he had adopted and kept close to his heart, wounded. Minh the Wounded, I began calling him in my prayers.

Old Chaboux died, and a young Jean Blériot arrived from France to don the covered title. Now only an act of god, a bout of malaria, or a lustful look at Madame would hasten the departure of

19

Chef Blériot, as he insisted on being called. May 11, 1923, began his reign. Anh Minh stayed on in the kitchen of the Governor-General's to serve under yet another French chef, to cover for him once he began to reek of rum, to clean up after him once he could no longer find the rim of the pot, handfuls of shallot and dashes of oil seasoning the tile floor.

And, me, what was I supposed to do? Twenty years old and still a *garde-manger*, sculpting potatoes into perfect little spheres, carving chunks of turnips into swans, the arc of their necks as delicate as Blériot's fingers, fingers that I wanted to taste. Equipped with skills and desires that no man would admit to having, what was I supposed to do?

"Two American ladies wish to retain a cook—27 rue de Fleurus." Prosperous enough area of town, and two American ladies must have enough to pay a nice wage. One of the skills—it is more like a sleight of hand—that I have acquired since coming to this city is an acumen for its streets. I know where they reside, where they dissolve discreetly into one another, where they inexplicably choose to rear their unmarked heads. A skill born from the lack of other skills, really. When each day is mapped for me by a wanton display of street names congesting the pages of the help-wanteds, when I am accompanied by the stench of the unemployable, I am forced into an avid, adoring courtship with the boulevards of this city. I must admit that in truly desperate times, my intimate knowledge of the city has saved me. Paris is a Madame with a heart.

"Name any street. Go ahead, any street. I'll tell you where it is, Left Bank or Right Bank, exact locale even. Rue de Fleurus? It's a little street off of the boulevard Raspail, near the Jardin du Luxembourg." I have earned several dozen glasses of *marc* that way. Frenchmen, drunk men, love a challenge. The listeners, if any, often will ask me to repeat myself. It seems that my accented French is hard even on the ears of laborers. But once it is clear to them that I am there for their amusement, the rest is an enthralling performance. Fortunately for me, I have no idea how to say "enthralling" in French because otherwise I would be compelled to brag and ruin the surprise. And they are always surprised. And they always try again. They will name the street where their great-aunt Sylvie lives, where their butcher is located, where they last got lost, and, when truly desperate, they will name a street on one of the islands that cleave this city. By then I am gone because too often their surprise deviates into anger: "How can this little Indochinese, who can't even speak proper French, who can't even say more than a simple sentence, who can't even understand enough to get angry over the jokes that we're making at his expense, how can *this* Indochinese know this city better than we?" All I need is a little monkey dressed in a suit more expensive than my own, and I could join the ranks of the circus freaks. "Come one, come all. See the Half-Man-Half-Woman Sword Swallower, the Bearded Lady, and, now, introducing the Little Indochinese Who Knows This City Better Than Any Parisian!" But this is hardly a skill to impress a potential Monsieur and Madame.

I have been in this city for over three years now. I have interviewed with and even worked for an embarrassing number of households. In my experience, they fall into two categories. No, in fact, there are three. The first are those who, after a catlike glimpse at my face, will issue an immediate rejection, usually nonverbal. A door slam is an uncommonly effective form of communication. No discussion, no references required, no "Will you want Sundays off?" Those, while immediately unpleasant, I prefer. Type twos are those who may or may not end up hiring me but who will, nonetheless, insist on stripping me with questions, as if performing an indelicate physical examination. Type twos behave as if they have been authorized by the French government to ferret out and to document exactly how it is that I have come to inhabit their hallowed shores.

"In Paris, three years," I tell them.

"Where were you before?"

"Marseilles."

"Where were you before that?"

"Boat to Marseilles."

"Boat? Well, obviously. Where did that boat sail from?"

And so, like a courtesan, forced to perform the dance of the seven veils, I grudgingly reveal the names, one by one, of the cities that have carved their names into me, leaving behind the scar tissue that forms the bulk of who I am.

"Hmmm . . . you say you've been in Paris for three years? Now, let's see, if you left Indochina when you were twenty, that would make you . . ."

"Twenty-six, Madame."

Three years unaccounted for! you could almost hear them thinking. Most Parisians can ignore and even forgive me for not having the refinement to be born amidst the ringing bells of their cathedrals, especially since I was born instead amidst the ringing bells of the replicas of their cathedrals, erected in a faroff colony to remind them of the majesty, the piety, of home. As long as Monsieur and Madame can account for my whereabouts in their city or in one of their colonies, then they can trust that the République and the Catholic Church have had their watchful eyes on me. But when I expose myself as a subject who may have strayed, who may have lived a life unchecked, ungoverned, undocumented, and unrepentant, I become, for them, suspect. Before, I was no more of a threat than a cloistered nun. Now Madame glares at me to see if she can detect the deviant sexual practices that I have surely picked up and am now, without a doubt, proliferating under the very noses of the city's Notre-Dames. Madame now worries whether she can trust me with her little girls.

Madame, you have nothing to worry about. I have no interest in your little girls. Your boys . . . well, that is their choice, she should hear me thinking.

The odds are stacked against me with this second type, I know. But I find myself again and again shamefully submitting. All those questions, I deceive myself each time, all those questions must mean that I have a chance. And so I stay on, eventually serving myself forth like a scrawny roast pig, only to be told, "Thank you, but no thank you."

Thank you? Thank you? Madame, you should applaud! A standing ovation would not be inappropriate, I think each time. I have just given you a story filled with exotic locales, travel on the open seas, family secrets, un-Christian vices. *Thank you* will not suffice.

My self-righteous rage burns until I am forced to concede that I, in fact, have told them nothing. This language that I dip into like a dry inkwell has failed me. It has made me take flight with weak wings and watched me plummet into silence. I am unable to tell them anything but a list of cities, some they have been to and others a mere dot on a globe, places they will only touch with the tips of their fingers and never the soles of their feet. I am forced to admit that I am, to them, nothing but a series of destinations with no meaningful expanses in between.

Thank you, but no thank you.

The third type, I call the collectors. They are always good for several weeks' and sometimes even several months' worth of work. The interviews they conduct are professional, even mechanical. Before I can offer the usual inarticulate boast about my "good omelets," I am hired. Breakfast, lunch, and dinner to be prepared six days a week. Sundays off. Some immediately delegate the marketing to me. Others insist on accompanying me for the first few days to make sure that I know the difference between a *poularde* and a *poulette*. I rarely fail them. Of course, I have never been able to memorize or keep an accurate tally of the obsessive assortment of words that the French have devised for this animal that is the center, the stewed, fricasseed, sautéed, stuffed heart, of every Frenchman's home. Fat chickens, young chickens, newly hatched chickens, old wiry chickens, all are awarded their very own name, a noble title of sorts in this language that can afford to be so drunk and extravagant toward what lies on the dinner table. "A chicken" and "not this chicken," these are the only words I need to navigate the poultry markets of this city. Communicating in the negative is not the quickest and certainly not the most esteemed form of expression, but for those of us with few words to spare it is the magic spell, the incantation, that opens up an otherwise inaccessible treasure trove. Wielding my words like a rusty kitchen knife, I can ask for, reject, and ultimately locate that precise specimen that will grace tonight's pot.

And, yes, for every coarse, misshapen phrase, for every blundered, dislocated word, I pay a fee. A man with a borrowed, ill-fitting tongue, I cannot compete for this city's attention. I cannot participate in the lively lovers' quarrel between it and its inhabitants. I am a man whose voice is a harsh whisper in a city that favors a song. No longer able to trust the sound of my own voice, I carry a small speckled mirror that shows me my face, my hands, and assures me that I am still here. Becoming more like an animal with each displaced day, I scramble to seek shelter in the kitchens of those who will take me. Every kitchen is a homecoming, a respite, where I am the village elder, sage and revered. Every kitchen is a familiar story that I can embellish with saffron, cardamom, bay laurel, and lavender. In their heat and in their steam, I allow myself to believe that it is the sheer speed of my hands, the flawless measurement of my eyes, the science of my tongue, that is rewarded. During these restorative intervals, I am no longer the mute who begs at this city's steps. Three times a day, I orchestrate, and they sit with slackened jaws, silenced. Mouths preoccupied with the taste of foods so familiar and yet with every bite even the most parochial of palates detects redolent notes of something that they have no words to describe. They are, by the end, overwhelmed by an emotion that they have never felt, a nostalgia for places they have never been.

I do not willingly depart these havens. I am

content to grow old in them, calling the stove my lover, calling the copper pans my children. But collectors are never satiated by my cooking. They are ravenous. The honey that they covet lies inside my scars. They are subtle, though, in their tactics: a question slipped in with the money for the weekly food budget, a follow-up twisted inside a compliment for last night's dessert, three others disguised as curiosity about the recipe for yesterday's soup. In the end, they are indistinguishable from the type twos except for the defining core of their obsession. They have no true interest in where I have been or what I have seen. They crave the fruits of exile, the bitter juices, and the heavy hearts. They yearn for a taste of the pure, sea-salt sadness of the outcast whom they have brought into their homes. And I am but one within a long line of others. The Algerian orphaned by a famine, the Moroccan violated by his uncle, the Madagascan driven out of his village because his shriveled left hand was a sign of his mother's misdeeds, these are the wounded trophies who have preceded me.

It is not that I am unwilling. I have sold myself in exchange for less. Under their gentle guidance, their velvet questions, even I can disgorge enough pathos and cheap souvenir tragedies to sustain them. They are never gluttonous in their desires, rather the opposite. They are methodical. A measured, controlled dosage is part of the thrill. No, I am driven out by my own willful hands. It is only a matter of time. After so many weeks of having that soft, steady light shined at me, I begin to forget the barbed-wire rules of such engagements. I forget that there will be days when it is I who will have the craving, the red, raw need to expose all my neglected, unkempt days. And I forget that I will wait, like a supplicant at the temple's gate, because all the rooms of the house are somber and silent. When I am abandoned by their sweet-voiced catechism, I forget how long to braise the ribs of beef, whether chicken is best steamed over wine or broth, where to buy the sweetest trout. I neglect the pinch of cumin, the sprinkling of lovage, the scent of lime. And in these ways, I compulsively write, page by page, the letters of my resignation.

"Yes, yes, they're still looking for a cook," confirms the concierge. "You'll have to come back in an hour or so when they've returned from their drive. Just knock on that door to your left. It leads to the studio. What did you say your name was?"

"Bình," I answer.

"What?"

"Bình."

"Beene? Beene, now that's easy enough on the tongue. You seem like a nice boy. Let me give you a bit of advice—don't blink an eye."

"What?"

"Don't blink an eye," repeats the concierge, raising his brows and his voice for added emphasis. "Do you understand?"

"No."

"The two Americans are a bit, umm, unusual. But you'll see that for yourself as soon as the door to the studio is opened."

"Studio? Painters?"

"No, no, a writer and, umm, a companion. But that's not the point! They are nice, very nice."

"And?"

"Well, no point really. Except. Except, you should call her by her full name, Gertrude Stein. Always 'GertrudeStein.' Just think of it as one word."

"Is that it? What about the other one?"

"Her name is Alice B. Toklas. She prefers 'Miss Toklas.'"

"And?"

"Well, that's it. That's it."

"I'll be back in an hour, then. Good-bye, Monsieur."

CHAPTER 3

This is a temple, not a home.

The thought—barely formed, fluid, just beginning to mingle with the faint smells introduced by the opening door—changes so quickly from prophecy to gospel that I am for a brief moment extricated from my body, made to stand beside myself, and allowed to serve as a solemn eyewitness. Ordinarily, I am plagued, like the Old Man, with a slowness. In him, it was triggered by cowardice. In me, it is aggravated by carelessness. Ours is a hesitancy toward an act that is habitual and common to those around us: the forming of conclusions. We are, instead, weighted and heavied by decades of observations. We gather them, rags and remnants, and then have no needle and thread with which to sew them together. But once they are formed, ours become the thick, thorny coat of a durian, a covering designed to forestall the odor of rot and decay deep inside. But to the neighbors whose prying eyes were members of our extended family, the Old Man was a person of sure-footed opinions, a man of unwavering morals, a man who laid down

30

judgments with the ease of an ox marking its path with piles of its own dung. Since my first night away from home, I have been suffering through a dream, sad and naked. I am standing in front of the Old Man's coffin, which has been laid out in front of his house underneath the morning sun, and I am saying, as if in a trance: "This was a man who benefited from a long life. Over the course of his many decades, he had reached a handful of conclusions about the world around him. In his hands they, the coarse sediments of his life, lost their natural complexities, became a string of pearl-like truths, a choker for the necks of those who share his name." Taking a deep breath, I then solemnly declare, "He was a coward who finally had the courage to die, knowing that in the silence that he leaves behind him, I would have the last word, would come forward to ensure that his reputation dies along with his body." In my dream, I am saying all of this in French, though I know that this is impossible. But in my dream, cruelty greases my tongue and I am undeniably fluent.

This is a temple, not a home.

The thought—growing stronger with the scent of cloves and sweet cinnamon in the air—takes me out of the past, a borderless country in which I so often find myself, and returns me to Paris, to the rue de Fleurus, where a door, joints rusted red but otherwise unadorned, is opening. A woman with the face of an owl emerges and positions herself inside of a wedge of light. The woman, I think, has the face of an "Ancient." This is not to say that her face is wrinkled or dulled. Ancients, according to Bão, my bunkmate on board the *Niobe*, wear faces that have not changed for centuries. To look at them, he said, is to look at a series of paintings of their ancestors and their descendants, as when two mirrors endlessly reflect each other's images. Bão said that Ancients possess features so strong and forceful that they can withstand generation after generation of new and insurgent bloodlines. Women, who are accused of adultery because the faces of their children refuse to resemble those of their husbands, are often Ancients. In a firefly moment of introspection, Bão said that these women are feared because they make a mockery out of the marriage union, that their children's preordained faces proclaim too loudly that the man is irrelevant, that maybe he is not needed at all. Bão, of course, did not say it in exactly these words. His were more immodest, recalling with photographic details the acts performed by Serena the Soloist, a mixed-blood beauty from Pondicherry who commanded half a week of his wages, money he now thought was well spent, for a glimpse of his own irrelevancy. Money well spent, indeed. Serena and her talented fingers and toes have become for Bão a supple example, a sort of explicit device, that helps him to explain everything he knows in life, from how to bargain for a few extra slices of beef in his bowl of *phở* to the difference between serving under English ship captains and French ones. But no matter why Serena was introduced, after each encore Bão without fail would offer this advice: "Remember, as Serena the Soloist showed me, there are just *some* things a man can't do!" Bão's eyes would then open wide, and his body would remain perfectly still, as if he were removing all distractions so that the indelicate meaning of his words could be fully savored. Bão's own convulsive, silent laughter would then officially end the show. When we first met, I asked Bão why he became a sailor when his name meant "storm." He responded with a rhythmless shaking, an open-mouthed silence, that I would only later learn to equate with laughter.

As I slipped into the South China Sea, as water erased the shoreline, absolving it of my sins, I began to believe that conflict and strife were landlocked. Too sweat-stained and cumbersome for sea travel, I thought. So during our time together, Bão and I developed a tacit understanding that everything he said was true. A covenant easily kept because there were few on board the *Niobe* with the authority to contradict, to say "No, that is not true," who understood the sounds that we made. The First Officer, according to Bão, knew a few words of Vietnamese, but the woman who sold them to him was from the old Imperial City of Hue. His ears were trained only to respond to her Hue cadence, with its twists and undulations, like the wringing of wet silk, regal even as she sat naked asking for the money she had just earned. The First Officer heard in our southern market banter the unfamiliar language of a lower class of whores. This is all to say that Bão and I had built a safe house, and we were its only inhabitants. We were also the fatal flaws in its design. Arms raised, palms opened, giving ourselves up to the Indian Ocean winds that carried with them traces of loneliness like airborne granules of pollen, we were its only pillars, absorbing the whole of its weight. As long as we were together, we had shelter. The day that the *Niobe* docked in Marseilles, Bão collected his pay and waved good-bye from a ship heading for America. "As long as we are together, we have shelter," I mouthed to him, but he was already at sea.

The woman with the face of an owl repeats her question. My memories of Bão must have been swallowing me whole. How long have I have been standing there, silent? My delay in responding, even when what is posed is simple and direct, can usually be shrugged away with a smile and a "My French is not very good." But this afternoon I cannot deliver either one. I cannot respond to any of the woman's jangly French words because I am too enthralled by her upper lip with its black hairs twitching gently as she speaks. Her mustache, I think, would be the envy of all three of my brothers, who could only aspire to such definition after weeks' worth of unfettered growth. The arc of hair, like a descended third eyebrow, is topped by a solemn monument to the god of smells.

Protruding from her forehead, abruptly billowing out as it reaches her eye sockets, it is not so much a nose as an altarpiece that segregates the left side of her face from her right. Moving northward, her facial features disappear underneath a skullcap of hair, dark, absorbing the late-afternoon light. I am overwhelmed by the intrusiveness of it all until I look into her eyes. They live apart from their housing. Chasing the light that gilds this city in early autumn, her irides are two nets gently swooping over a band of butterflies. Catching the light, the circles erupt, bright with movement, the flapping and fanning of many colored wings. We stand looking at each other, waiting for my response. I am here to inquire about the position as a cook, I want to say, but lacking the finer components, I offer instead, "I am the cook you are looking for." Her eyes flicker with recognition and respond with an implicit "Of course."

I have been behind the temple door longer now than any other in this city. I have been given my own set of keys. I know the arrangement of the rooms that the door once concealed. I have been given a room to call my own. I have slept soundly, dreamed deeply, inside it. I can walk through the others with my eyes closed. I can walk through them without being seen. I have heard all the stories that inhabit them, know the colorful faces that line their walls. I can imagine my Mesdames waiting here for me from the very beginning. Life at 27 rue de Fleurus, believe me, has the ebb and flow of the sea, predictable, with reassuring periods of calm.

I had arrived on a Sunday afternoon, after all. Miss Toklas would have been nowhere else but firmly planted in the kitchen. Enrobed in thick woolen socks, secured underneath the leather straps of her sandals, her feet would have stood slightly apart as she peeled the tart green apples that would later that night soothe the GertrudeStein's periodic hankering for her childhood in America. Miss Toklas always stands when she is in the kitchen. Cooking, she thinks, is not a leisure activity. But for her, it has become just that, and she is keenly aware of it. She keeps a cardboard box filled with recipes, like other women keep love letters from their youth. She is afraid that she will forget the passion. She now cooks for GertrudeStein only on Sundays. In their household, like others in Paris, the cooks are granted Sundays off. At the end of each week, Miss Toklas by necessity and by desire steps back into the kitchen, gets butter and flour underneath her fingernails, breathes in the smell of cinnamon, burns her tongue, and is comforted. They never dine out on Sundays. No exceptions. No visitors at the studio door with letters of introduction. No requests granted for a viewing of the paintings. On Sundays my Madame and Madame are safely settled in their dining room with their memories of their America heaped onto large plates. Of course, Miss Toklas can reach far beyond the foods of her childhood. She is a cook who puts absinthe in her salad dressing and rose petals in her vinegar. Her menus can map the world. But lately the two of them have shared a taste for the foods that fortified them in their youth. Neither of them seems to notice that Miss Toklas's "apple pie" is now filled with an applesauce-flavored custard and frosted with buttercream or that her "meat loaf" harbors the zest of an orange and is bathed in white wine. GertrudeStein thinks it is unfathomably erotic that the food she is about to eat has been washed, pared, kneaded, touched, by the hands of her lover. She is overwhelmed by desire when she finds the faint impressions of Miss Toklas's fingerprints decorating the crimped edges of a pie crust. Miss Toklas believes that these nights are her reward. She is a pagan who secretly yearns for High Mass. To her, there is something of both in their Sunday nights that lets her spirit soar.

"Pussy, there is someone at the studio door," GertrudeStein would have called out from her chintz-covered armchair.

There are two of these armchairs at 27 rue de Fleurus, and both of them are located in the studio. They were made-to-order and therefore could accommodate both the fullness of GertrudeStein's girth and the conciseness of Miss Toklas's stature.

"Lovey, I am *tired* of dangling my feet in the air. A woman of my age should be able to sit down without having to look like a misbehaving child," Miss Toklas must have declared.

"All right, Pussy, all right," GertrudeStein must have agreed.

And their debate about the costly armchairs must have ended just like that. Because Miss Toklas, I know, rarely has to say more than "Lovey" to triumph.

GertrudeStein, accustomed by now to her comfy throne, would have called out again, "Please, Pussy, please. There is someone at the studio door."

"But, Lovey, *you* are right there!" Miss Toklas, from her position at the kitchen sink, would have stated the obvious, knowing all the while that it was of no use. GertrudeStein will not answer her own door today or any other day. GertrudeStein has in recent years begun to conclude that those who deliberately seek her out are god-awful nuisances, unless they were willing, of course, to recognize her genius. She, it must be acknowledged, is the brightest star in the Western sky. Though in truth, I think GertrudeStein is more of a constellation. She is about the same height as Miss Toklas, but she has a sturdy build, storing most of her weight in her bosom and hips. GertrudeStein is a great beauty, both Miss Toklas and I believe. No, for me, not at first. Only Miss Toklas could claim such immediate clarity. GertrudeStein's features are broad, unmistakable, a bit coarse. Her nose and ears appear to be disproportionately larger than the

38

rest of her face. She, though, carries herself as if she is an object of desire. She carries herself as if she is her own object of desire. Such self-induced lust is addictive in its effect. Prolonged exposure makes those around them weak and helpless.

I have seen scattered around the apartment photographs of a GertrudeStein who wears her hair in a massive topknot, loose, blowzy, somewhat in disarray. The total effect, however, is heroic. The GertrudeStein I know has less hair on her head than I do. The story of her transformation began, I would imagine, around noon, as she is rarely awake until then:

GertrudeStein looks at her reflection floating on the surface of a silver teapot and concludes that the pile of hair on top of her head is unacceptable. It is, she thinks, disrupting the continuity of her face. Shearing it, she tells Miss Toklas, will be an important act. Pointless overdecoration, GertrudeStein explains, thinking of the commas and periods that she has plucked from the pages of her writings. Such interferences, she insists, are nothing more than toads flattened on a country road, careless and unsightly. The modern world is without limits, she tells Miss Toklas, so the modern story must accommodate the possibilities—a road where she can get lost if she so chooses or go slow and touch each blade of grass. GertrudeStein should know. She is an excellent driver. She lapses, however, when she has to go in reverse. She would rather keep on driving until she can turn the automobile

39

around, a 360-degree arc of obstinacy. That way, she is technically always going forward.

Miss Toklas likes the wind in her face.

It takes Miss Toklas nearly two days, interrupted only by their mutual desire to eat, to cut off GertrudeStein's hair. As each lock is slipped between the blades of her scissors, Miss Toklas smiles, and says, "Oh, this is so Spanish!" That is her highest compliment for any situation. Spain, Miss Toklas thinks, is where her soul first emerged, fully formed. Spain is where she first experienced Passion, without GertrudeStein. Every town has at least one house, marked by the sign of a cross, in which she could meet Her. Her flirtation, her lover, her Virgin. On their first visit to Ávila, she begs GertrudeStein to stay, to linger in the shadows of the city's cloistered walls. GertrudeStein suspects that on Spanish soil, Miss Toklas would become another's devotee. GertrudeStein could not bear such disgraceful competition. Paris, she knows, has its share of seductions, but those are at least corporeal in form. Miss Toklas is moved by the sight of GertrudeStein's shoulders as they are being eased into a shawl of newly clipped hair, lacelike, covering and revealing all at once. Miss Toklas keeps on cutting, remembering the monks who wound through the streets of Valencia, a slow-moving, deliberate act. She keeps on cutting, losing herself in GertrudeStein's conversion. After her two-day sitting, GertrudeStein is left with a patch of closely cropped hair that stops just at her earlobes, a mantle intended to be demure but instead alludes to the skin, bare and lurking below. She holds Miss Toklas in her arms, placing thank-you kisses in her palms. Miss Toklas remembers the children in Burgos who mistook GertrudeStein for a bishop and begged to kiss her ring.

Wiping her hands off on her apron, Miss Toklas would have walked down the hallway toward the studio door. She would have passed by her Lovey sitting deep within the shadows of yet another detective story. GertrudeStein is very democratic in her reading choices. She delights in the clipped prose, the breakneck speed at which she turns the pages, the steamy mix of petty crimes and bad love affairs. She is especially addicted to the flagrant use of a distinctly American English, a language that she thinks ignites these stories with their vigor and vim. Over two decades in Paris, and yet with each day GertrudeStein believes that she is growing more intimate with the language of her birth. Now that it is no longer applicable to the subjects of everyday life, no longer wasted on the price of petrol, the weather, the health of other people's children, it has become for her a language reserved for genius and creation, for love and devotion. As she is destined now to see it more often than to hear it, GertrudeStein has also grown to appreciate its contours and curvatures, captured and held steady on the pages of the books and letters that cross her lap. The words provoke the scientific in her,

41

remind her of her days in medical school, dissecting something live and electric, removing vital organs from a living animal and watching the chaos that ensues.

Miss Toklas likes the smell of fresh ink on fingertips.

She types and proofs all of GertrudeStein's writings. The intimacy that she has with these written words cannot be had, she thinks, by merely reading the finished, typewritten pages. She longs for the scrawl, the dark, dark lines where her Lovey has pressed firmly, deliberately. She recognizes each break in the flow of the ink, sometimes in midword, pauses for her pleasure. Not until she cries out "Mercy, please have mercy!" does the ink resume its flow. When Miss Toklas first moved into 27 rue de Fleurus, there were other women typing and proofing for GertrudeStein. Miss Toklas immediately recognized the familiarity that such acts bestow. She did not want to see the unfamiliar pairs of white kid gloves lying on the table, a shed serpent skin, fingers poised for the cool touch of the typewriter keys. She thought she smelled their sweat corrupting the ink on the pages. She needed to know that this was not so. Miss Toklas has long since made herself indispensable to GertrudeStein. She is as much a guardian of their temple as the solid door to the studio. She is the first line of defense, the official taster of the King's food, the mother hen. Miss Toklas throws open the studio door with a single flick of her wrist, a revelation in the strength of her hands. She sees my face, and says, "I am Alice B. Toklas, and who are you?"

CHAPTER 4

"Thin Bin," says GertrudeStein, merrily mispronouncing my name, rhyming it instead with an English word that she claims describes my most distinctive feature, declining to share with me what that feature would be. I have learned that my Madame, while not cruel, is full of mischief. She never fails to greet me with a smile and a hearty American salutation: "Well, hello, Thin Bin!" She then walks on by, leaving me to speculate again on what this "thin" could be.

Short, I think, is the most obvious answer.

"Stupid," the Old Man insists.

Handsome, I venture, is the better guess.

All my employers provide me with a new moniker, whether they know it or not. None of them—and this I do not exaggerate—has called me by my given name. Their mispronunciations are endless, an epic poem all their own. GertrudeStein's just happens to rhyme. Every time she says my name, I say it as well. Hearing it said correctly, if only in my head, is a desire that I cannot shake. I readjust and realign the tones that

44

are missing or are sadly out of place. I am lonesome all the same for another voice to say my name, punctuated with a note of anticipation, a sigh of relief, a warm breath of affection.

"Thin Bin," says GertrudeStein, "how would *you* define 'love'?"

While my Madame begins her question with what I have to come to accept as my American name, she has to deliver the rest of it, the meat of it, to me in French. It is, after all, the only language that we have in common. And GertrudeStein's French is, believe me, common. It is a shoe falling down a stairwell. The rhythm is all wrong. The closer it gets, the louder and more discordant it sounds. Her broad American accent, though, pleases her to no end. She considers it a necessary ornamentation, like one of the imposing mosaic brooches that she is so fond of wearing. She uses it freely on her daily stroll around the neighborhood with Basket pulling at her by a red rope leash. GertrudeStein never walks the Chihuahua. Pépé does not perform well when there is dirt or stone underneath his stiletto paws. First he shakes and then he passes gas. For a dog the size of a guinea hen, he passes more than can be imagined. GertrudeStein prefers the goat-sized poodle. Basket's cape, she believes, gives him a sensible air. Together these two ample ambassadors of American goodwill canvass the streets of the Left Bank, engaging the shopkeepers in their doorways, the old men walking their tiny dogs, the kind that, like Pépé, shiver all year round. It is always surprising for me to see Basket strolling with GertrudeStein. For all of His Highness's haughtiness when he is home alone with me, the poodle Basket on the streets of this city is reduced to yet another tongue-lolling, rear-end-sniffing, pee-spraying object of undue affection. I am not the jealous type. It is just that dogs, or rather Madame and Madame's love relationships with them, are more foreign to me than their language could ever be. As Anh Minh would say, "Only the rich can afford *not* to eat their animals."

GertrudeStein is fully versed in the language of canine appreciation. She uses it and Basket, panting and pink, to befriend even the surly butcher on the boulevard Edgar-Quinet, a man with one glass eye constantly trained on the rows of small stripped carcasses hanging in his shop windows. She uses it and Basket to sweet-talk the long-lashed Gypsy girl on the rue de la Gaîté who hawks bundles of rosemary or violets, depending on the season, when Basket bounds over and licks her hands and sniffs underneath her skirts. My Madame uses it and Basket because her French, like mine, has its limits. It denies her. It forces her to be short if not precise. In French, GertrudeStein finds herself wholly dependent on simple sentences. She compensates with the tone of her voice and the warmth of her eyes. She handles it with stunning grace. When I hear her speak it, I am filled with something very close to joy. I admire its roughness,

46

its unapologetic swagger. I think it a companion to my own. I think we will exchange one-word condolences and communicate the rest with our eyes. I think *this* we have in common.

GertrudeStein has, in turn, taken an interest in my, well, interpretation of the French language. She is affirmed by my use of negatives and repetitions. She is inspired by witnessing such an elemental, bare-knuckled breakdown of a language. She is a coconspirator. She would, of course, enjoy the show. I remember that on the day that I was hired GertrudeStein was present for my first discussion with Miss Toklas about the menus for the coming week. That conversation took place then, as it does now, in the kitchen. GertrudeStein, I now know, never goes into the kitchen. She must have sensed the potential in me from the very beginning. I wanted that afternoon to ask Miss Toklas whether the household budget would allow for the purchase of two pineapples for a dinner to which my Mesdames had invited two guests. I wanted to tell her that I would cut the first pineapple into paper-thin rounds and sauté them with shallots and slices of beef; that the sugar in the pineapple would caramelize during cooking, imparting a faint smokiness that is addictive; that the dish is a refined variation on my mother's favorite. I wanted to tell her that I would cut the second pineapple into bite-sized pieces, soak them in kirsch, make them into a drunken bed for spoonfuls of tangerine sorbet; that I would pipe unsweetened cream around the edges, a ring of ivory-colored rosettes. And because I am vain and want nothing more than to hear the eruption of praises that I can provoke, I wanted to tell her that I would scatter on top the petals of candied violets, their sugar crystals sparkling.

"Madame, I want to buy a pear . . . not a pear."

Miss Toklas looked at me, recognition absent from her eyes.

I, yes, lost the French word for "pineapple" the moment I opened my mouth. Departing at their will, the words of this language mock me with their impromptu absences. When I am alone, they offer themselves to me, loose change in a shallow pocket, but as soon as I reach for one I spill the others. This has happened to me many times before. At least I now know what to do, I thought. I repeated my question, but this time I had my hands on top of my head, with only the bottom of my palms touching my hair. My fingers were spread like two erect, partially opened fans. Complete with my crown, I stood in front of my new Madame and Madame the embodiment of "a-pear-not-a-pear." I remember seeing GertrudeStein smile. Already, my Madame was amusing herself with my French. She was wrapping my words around her tongue, saving them for a later, more careful study of their mutations.

GertrudeStein has since made it her habit to test my skills. At first she was satisfied with my resourceful renaming of foods, animals, household objects. But as it was also her habit never to master any language but her own, she first has to compile her list in English, rummage through Miss Toklas's dictionary for the French equivalent, and then locate an illustration or physical sample for me to examine. This is an after-dinner activity for GertrudeStein. She devotes no more than half an hour to it, a diversion before she cracks open a broad-spined book for the remainder of the night. Miss Toklas is always nearby, her needlework bobbing in her hands. Recently GertrudeStein has decided that it would be more efficient if she begins with the last step of her formula. To do otherwise, she now thinks, is simply too impractical, like an artist who paints a portrait and then roams the world searching for its model. Conveniently for GertrudeStein, she already has a whole world stashed away in the rooms of 27 rue de Fleurus. Buttons, seashells, glass globes, horseshoe nails, matchboxes, cigarette holders—the last inspired by Miss Toklas, whose voice reveals her habit—are deposited throughout the apartment. Some are grouped by types, some by years of acquisition, others by sentiment. By the time Miss Toklas moved into the rue de Fleurus, GertrudeStein had already acquired a sizable collection. Miss Toklas immediately understood. She did not have to be told that the objects of everyday life become relics and icons once they have touched GertrudeStein's hands. She already believed it.

The dinner dishes have been cleared and washed, and I have been again summoned to the studio. Surely after four years of this game, I think, there cannot be anything left in this apartment that we have not named. Last week, for instance, I had to inform GertrudeStein for the third time this year that Basket is "a-dog-not-a-friend" and that Pépé, well, Pépé is "a-dog-not-a-dog."

"Thin Bin, how would *you* define 'love'?"

Ah, I think, a classic move from the material to the spiritual. GertrudeStein, like the collectors who have preceded her, wants to see the stretch marks on my tongue. I taste a familiar drop of bitter in the back of my throat. I point to a table on which several quinces sit yellowing in a blue and white china bowl. I shake my head in their direction, and I leave the room, speechless.

Paper-white narcissuses, one hundred bulbs in shallow pools of moistened pebbles, their roots exposed, clinging, pale anchors steadying the blooms as they angle toward the sun. The windows are never completely closed because the sweet powdery scent would be unbearable. In those corners where sunlight is an unfulfilled promise, there are bowls of varying sizes holding hydrangea clusters, dried, the color of barely brewed tea. With no water to weigh them down, the blooms rattle against their china vessels whenever a draft sidles through the garret. The petals scraping lightly against the bone-enriched walls sing the song of

50

a rainfall. I choose to remember these things only. The rest I will discard.

I will forget that you entered 27 rue de Fleurus as a "writer" among a sea of others who opened the studio door with a letter of introduction and a face handsome with talent and promise. You stood at the front of the studio listening to a man who had his back to me. I entered the room with a tray of sugar-dusted cakes for all the young men who sit and stand, a hungry circle radiating around GertrudeStein. After years of the imposed invisibility of servitude, I am acutely aware when I am being watched, a sensitivity born from absence, a grain of salt on the tongue of a man who has tasted only bitter. As I checked the teapots to see whether they needed to be replenished, I felt a slight pressure. It was the weight of your eyes resting on my lips. I looked up, and I saw you standing next to a mirror reflecting the image of a wiry young man with deeply set, startled eyes. I looked up, and I was seeing myself beside you. I am at sea again, I thought. Waves are coursing through my veins. I am at sea again.

I will forget that you whispered to Miss Toklas that you were looking for a cook. You accompanied my Madame into the kitchen, bestowing upon her all the while compliments and congratulations for the composition of her tea table. The cakes are almost as sublime as their setting, you said. Honeysuckle roses and acacias, you lied, are your favorite floral combination. Leaning in, you explained in a conspiratorial tone that some friends are visiting and that you want to host a dinner party in their honor. I hope that I may impose upon you for a bit of advice, you murmured into the curving canals of my Madame's ear, and in that polite but intimate way you began the story that you were telling for me.

Miss Toklas admired the timbre of your voice. She wondered if she were hearing bells. She thought that you resembled a young novice whose face she once had glimpsed through the crumbling, honeycombed walls of a Spanish convent. Something feral and fast underneath the gentle garb, she recalled. Her eyes lingered on the cut of your suit. So American in its forthrightness, she thought. No bells and whistles, she thought. Miss Toklas approved of the scent of bay and lime on your skin. Like a Frenchman, she thought, announcing himself even before he enters the room, making an impression even after he is gone. With each breath my Madame was taking you in, and you knew it.

Later that night Miss Toklas asked me what I did with my Sundays. I had been in their household for over four years, and that night was the first time, the first time either one of my Mesdames had asked me about my one day away from them. My Sundays belong to me, I thought.

"Nothing," I said.

"Nothing," Miss Toklas repeated with a smile.

Are you mocking me, Madame? I thought.

"Why?" I asked.

"Do you remember the young man who came into the kitchen with me this afternoon?"

Remember him? If I am fortunate, I will think of nothing but him all night long, I thought.

"Yes," I said.

"He is looking for a cook for this Sunday."

I am the cook he is looking for, I thought.

"Oh," I said, without blinking an eye.

Miss Toklas explained to me that you were a young bachelor who would allow me free reign with planning the menu. An American, but one who could still afford to pay a premium, she assured me, for the inconvenience created by such short notice. She handed me your calling card and told me to meet you the following day at a quarter past two.

"Did I mention that he complimented you on those lovely, actually, I think he said 'sublime,' cakes that you served this afternoon?" Miss Toklas added, knowing that I am vain and that my vanity would understand the honey in her voice, even if I had to flick aside her hollow words like ants.

I had no hope, so I had no suspicion. I looked at the name on the card and saw nothing there but a fine pair of boots for the winter. My shirt cuffs are worn. Frayed edges are the telltale filigree of secondhand garments. My gloves bare the tips of my fingers to cold, observant eyes, but my shoes, my shoes belong to a man who does not think twice about strolling through life on the heels of luxury. Supple leather, hand-stitched details, eloquent in form and function and, yes, they gleam. I shine them each day with the sweat of my labor. I shine them each night until I can see my reflection, muddied and unpolished. I had arrived fifteen minutes early, and there was no one home.

I sat in the doorway of 12 rue de l'Odéon and lost myself in the passing street life. In this way, I am afraid, I am very French. I am entertained best by the continuous flow of people whom I do not know. I am amused by the faces that fade in and fade out as they pass me by. What these Parisians will declare out loud under their blue-tented sky, I will never fully understand, but I do not need their conversations. There are always the stock characters with their classic poses, which even I can comprehend: lovers, best when configured in threes, two locked in a visual embrace, the third trailing, losing self-respect but not hope with each frantic step; students, traveling in a band of fours and fives, eyes bloodshot from endless nights of too many books or too many drinks but rarely both; poets, always alone even when they are accompanied by their muse, casting long shadows in long coats with too many holes and patches, carefully cultivated emblems of creativity that disqualify them from pity.

From the other side of the street you approached holding two books in one hand and in the other, dangling from one finger, a white paper box tied with some red string. Sweets, I thought. My eyes fell into the rumpled folds of your coat, the waves of your hair. I want to be at sea again, I thought. I want to be at sea again.

Your hair looks clean and freshly washed, I thought. An important indicator of anyone's over-all cleanliness. You wear it parted on the left-hand side. A personal preference of mine as well. Your tie is tucked into the V of your sweater. I too prefer a sweater's soft drape to the buttons and bulk of a vest. Your coat looks warm. I would look good in it. Your hands . . . your hands? But where are your gloves? Ah, hands like yours will not stay cold for very long. Your eyes, coffee and cinnamon. An infusion to wake me from sleep.

"Well, are you coming in with me, or shall we conduct our interview here in the doorway?"

Your French was flawless but with a slowness to its delivery, unctuous and ripe. I wanted to open my mouth and taste each word. "Interview," though, slapped me in the face. The word was a sharp reminder that I was a servant who thought himself a man, that I was a fool who thought himself a king of hearts. I got up and walked with you into a stairwell paneled with sheets of sunlight, slipped one by one through the dusty windowpanes. I followed you up four flights of stairs, and with each step I was a man descending into a place where I could taste my solitude, familiar and tannic.

★   ★   ★

Quinces are ripe, GertrudeStein, when they are the yellow of canary wings in midflight. They are ripe when their scent teases you with the snap of green apples and the perfumed embrace of coral roses. But even then quinces remain a fruit, hard and obstinate—useless, GertrudeStein, until they are simmered, coddled for hours above a low, steady flame. Add honey and water and watch their dry, bone-colored flesh soak up the heat, coating itself in an opulent orange, not of the sunrises that you never see but of the insides of tree-ripened papayas, a color you can taste. To answer your question, GertrudeStein, love is not a bowl of quinces yellowing in a blue and white china bowl, seen but untouched.

CHAPTER 5

The last time I saw Anh Minh, we met at the back gate of the Governor-General's house. I remember looking inside the brightly lit kitchen and seeing the ceiling fans whirl, pushing hot currents of air out the windows. It was two o'clock in the morning, but the kitchen was all oven heat. Chef Blériot had fired up all four of the coal ovens and stuffed them with slender loaves, their smooth surfaces slashed at even intervals. The rest of the house was dark, except for a dim glow coming from the window of the chauffeur's room.

Years ago when I had just joined the Governor-General's household, Anh Minh told me that the chauffeur was the first son of a rich merchant, had studied in Paris, returned to Vietnam to see his father smoke away all of the family's fortune in puffs of opium, lost his automobile to a gambling debt, and spent hours now, when he was not driving Monsieur and Madame's Renault, writing poems about Madame's secretary, a slightly cross-eyed girl who was half-French and half-Vietnamese. All this, my brother said to me without a breath or a pause. He ran in a similar speed through the life stories of the others who made up the household staff of fifteen. He was motivated by a sense of duty and not by a love of gossip. He knew that I would need these facts in order to survive. That they would help me to avoid the pitfalls of those personalities who ranked higher up than I. I was told these stories so that I could think of them before I opened my mouth. At the Governor-General's, a servant whom Monsieur and Madame disliked would need to be careful, but one whom his fellow servants disliked would not last the night. Think of it as having thirteen enemies as opposed to two, Anh Minh told me. He had kindly excluded himself from the count of possible assassins, and that fact I also stored away. Overall, my oldest brother preferred to limit his lessons to the goings-on of the kitchen. I always knew when Minh the Sous Chef was preparing to teach. First he would wipe his fingers on the handkerchief that he always kept in his pocket, then he would throw his head back, tendering his throat to the blades of the kitchen's ceiling fans. From out of his mouth then came praise for the merits of Breton butter, heavily salted and packed in tins, which was served to Monsieur with his morning baguettes. Madame preferred preserves, in thick glass jars with hand-lettered labels, made from yellow plums that have the name of a beautiful French girl. "Mirabelle," Anh Minh repeated so that I, too, could see her. When old Chaboux passed away and young Blériot arrived to take his place, my brother told me that these French chefs were purists, classically trained, from families of chefs going back at least a century. Minh the Sous Chef agreed that it was probably better this way. After all, the *chef de cuisine* at the Continental Palace Hotel in Saigon—a man who claimed to be from Provence but who was rumored to be the illegitimate son of a high-ranking French official and his Vietnamese seamstress—had to be dismissed because he was serving dishes obscured by lemongrass and straw mushrooms. He also slipped pieces of rambutan and jackfruit into the sorbets. "The clientele was outraged, demanded that the natives in the kitchen be immediately dismissed if not jailed, shocked that the culprit was a harmless-looking 'Provençal,' incensed enough to threaten closure of the most fashionable hotel in all of Indochina, and, yes, the Continental sent the man packing!" said Anh Minh, delivering another lesson in the shortest amount of time possible.

Anh Minh believed that if he could save three minutes here, five minutes there, then one day he could tally them all up and have enough to start life all over again. Even then, I knew that every night those minutes saved were squandered away in a deep sleep from which my brother awoke with nothing but the handkerchief in his pocket. But in the kitchen with Minh the Sous Chef, I was content just to listen. Anh Minh, being the first, had inherited the voice that we, the three brothers who followed, coveted. If I closed my eyes, the Old Man was there with his river tones, low and close to the earth, a deep current summoning me from ashore. He was there without the floating islands of sewage, the half-submerged bodies of newborn animals, the swirling pools of dried-up leaves and broken branches. Making its way through Anh Minh's parted lips, the Old Man's voice, purified, said, "I believe in you." In the kitchen of the Governor-General, I learned from my brother's words and found solace in the Old Man's voice. I received there the benediction that I would otherwise never hear.

"Stupid! Hey, Stupid, get me my box of chew." The Old Man was talking to me all right, but he could have been talking to any of my brothers instead. By the time we were able to walk, we had learned our name. "Stupid" was shared by us like a hand-me-down. We were all the same until one of us redeemed himself, collecting small tokens, brief glimpses of the man whom the Old Man wanted us to be.

One became a porter for the railroads, second-class, but he hoped to see the interior of first before too long. The French had tattooed the countryside with tracks, knowing that mobility would allow them to keep a stranglehold on the little dragon that they called their own. Every day, mobility pounded on the shoulders of my second oldest brother. Every day, Anh Hoàng was shoved into the ground by the weight of the vanity cases of French wives. They, with their government-clerk husbands, were touring their colony, forgetting who they were, forgetting that they had to cross oceans to move up a class.

My third oldest brother worked at a printing press. He cleaned the typeset sheets, ready to be dismantled, voided by the next day's news. He removed each block and cleaned the letters while they were still warm and cloaked in a soft scab of ink, getting his brush into the sickle moons of each "C," the surrendering arms of each "Y." In his hands were the latest export prices of rubber, profitable even though the natives had delayed the caoutchouc harvest with their malaria and dysentery. In his hands were the numbers of heads guillotined for a foolhardy assassination attempt—the lone Nationalist did not even reach the gates of the villa, but justice demanded that an example be firmly set. Anh Tùng looked down and saw only the "O" roar of a lion's mouth, the "T" branches of a tree, the "S" curve of the Mekong. Anh Tùng smiled to himself thinking how the heat of the presses was not as bad as his friends had warned him, how the taste of ink *can* be washed away by a cup of tepid tea, how he would just hide his graying fingernails in his pockets when he went courting.

Minh the Sous Chef was the undeniable success. He should have been born in the Year of the Dragon, the Old Man said. A dragon in a long white apron was an irony forever lost on the Old Man. To him, the apron was a vestment, embroidered, consecrated by the outstretched hands of his god. No blotches of chicken grease, no stench of onions, no smears of entrails and fish guts, only the color of success in the Old Man's eyes. He often speculated that Anh Minh, being the firstborn, must have inherited the full measure of his own intelligence, talent, and ambition. When men of his own age were present, the Old Man declared that Anh Minh, being *the first*, must have soaked up all that my mother's womb had to offer. I can still see these strangers licking their lips, hear their low laughter, as they all shared in the thought of my mother at fourteen, at being her first, at soaking her up. Worse, I can still hear the Old Man's words:

"Look at Stupid over there. Good thing she dried up after him. The next one would have been a girl for sure!" the Old Man says, as he spits out the thin red juices flooding his lips. The betel nut and the lime paste that he constantly chews are dissolving in the heat of his mouth. He misses the spittoon. I jump up to wipe the floor clean. It is the reason that he keeps me around. He points his chin at me, offering me up to his cohorts as he had my mother. The laughter is now high and pitched. I am six years old. I am standing in the middle of a room of men, all drunk on something cheap. I am looking at the Old Man as he is spitting more red in my direction. The warm liquid lands partly in the brass pot and partly on my bare feet. I am six years old, and I am looking up at this man's face. I smile at him because I, a child, cannot understand what he is saying to me.

The last time I saw Anh Minh, he was in the garden behind the Governor-General's house with a crew of his strongest men, beating buckets of egg whites and shovels of white sugar in oversized copper bowls. Worktables had been set up just steps away from the door to the kitchen. On a night like this, Anh Minh knew that it was better to labor under the open sky. A breeze might blow through, and the leaves on the branches overhead would fan his men as they worked. On a night like this, the kitchen fans—giant star anises suspended from the ceilings—did little to lessen the heat coming from the ovens. If they had stayed inside, the egg whites, my brother knew, would have cooked solid. He had seen it happen to French chefs, newly arrived, who had no idea what can happen in the kitchens of Vietnam. The egg whites hit the side of the bowl, the wire whisk plunges in, and before the steady stream of sugar can be added, the whites are heavy and scrambled, a calf's brain shattered into useless lumps. In comparison, the garden was an oasis but still far from the ideal temperature for beating air into the whites until they expanded, pillowed, and became unrecognizable. Anh Minh compensated by setting each fire-colored bowl in a tray of chipped ice, a fortune disappearing before our eyes. Except for the "whoosh whoosh" of air

63

whisked by taut forearms, there was silence. Sweat beads descended from necks, arms, and hands and collected in the bowls. Their salt, like the copper and the ice, would help the mixture take its shape.

Sixty-two guests were expected that night at Madame's birthday dinner. One hundred twenty-four turban-shaped islands of meringue, criss-crossed by fine lines of caramelized sugar, would bob two by two in crystal bowls brimming with chilled *sabayon* sauce. Anh Minh claimed that this was the one dish that proved that old Chaboux had been worthy of the chef's toque. His replacement, Chef Blériot, must have agreed, as this was the one recipe from the former regime that he followed without change. Even though it was highly unorthodox, said Anh Minh, a clear deviation from the classic recipe for *oeufs à la neige*. "Eggs in the snow," Anh Minh had translated for me, like it was the first line of a poem. He, like Chef Blériot, refused to condemn old Chaboux's actions. "Poor Chaboux," Anh Minh said, "no one had been more surprised by Madame's command than he."

After all, "As if in France!" was Madame's unflinching rallying cry, one that had never failed to set old Chaboux's Gallic heart pounding. "The Governor-General's household has the duty to maintain itself with dignity and distinction. Everything here should be *as if in France!*" Madame commanded, failing to note that in France she would have only three instead of fifteen to serve her household needs. "As if in France!" ended each sharp command, a punctuation that Madame inserted for our benefit. Even the oldest member of the household staff, the gardener's helper with his stooped back and his moss-grown tongue, could mimic it. Every afternoon when Madame donned her tennis whites and departed for the club, we would let it slip from our lips, an all-purpose complaint, a well-aimed insult, a bitter-filled expletive. Madame's phrase had so many meanings, and we amused ourselves by using them all. Accompanied by our laughter, "As if in France!" barreled through the house, hid itself inside closets, slept behind curtains, until Madame returned, her face flushed from lobbing a little ball to and fro, to reclaim the words as her own. "As if in France!" lost its power over Madame, though, when the topic at hand was her growing distrust of cows' milk. "In this tropical heat," Madame had been told, "it is not unheard of for the milk to spoil as it is leaving the beast's sweaty udder."

"Imagine living among a people who have tasted only mother's milk," the chauffeur overheard Madame exclaiming as she dictated a letter. "Before we arrived," Madame continued, "what the Indochinese called 'milk' was only water poured over crushed dried soybeans!" Madame knew that this would set her sister's head shaking, thinking of how fortunate she was to have married a man with no ambition. Madame ended her letter, which was to be typed by her secretary onto the

Governor-General's official stationery, with a few parting lines about the managerial difficulties of overseeing a household staff of fifteen. This, explained the chauffeur, was just in case her sister lingered too long on such unenlightened thoughts.

Madame's orders to old Chaboux were clear. The *crème anglaise*, the surrogate snow, a concoction of egg yolks, sugar, and milk, had to be replaced. For her birthday dinner, Madame wanted her eggs in the snow, but she would not have any of Indochina's milk in the snow. "Simply too much of a risk," she said. "I've heard that the Nationalists have been feeding the cows here a weed so noxious that the milk, if consumed in sufficient amounts, would turn a perfectly healthy woman barren." The "woman" that Madame and old Chaboux had in their minds was, of course, French. Madame added this piece of unsolicited horror and bodily affront to Mother France just in case old Chaboux dared to balk at his task. It was all up to him. He was the intrepid explorer dispatched to honor and to preserve the sanctity of Madame and all Mesdames who would receive the embossed dinner invitations. In a country hovering at the edge of the equator, in a kitchen dried of the milk of his beloved bovine, this beleaguered chef had to do the impossible. Old Chaboux had to find new snow.

"*Sabayon* sauce instead of *crème anglaise!*" Anh

Minh repeated the now departed chef's dramatic solution. Every year Minh the Sous Chef's retelling of the ingredients, while guarding their exact proportions as his secret, signaled that the all-night preparation for Madame's dinner had begun. "Over the lowest possible flame, whisk egg yolks with sugar and dry white wine," my brother, standing in a makeshift kitchen lit by stars and a barely present moon, explained the recipe to me one more time, knowing all the while that this would be his final lesson, regretting that in the end it had so little meaning.

Misfortune and despair have always propped the Old Man up like walking sticks, like dutiful sons. Not his own but other people's. The Old Man built a business off of other people's last resorts and broken spirits. He delivered them to the open arms of His Savior, Jesus Christ, and, to a lesser extent, the Virgin Mother. Virgin Mother, indeed. Only men who have taken a vow of celibacy could conjure her up, a hallucination who comes to them in the votive-lit nights, who tells them to place their weary heads on her bosom, draped in chaste cloth but ample all the same. The Old Man had no patience for Her. He had felt that way from the very beginning, from the day that he was led to Saigon's Notre-Dame and told to kneel, to turn his face toward the cathedral doors and away from the woman who had to peel his small pleading fingers from her own. From that day, from the moment when he became a Catholic, She was to him an unnecessary attachment, a weak character in a story that he would otherwise come to believe.

A cathedral, even one so close to the equator, can still cause a young boy to shiver. In a country with only two seasons, sun and rain, a cold day if it arrives can rarely survive. The houses of his Lord are a favorite resting place, where the cold is hoarded and stored away in the curtained confessionals, the cathedral's stone floor, the marble Christ, crucified and veined, the gold chalices, icier than their burnished colors would imply. In a cathedral, shuddering, a young boy, who would one day become the Old Man, spent his youth advancing from choirboy to altar boy to seminarian, dutifully living the life that the holy fathers had chosen for him. But when it came time for his ordination, the young man announced that the Virgin Mother had come to him and told him to take a wife. The holy fathers were stunned. Many wondered why She had never said the same to them. The young man had lied, but his words were precise. He wanted not just a woman but a wife. After all, he could join the priesthood and still have a woman. Some of the holy fathers had two or three. It seemed that their vow of celibacy made many women feel utterly at ease. Baring their souls led to the baring of other things as well. When I am feeling generous, I tell myself that he wanted a wife because he wanted something to call his own. More accurately, he wanted something he could own, property that could multiply, increase in worth every nine months. The holy fathers walked away, heads bowed, claiming that they knew nothing about such things.

The young man went to see a matchmaker who told him not to worry. Even a man with no money, property, or a family name could procure a wife. Being a man is already worth enough, he was told, and the rest are extras, baubles for the lucky few. "The trick," said the matchmaker, "is to find a girl worth less than you." For the young man, that meant she had to be worth nothing at all. Sadly, there were a number of suitable candidates. The young man walked away from the holy fathers and from a life garbed in tunicles, chasubles, palliums, and miters, but he did not go far. He found a small house on the outskirts of the city, a good distance from the cathedral but still close enough to hear its carillon bells. He chose it for its location. In order for his new business to thrive, he needed to be within walking distance of poverty. Abject was not required. That would be overdoing it. He needed just a paid-on-Saturday, broke-by-Sunday kind of poverty, a deep-rooted not-going-anywhere-soon kind of insolvency. Given his particular area of expertise, he also needed to find a neglected, preferably withering, outpost of his Lord. The young man soon found all that he was looking for. He walked into a wood-framed church equipped with a native priest and little else and offered to keep that congregation alive, for a fee of course, paid upon delivery, per newly bowed head. Father Vincente, né Vũ, who had celebrated Mass only as a lonely affair between himself and the occasional visiting seminarians, agreed and did not bother to ask how.

The young man was not brilliant. He was not even clever. He was gifted, though, with a singular insight: "Where there is gambling, there is faith." This was the gem that his god had unwittingly placed inside his mouth. He, in turn, devised a ritual that made it easier for the two to meet: late-night card games at his house and early-morning prayers at His house. When the gamblers won, they prayed, and the newly converted always won at least once or twice, a hook lodged painlessly inside their cheeks. When the gamblers lost, they prayed. Either way, the young man—as he always got a healthy cut of the pot in addition to the usual per-head fee from Father Vincente—and to a lesser extent the Catholic Church, won. Would Father Vincente have fainted or at least blushed if he had known? But why ask questions when the diocese rewarded him for the steady rate of conversions, the monthly baptismals that multiplied his parishioners, giving him finally a flock.

As the years went by, there developed, however, an increasingly rapid migration from pew to grave in Father Vincente's church. Even Father Vincente acknowledged the irony. "No sooner did they come looking for salvation than salvation came looking for them" became the signature line in his otherwise unremarkable delivery of the last rites. With each passing year Father Vincente noted with growing regret that the young man, who was now the Old Man, could no longer deliver to him that segment of the population that had been the life-blood of the church. Young men, Father Vincente had been pleased to observe, had a tendency to marry and therefore could contribute wives and offspring to the congregation. Father Vincente eventually understood that the Old Man's appeal was limited to men his own age. "You have to know your customers," the Old Man said with a shrug, his speech slurring, words slipping off his spirits-slick tongue. Father Vincente held his breath and turned his face the other way.

The last time I saw Anh Minh, he closed his eyes and said that he had seen everything, my foolish grin, the stream of red, the open mouths, the white cloth limp in my hand. He dropped his head and said he could save me then but not now. He confirmed for me what I had always suspected. Anh Minh had a weakness for small animals. He could never cut a chicken's neck and hold it over a bowl and watch the blood drain. He understood life through the parables of his chosen trade, and what he witnessed fourteen years ago in the Old Man's house was a blade being sharpened. What he felt shook his body.

On the day when my six-year-old feet bore stains

of red, Anh Minh convinced the Old Man that within a few years he would be able to secure a position for me in the Governor-General's kitchen. "Even the lowest-paid helpers get two meals a day and a chance to wear the long white apron someday," Anh Minh said. "But the competition is stiff," he told the Old Man. "Now, every kid who waits outside the back gate knows a mouthful of French, has worked in a plantation kitchen, has a distant cousin or two within the ranks of the household staff. Now is the time to get started."

"He could first get some experience by helping Má out with her business. I mean with her chores in the kitchen. Of course, Má's kitchen is nothing like the Governor-General's," Anh Minh quickly added, upon seeing the glint that had cracked open the Old Man's eyes. "At most, he could learn from Má how to hold a knife, how to chop and peel, work his way around a hot stove. He'll learn the finer points when he comes to work with me. Má can just get him started with the basics," Anh Minh proposed, hoping that our mother was not listening behind the closed door, hoping that her heart was still whole. No matter how many steamed packets of rice she sold, my brother knew that the Old Man would never tolerate it being called a "business." That was *his* word. Anh Minh deferred to him even though he knew that it was the proceeds from our mother's kitchen that kept rice on our table, that the Old Man's income only kept his bottles from going dry. "Can't be helped," the Old Man had said. "A necessary business expense," he claimed.

"As for the French, I can teach him enough to impress Monsieur and Madame, but I'd have to begin now. Every day once he's done with Má, he can come to the Governor-General's. I'll teach him a few words during my breaks. Anyway, it'll do him good to see how a *real* kitchen is run."

A smile appeared on the Old Man's face, like a sudden blistering of the skin. Again, his oldest son was making him proud. Minh the Sous Chef was thinking like a man, thinking of how to turn a profit from a loss, the Old Man thought. He was right. Anh Minh was thinking like a man, thinking of how to hide away a pain he could not bear. Anh Minh sent his words swirling through the Old Man's house, searching. They found for me there a room that the Old Man never deigned to enter, the only room in the house with a dirt floor. "Good enough for her," the Old Man had said, casting a sideways glance at my mother. The gesture had the same careless force as the spittle that shot from his mouth.

The last time I saw my oldest brother, he revealed to me the heroic deeds of his spent words, how they foretold the story of my life, kitchen-bound and adrift at sea. "I have given you everything," Anh Minh said, "and you have wasted it."

Both of us were raised by the Old Man, after all. Anh Minh, like me, was always looking for something more, and he had found it, I am afraid, in the darkness of the Governor-General's kitchen. Anh Minh, what did you think you would find there? Chef Blériot and Madame's secretary, a bit of fallen cleavage, a knot of lace underclothing wrapped around her bloodless ankles, a bit of sex to leverage into something more? My dear brother, I did not waste the life that you gave me. I traded it away for Blériot's lips counting down the notches of my spine, parting at the small of my back, for my fingers wrapped inside the locks of his hair, guiding his mouth as it arched my back, as he brought us both heavenward without shame, as he made me cry "Mercy, please have mercy!"

The last time I saw Anh Minh, he stood with a fingernail moon at his back, with his heart in his throat. "How can I save you now?" he asked, repeating the only words that he had left for me that night.

CHAPTER 6

While we were aboard the *Niobe*, laboring the distance between Saigon and Marseilles, Bão told me about a sailor who came from a family of basket weavers going back many generations. In the beginning their ancestors had tried to sow their land with rice shoots, but the water hyacinths that grew first in those flooded fields refused to give up their claim. For three seasons, the family struggled and the water hyacinths won. When they looked around them, these people felt mocked, cursed even, because all of the neighboring plots were a rich rice-paddy green. Desperate and starving, the sailor's ancestors said so many prayers to their ancestors that finally they received a response. The matriarch of the family one morning announced that she had had a vision, which was particularly unexpected as she had been blind from birth. She said that from now on they would harvest the water hyacinths and dry their stalks for weaving baskets. According to Bão, she even showed them how, devising a pattern so intricate and tight that the baskets held water. Their neighbors thought them very useful and gladly traded some rice for a basket or two. In this way, the family no longer starved. In fact, by the time that the boy who would become the sailor was born, his family knew of no other way to make a living.

On his fifteenth birthday, the boy stopped his weaving and announced that he would travel to the next village over. When his family asked him why, he said, "Just to see." It was the anniversary of his birth and he was the oldest son, so his family packed him some rice, enough for the four-day journey to the next village over. Eight days later, the boy returned to his family's house, surrounded by water hyacinths in full purple bloom, and he told his family that he wanted to move to the next village over. When they asked him how he would survive, he said he would take some water hyacinth cuttings with him and begin a weaving business of his own. Four days away is not so far, and he *was* the oldest son. The following day the boy departed his family's land with a basket filled with cuttings, poised upon his right shoulder. With each forward stride, he left behind the impression of a slightly tipping scale.

"Can you guess what happened when he got to the next village?" Bão asked.

"He forgot the pattern," I answered.

"No, you ass! A person can't forget a skill like basket weaving because he moves from one village to another."

"Oh."

Bão's words can often be unkind, but I did not mind because he himself was never that way. That is not an implausible thing. Believe me, I am the one who knew him, shared the darkness of sleep with him, heard him humming during the hours before light. So I am the one, really the only one, who is qualified to say what is implausible about Bão.

"Come on, try again," he beckoned.

"The basket weaver didn't have any land," I guessed.

"No, he wasn't the village idiot like you. He bartered his labor during the rice harvesting season for the right to work on a small parcel of his neighbor's land."

"Just tell me then, Bão."

"No water hyacinths!"

"What?"

"No . . . water . . . hyacinths!" Bão repeated, as if the pauses, the added silence between his words, could also confer meaning.

According to Bão, the family's cuttings would not take to the new land, even though the field was suitably waterlogged and growing conditions were in all other ways favorable. The basket weaver had to pull the cuttings from the mud and the water and replant the plot with a local variety, which soon flourished under his care. He harvested them and dried them, but when he went to weave them, they broke apart in his hands. When the next growing season came along, the basket weaver brought his

77

family's water hyacinth cuttings to the next, next village over and attempted to plant them in another small parcel of land. Again, there was not even a tiny shoot. Again, he tried the local variety, but the stalks proved brittle or, worse, they would hold the pattern of the weave only until he was done, and then they pulled themselves apart. The basket weaver, Bão said, continued his travel from village to village, hugging along the southern coast of Vietnam, only to find that there was not one place where his family's water hyacinth cuttings would grow. Exhausted and literally running out of land, the man ended up at sea.

"There must be another place," the basket weaver said to Bão after weeks and weeks at sea.

"I told him to try Holland!" Bão said, evidently proud of himself for ending the weaver's journey and his story with such practical advice. That, for Bão, was of course the point of telling the basket weaver's story. No matter who else may be present, Bão was the hero in all of his stories.

I think about him now usually when I am between jobs, which, granted, is often. About the basket weaver, not Bão. (Well, yes, him too.) For me, it is more than just the differences, the obvious contrast between the nature of the weaver's livelihood and mine. I am struck by how nonexportable it is, how it is an indigenous thing, requiring as it does the silt of his family's land. But this is not why I return to the basket weaver's story again and again. I keep him with me because I want to

78

know the part of his story that Bão did not tell me. What happened in the house, surrounded by water hyacinths in full purple bloom, that made him go? "Just to see" sounds to me like something Bão would make up, substituting his own vagueness for something twisting and more difficult to say. I can imagine the weaver's desire, all right, the geography of it reasonably extending to the next village over and, maybe, one or two after that. But to take one's body and willingly set it upon the open sea, this for me is not an act brought about by desire but a consequence of it, maybe.

When I first heard the weaver's story, I was twenty years old, seasick but otherwise healthy. I was a very healthy twenty-year-old man, in fact, full of sex and pride, full of these things that my brothers had exhibited before me like brave medals for wars that they had never fought. But there was a place and a time. Pride, for instance, was never worn to work. Minh the Sous Chef had taught us that. Monsieur and Madame are very sensitive to the sight of it, an eyebrow cocked too high, lips crooked in irony, shoulders pulled straight by sinews and unbroken bones. Sometimes even before the servant realizes that he is exhibiting it, Monsieur and Madame have detected it, like something alive underneath their bed. They, of course, would be the first to know. Unemployment is inevitable, so why not just get it over with now? I imagine that is their rationale for the resulting automatic dismissals. Monsieur and Madame think it is like training an animal, a dog maybe. Once we learn that certain actions have no consequences, we are useless. Our arms and legs, moved by our own free will, can no longer respond quickly enough, obediently enough, to the sound of our master's voice. Every Monsieur and Madame knows that pride carries with it danger. They think of it as a slight foaming around the mouth. Pride is, therefore, reserved for the home, if you are a Vietnamese man, a father or the oldest son. Otherwise, take it out into the street. Strut it in the alleyways, where girls hang their laundry and young men show off the pomade in their hair. That, of course, brings me to the subject of sex. Yes, sex. Why else would someone put pomade in his already greasy hair or lay bare her undergarments in the slow, baking heat of a Saigon sun?

As we all had heard from the Old Man, my brothers Tùng and Hoàng were not the brightest ones in the family, but they never needed his malicious pucker of a mouth to tell them that they were the handsomest. Young girls, our mother, the neighborhood ladies of all ages, sang songs to them, secret notes of desire hidden inside everyday greetings and pleasantries. Tùng and Hoàng have always been beautiful, but as they grew older their beauty changed from an almost girlish thing into something completely their own, a thing that hovered around them, not quite touching the still wet canvas of their skin. These two, believe me, never had to look for sex, search it out like scavengers. When we would walk the alleyways, the girls, in their rush to get noticed, hung out clothes still dripping with water, so heavy that they sagged the lines. My brothers noticed them, all right, the sheerness of their wet clothes, the way the water ran down their arms, the steam that rose from them. Tùng and Hoàng would harvest these scenes for all that they had to yield. Memories of these girls would feed them during the night, very well from what I could hear, a gruff moan for each imagined nibble and bite. But these two would not have to rely on their imagination for very long.

From the beginning the things that kept me up at night were, well, less defined. I noticed the clothesline girls, a blind man would have noticed them, but the effect for me was not the same. When I closed my eyes, their bodies melted away, leaving behind just their desires, strong, pulsating. Now *that* I could feel, and prophetic of this life that I now live, this trade that I now practice, I could taste it too. The last peaches of the season honeyed by the sun, the taste of my own salt on my fingers, it was a cross between the two. As I grew older, my desire filled itself in. It found a face and a body, not so different from that of Tùng and Hoàng's. That was the problem. I will not call it a curse because it is not. A curse is a father in name only or the tightness of Monsieur and Madame's hands around my neck even when they are not there. A curse, I remembered thinking when I first heard the basket weaver's story, was that man's boundless search or, perhaps, his steadfast belief that there existed an alternative to the specific silt of his family's land.

When I first heard the weaver's story, I was twenty years old and in love. I mean *in* love, painfully, involving every part of my body except for my head, in a way that I now suspect only a twenty-year-old man can be. Not so much a fever but a quake, a continuous tremor that made it difficult or just unnecessary to think. Talking was difficult as well. Speech was definitely one of the first things to go, as this sort of feeling can be better expressed in other ways. I had been working at the Governor-General's house for about seven years by then. He had been there for less than a month, but he arrived as the *chef de cuisine* and was, of course, French. Both things added up to a seniority beyond any of my earthly years. "So much power bestowed on someone so young!" was the refrain coursing through the Governor-General's house on the day that he arrived. "Abuse and waste," those of us within the ranks of the household staff predicted, "will soon follow." But Chef Blériot made up for his youthful appearance with a harshness of manner that surprised even us. We would have called him Napoleon, except that he defied us by being neither short nor pudgy around the waistline. No, Blériot was as commanding in his looks as in his manners. He was a remarkable specimen of French manhood, we all had to admit. His hair, "chestnut" brown, according to the chauffeur, held the beginnings of several strategic curls that would now and then fall, slightly grazing the arch of his brow, a lyrical move that impressed us in spite of ourselves. And who among us did not look a moment too long into his eyes, blue with black bursting stars inside? "Cow's milk in its immeasurable forms," said the chauffeur, "was responsible for the rest." That, however, was an open topic for debate. We in the household staff often sat and speculated upon the substance of this man. We cursed his name and blessed his body with words of our desires, all different. The gardener's helper wanted his youth. The chauffeur envied his height. Madame's secretary, we could all tell, was in need of everything that Chef Blériot had to offer. I, of course, was predisposed against him from the start. My oldest brother, after all, would have to settle for the title of Minh the Sous Chef for yet another lifetime of years.

On the day of Chef Blériot's arrival, Anh Minh sat in a corner of the kitchen, this vastness that he had called his own for two unprecedented weeks, with his hands resting on his lap. There was nothing left for him to do. The pots and pans had been scrubbed and rescrubbed and were as shiny as they could ever be. The larder had been swept and cleaned. The sous chef had already taken off the chef's toque and had had it laundered and starched. The sight of my brother sitting, bareheaded, stilled by disappointment, taught me lessons he never intended. This man, who at home was the subject of boasts and the object of praise, was here nothing. Less than nothing, he was just another servant in waiting. I am certain that the rest of the household staff remembered the expression on my brother's face, but I cannot. When I close my eyes and see him now, I see his hands. Hollow, they seem to me. Flimsy enough to be thrown from his lap by the breeze of a slamming door. By the time sorrow shows itself in the hands, it is deep and infinite, no longer a wash but an out and out drowning. This is what I have taken with me, these hands that I now periodically look for in my own. The sight of them should have put an end to the story or there should have been no story at all, but then Blériot chose such a subtle, almost forgettable beginning. How was I to know?

"Chef Blériot wants you to go with him to the market," said Anh Minh, or Minh *Still* the Sous Chef, as I had begun to call him.

"Why me?" I asked.

"He wants you to show him around, translate when necessary."

"Translate? Did you tell him I could speak French?"

"I said that you've been learning. Don't worry about it. You know more French words than

Blériot does of Vietnamese. Here that makes you a translator."

"Oh."

"Remember, just don't lie."

"What do you mean? I haven't—"

"Of course not, I only meant that if you don't know the word in French, just say so. Don't lie. They always figure it out, and then they are pissed when they do."

"Oh."

"I'm serious. There is no kidding around with this guy. Remember to call him 'Chef' Blériot and remember that what you do reflects back on me."

Anh Minh's words were always considered but often trite. This language of mirroring was overused, especially within the confines of our family. It sounded like something the Old Man would say, except his version would have a swearword at the beginning and at the end. Either way, the threat of having all my indiscretions paraded on the surface of my brother's skin was still not enough to keep me away.

"Slower, slower. Chef Blériot, please, speak slower. My French is not very good."

He smiled, a closed-mouth movement that concentrated attention in the curves of his lips. At first I saw it as a smirk, a mocking pockmark of an expression, but somewhere between the woman selling bitter melons and the blind man selling onions and garlic, I saw the curves and I saw the lips.

"How old . . . are . . . you?"

"Nineteen, twenty soon, Chef Blériot."

He smiled again. This time there was nothing that I could do. This image of him shading his blue eyes, each with a black bursting star inside, from the yellow of the early morning sun had already archived itself in me. Somewhere between the twin sisters selling mangosteens and the old woman selling whatever she had in her garden that day, I asked him the same question.

"Twenty-six," he answered.

"Oh."

"Tomorrow, you'll show me the fish market."

"Yes, tomorrow, the fish market I'll show you."

A promise sealed in the language of commerce, in a place of barter and trade.

"Sole?" Blériot asked.

"Sole," I translated.

"Catfish?"

"Catfish."

"Shark?"

"Shark."

A slow seduction, now that I think about it, amidst the fruits of the sea. But back then, well, back then there was nothing to think about. It was already impossible. Blériot, though, took his time. He was a cook, after all. For tenderness, we all know that braising is better than an open flame. At first I met him at the back gate of the Governor-General's house at five-thirty in the

86

morning. By the time we reached the central market, the vendors were just about done setting up. By the end of the first week, all the vendors knew his name, even the blind seller of onions and garlic. I told Blériot that it is not coincidence that this man sells what he does. With onions and garlic, he can protect himself from thieves, because he can always smell them walking away. A little lie makes for a good story. Blériot looked at me as if he agreed. All the market vendors also knew his position—Chef Blériot, the *chef de cuisine* at the Governor-General's house, a man who was more important to them than the Governor-General would ever be. They competed for his biweekly purchases of chicken eggs by the cartful. They saved their wormless tomatoes for him, put aside cucumbers the size of their fingers for him. They agreed to grow spinach for him. They traded their scallions for leeks grown in the central mountain region for him. They learned that he would not barter, and so they always quoted him their most optimistic price. Either he would buy or he would walk. It was the gamble they took for a chance at an easy week's profit. As for me, they had seen me before, but now they really looked at me, wondering where my allegiance lay. Whether I was the kind who would betray his own to save his Monsieur the equivalent of a couple of centimes. Whether I lived off of their blood or his money. Neither, thank you. After the third week Blériot told me to meet him at five. In the half-light of morning, everyone looks beautiful, I remembered thinking, even the twin sisters selling mangosteens. We took the half of an hour, the half of a waxing moon, and roped it around the city's still, blue streets. Intimacy, or something very close to it, was spun and webbed this way. Every week brought with it another half-hour, another sliver of the moon, till he had the entirety of a night. Naturally, the space between our bodies began to disappear. Effortlessly, we began to touch.

Men like Bão always think that *this* is when the story really begins. But there is no narrative in sex, in good sex that is. There is no beginning and there is no end, just the rub, the sting, the tickle, the white light of the here and now. That is why it is so addictive, so worth the risk. That is why men like me brave ourselves for it. It is a gamble worth taking. I brace myself for the Old Man's words, his lips sucking their marrow dry: "Where there is gambling, there is faith." Anytime that he has said anything truthful to me, I have come to regret it, because with him truth comes barbed in judgment, thick in condemnation. Truth is something strapped to a man's body before he is led to the water's edge and pushed. Yes, the Old Man was right, but not for the reasons that his sour heart attributed to me. In me, faith did flourish and, like the basket weaver, it was with faith that my story began. When I first heard the weaver's story, I did not see that we had more in common than this. No, I did not think to ask, What keeps him from returning home, to a house surrounded by water hyacinths in full purple bloom?

CHAPTER 7

Most Messieurs and Mesdames do not want to think about it. They would prefer to believe that their cooks have no bodily needs, secretions, not to mention excrement, but we all do. We are not all clean and properly sterile from head to toe. We come into their homes with our skills and our bodies, the latter a host for all the vermin and parasites that we have encountered along the way. I have seen *chefs de cuisine* who never wash their hands, never, not even after they stick their fingers into a succession of pots and suckle on them like piglets at their mother's teats. I have seen pastry chefs who think nothing of sticking a finger into their ear, giving it a good swirl, and then working the wax into their buttery disks of dough. Merely a bad habit or a purposeful violation? The answer depends on their relationship with their Monsieur and Madame. When placed in such context, my habit is not so bad. I have, of course, thought about it. The satisfaction that could be drawn from it. Saucing the meat, fortifying the soup, enriching a batch of blood orange sorbet, the possible uses are endless, undetectable. But that is an afterthought. I never do it for them. I would never waste myself in such a way. It is only a few minutes out of my day, usually in the late evening hours when all the real work has been done. The extreme cold or the usual bouts of loneliness will trigger it. I want to say it is automatic, but it is not. I have to think about it each time, consider the alternatives, decide that there are none. I want to say it brings me happiness or satisfaction, but it does not. It gives me proof that I am alive, and sometimes that is enough. I want to say that it is more complicated than this, but it is not.

Most Messieurs and Mesdames never even notice, understandable given their preference for white-gloved servants. Believe me, underneath those cotton sheaths are the things that Messieurs and Mesdames should see, fish-scale cuticles, blooming liver spots, the pink and red ridges of scars and burns, warts like a sprinkling of morning dew. Or if they do notice, they think nothing of it. Most Messieurs and Mesdames are too engrossed by the food on their plates to take a good look at the hands that prepared and served it, a common mistake, an unfortunate oversight. Those with more experience in such matters know that closer attention must be paid. And according to Anh Minh, there is no one, not even the French, with more experience in such matters than the Chinese.

When I began working in the Governor-General's kitchen, Anh Minh told me about the "official tasters" who sat by the side of the Empress Dowager of China, right next to the little dog that lapped up the spit and the phlegm that this old woman in heavy silks would occasionally cough up. The tasters were assigned to eat a small morsel from every dish before the Empress would even place her nose among their wafting flags of steam. The tasters, according to Anh Minh, were chosen based on the refinement of their palates. They were men who could see with their tongues the grit of one grain of sand left clinging inside the frizzled lips of an oyster, the char of one ember tarnishing the skin of a river trout. They could detect the absence of the sun during the growing season and the presence of uncooked blood in the chambers of bones. "Imagine," Anh Minh said, "being the first." To hear him tell it, I thought that the official tasters had coveted positions indeed. With his usual rapidfire rhythm, Anh Minh evoked for me the epic balance of flavors in the dishes consumed by these long dead mandarins. When he spoke of bitter melons steamed with the brine-plumped tongues of one hundred ducks, I saw a landscape of greens and grays. I tasted parsimony and extravagance commingled on a single plate. Anh Minh, in this way, taught me what he understood to be the most important lesson of his trade. He knew that to be a good cook I had to first envision the possibilities. I had to close my eyes and see and taste what was not there. I had to dream and discern it all on my tongue. Slowly, gradually, I was able to do just that.

Anh Minh, of course, never mentioned the casualties who were carried out of the Empress's dining pavilion every few months or so. The limp bodies of the official tasters ravaged by poison, as flavorless as a mouthful of pure mountain snow, were buried with a pair of ivory chopsticks, a token of thanks from the Empress Dowager. Only after I heard the chauffeur's version of the story did I understand that the official tasters were men condemned to die for their culinary pleasures. The Empress, the chauffeur told me, had no need for gourmands. The Empress needed warm bodies who could absorb the poison and host death in her stead. The fact that these bodies belonged to men who appreciated good food was merely incidental. In fact, it was the result of a perverse sense of goodwill exhibited by the Empress's closest advisers. It was they, according to the chauffeur, who decided that the official taster positions would be awarded only to those who possessed an uncompromising ardor for the finest of comestibles. The advisers reasoned that the pleasure that these men could milk from each bite would surely be heightened, intensified to an almost excruciating degree, by their knowledge that each taste could be their last. When told of their imminent appointments, these men ate and drank continually for days and sometimes weeks, hoping for death to come to them in the dishes of their own choosing. It rarely did.

I suppose that the moral of the story was there

all along, but it took the chauffeur's rendition to make me understand. There is a fine line between a cook and a murderer, and that line is held steady by the men of my trade. Really, the only difference between the two is that one kills to cook while the other cooks to kill. Killing is involved either way. The wringing of feathered necks, the smothering of throats still filled with animal sounds, the examples are endless. Learning how to take away life while leaving the body whole and the flesh unbruised, that is how I began my apprenticeship. It is a delicate procedure that those who do not know how call by the misnomer "slaughter." That is, believe me, too harsh and grubby a word for such a finely coordinated set of movements, as graceful as death at someone else's hands can get.

"Unfortunately, you can see with your fingertips as well as your eyes," Miss Toklas says. "Press here," she continues on anyway, showing me the precise point on the neck before quickly looking away. The pigeon squirms under my fingers, its blood pumping hard, pressing through.

"Harder! Bin, you are letting it suffer."

How does she know? I wonder.

With her face still turned the other way, Miss Toklas lowers her voice and rounds it out into a coax. "Steady yourself. Stop shaking. Keep pressing down. Harder, that is right, harder."

She sounds like my mother, I think. The words are different, but that mix of gentleness and urgent

94

prodding is undeniably the same. After my mother stopped having babies of her own, she helped other women bring theirs into the world. I often heard her voice talking them through what their bodies were still reluctant to do. "Good job! The next one will be easier. Trust me."

Without looking back, Miss Toklas walks out of the kitchen, leaving me with five more to kill. She had said "Trust me" at the beginning of our lesson as well. "If you cut off their necks, you will lose all the blood. Done *this* way, those birds will come out of the oven plumper and tastier than you can ever imagine. Exquisite!" Doubt must have never left my face because Miss Toklas again said "Trust me" before continuing on: "You will need, when dealing with a larger bird, to feed it a couple of spoonfuls of eau de vie, cognac, or a bit of sherry. In my experience, ducks prefer the taste of eau de vie the most. It improves their flavor immeasurably, and it also braces them for what is to come. It will make your task, Bin, easier in every way."

"You will need . . ." is how Miss Toklas begins all of her recipes. It is a prophecy that always comes true. "Exquisite!" is how her recipes end. While that may sound more like an assertion than a line of instruction, she means it to be just that: Now *this!* is what "exquisite" tastes like is what she wants me to learn. Miss Toklas does not believe that there is an innate ability in every one of God's creatures to recognize perfection. Assistance is sometimes required. She feels that this was especially true of the cooks who have preceded me at 27 rue de Fleurus. According to the concierge, there have been many. Assistance, Miss Toklas must have felt, was too often required with these now departed cooks. I can imagine, though, that many of them left of their own accord after Miss Toklas showed them her recipe for smothered pigeons. She insists upon the technique for the preparation of all the other varieties of birds that can be purchased live from the Paris markets. The difference in the end result, I must admit, is spectacular, but the required act is unforgivable.

I have cut many necks. That is not the problem. Even before I pulled the first one back, aiming for that slight curve that forces the down to part and the skin to peek through, I had already watched my mother put a blade to many a chicken's neck. She would never cut it clean off. Her reasoning, unlike Miss Toklas's, was economical. First, my mother would nick the skin until the blood flowed. If the knife was inserted deep enough, there is a red arc that falls neatly from the notch to the awaiting bowl. A hesitant pair of hands would cause trickling and sputtering, a final messy insult to a body already sacrificed. It would also mean less congealed blood for the soup that night. Hesitancy does not complement death or hunger. Miss Toklas agrees wholeheartedly that speed and decisiveness are required. She believes that it is possible to be humane even when one is behaving brutally. This, I know, is her motto in other endeavors as well. I am fine when I have a knife in my hand, when it is the blade that delivers the *coup de grâce*. One of my favorite French phrases, I must admit. The "finishing stroke" is how it was taught to me, but I prefer the "stroke of grace." While I may never master the French language, I have learned that the true faces of its lofty expressions are often found on their most literal meanings. It is a perverse way of hiding something right in the open, very French in its contempt and cruelty for those who are not. Grace, believe me, is undoubtedly necessary when handling a knife. I can always tell a professional chef from a home cook. The knife work gives them away. There is an economy of movement coupled with a warriorlike aggressiveness that immediately identifies the chef. Such deftness is not required for the preparation of commonplace foods. When I began working at the Governor-General's, Anh Minh told me that I would have to relearn everything. "A knife in a professional kitchen is a cherished object," he said. The best ones are kept in their own canvas sheaths, locked away, and only the *chef de cuisine* has the key. There is one for every purpose, boning, skinning, disjointing, cleaving, the list goes on. It is their intended use, according to Anh Minh, that dictates their shape and the width of their blade. "A *chef de cuisine* always knows which one to use," he said. "You'll know too," he promised me. I was impressed. How could I not be? My mother had taught me to slice and chop, and I thought it was

97

an accomplishment in itself not to add my fingertip to the dish. Hers was the kind of knife that would have rusted except that it was continually in use. It was made from an indifferent material that became duller and duller with every cut. My mother always had her sharpening stone at the ready. A rebirth for the blade, she explained.

The difference, believe me, is this. With a knife, the blade is the surrogate executioner. It has no feelings and so cannot empathize with the slipping away of a life. But the fingers feel it all, the quickening of blood through the veins and arteries at the start, the faint fluttering at the end. Worse, they register the slight drop in temperature that accompanies the eventual calm. Miss Toklas is right. I can see with my fingertips as well as my eyes, and that is unfortunate, indeed.

I began with my habit. I said that it gives me proof that I am alive, but I have shared nothing but the details of the many small deaths that I have inflicted, of how many of them are required for a truly good meal. I do not mean to be coy. Who am I to hide? There is rarely anyone to notice what I have concealed or what I have left in plain sight. Though Miss Toklas, I must admit, had long ago taken me aside. I had been at the rue de Fleurus for only about a month. Of course, I was taken by surprise.

"Bin, have you been drinking?" my then new Madame wanted to know.

"No."

"Are you certain?"

"Yes."

"Have I not given you enough time? GertrudeStein and I do not mind waiting an additional quarter of an hour or so for our meals."

Yes, I nodded. It seemed appropriate for me to affirm even though Miss Toklas and I both knew that that statement was, in fact, not true.

Without taking her eyes off mine, Miss Toklas reached over and grabbed my hands. Wet from the breakfast dishes that I had immediately started to wash upon hearing her footsteps, my fingers rained all over the kitchen floor, the suds covering them dissolving in my Madame's warm hands.

"GertrudeStein and I tasted—"

"No—" I blurted out.

"Bin, I know what goes into my mouth," Miss Toklas interrupted what would have been my well-worn speech about a broken glass, an uncooked steak, or an unwashed mixing spoon. I never know which excuse I will use until it comes out of my mouth, slow and unconvincing. "Next time, Bin, you need to bandage them. Do you understand?"

"Yes," I replied.

My hands were still in hers, her blood pumping through. Miss Toklas, satisfied, released them. I held my hands behind my back. She wiped hers off on a dishtowel hanging from a nearby peg. She put her right hand into the pocket of her skirt and pulled out a roll of cotton gauze. "This is enough," she said.

"Enough," I repeated.

Again, Miss Toklas's words may have sounded like a suggestion, but they were a line of instruction, a warning even. I knew what she and GertrudeStein thought. They thought I drank, that I could not hold my liquor, that I was sloppy because of it. When I was inebriated and in their kitchen, a sort of knife fight with myself, they imagined, ensued, and they had tasted the aftermath.

In the years that we have been together since then, I have found that my Mesdames are often right and wrong. I am comforted by that and, in turn, am comforted by them. I have felt that way from the very beginning. I never did blink an eye, not even after I saw that 27 rue de Fleurus had a Madame and a Madame and not a Monsieur in sight. Though I know that for the concierge, GertrudeStein qualifies for that position. Either way, my Mesdames cohabitate in a state of grace. They both love GertrudeStein. Better, they are both *in* love with GertrudeStein. Miss Toklas fusses over her Lovey, and her Lovey lets her. GertrudeStein feeds on affection, and Miss Toklas ensures that she never hungers. In exchange, in the fairest of trades Miss Toklas has the satisfaction of being GertrudeStein's only one. No man's god can tell me that *that* is wrong. A kiss freely given is a wonder to watch, even if it is being seen through the slit of a partially closed door.

I must admit that at first I was curious. I never once questioned the substance of their love, but I did want to know whether their lovemaking was, well, the same. Yes and no. GertrudeStein is a boy, fifteen years of age to be exact, in her greediness. Miss Toklas gives a good chase, not literally of course. Remember my Mesdames were both in their fifties by the time I found them. For Miss Toklas, the hide-and-seek is all accomplished with her eyes. They retreat and are demure, charge and then acquiesce, close and give in. What comes next, I do not have to watch because I hear it. Every night, I hear it. Heat, believe me, has a distinctive sound. My Mesdames are very regular in all aspects of their domestic life. Since coming to 27 rue de Fleurus, I rarely go to bed cold anymore, though that may have less to do with my Mesdames' exploits and more to do with the electric radiators that they have installed. The radiators are smelly but warm, like too many of the men that I have been with. Humorous and true, sad all the same. As for being lonely, it will take more than electricity or my Mesdames to keep me from feeling that way. It will take a fire burning inside. The extreme cold or the usual bouts of loneliness will trigger my habit. I do not remember what happens next. I have a memory of it only from the first time:

I am nine and I am cutting scallions into little O's, green tips meeting the blade, sending it swiftly toward the pale rooted ends. There are five more bunches to go. My fingers, face, hair, stinking of raw scallions, all in exchange for my mother humming a tune that has no ending. I think this is an even trade. I have done this before and have often felt the slip of the knife as it is thrown off its course by the pungent slick that coats the inside of the O's. I grip the bunch with tighter fingers. I secure the cleaver's handle with my thumb. My mother is humming at a small piece of pork that will make the bowl of scallions into a feast. She is humming, and I think that I am hearing birds. I look up just to be sure, and I thread silver into my fingertips for the first time. Silver is threading my skin. Weightlessness overtakes me moments before my vision clears, my throat unclogs, and my body begins to understand that silver is threading my skin. I am floating away, and a sea of red washes me back. I shove my fingers into my shirt. I look to see whether the blood has dripped into and spoiled the bowl of O's. No, but without warning my instinct and my hunger give way, dislodged by something newer, stronger. A spiral swims away from the red mud seas and grows broader and hotter, and I cannot stop it. I cannot stop it.

My mother looks up and sees the color of my shirt, a color that is getting deeper and truer as I stand there looking down at my swaddled hand. She takes off her blouse and wraps it in tight circles around my fingers. Her eyes search for the contents of a shallow bowl, perched on the family altar that the Old Man allows her, a bowl that gathers dead flies and clumps of dust held together by kitchen grease. She tells me to sit down on the ground. Put the whole of my weight on top of that hand. She walks over to the altar, reaches inside the bowl, and takes out a small lime, a daughter's offering to the memory of a father and a mother whom she had not seen since she was fourteen. "No one wants a lime when they are dead," she apologizes every day to them. "Oranges, I know, are much preferred," she says. "They can be eaten alone. Sweet is good enough on its own. Sour requires salt and chili peppers, and I have none of that to spare." She rolls the lime on the table. Each rotation smashes the pulp inside. She does this until she feels the hardness of the fruit give way, sink into itself, drown in its own juices. A quick cut across its slackened belly, and she is crossing the kitchen with the halves still facing each other in the palm of her hand. She unwinds her blouse and sees that it will never be the same. Blood, she knows, changes everything. I see there on my fingertips a landscape that would become as familiar to me as the way home. She sits down and wraps herself around me, pressing my stooped back into herself. With one hand, she holds my fingers together. With the other, she squeezes the juice of the lime onto my fingertips. "Fire! Fire!" I yell. She blows them out and begins to hum a tune. My fingertips heal, despite the threat of rust on her knife.

Again lime juice has bleached the edges. Blood has drained, leaving rows of white cliffs flanking the sides of mud red seas. I look down and am amazed that even this landscape is dull compared to where I have just been. I remember, yes, a caress, a slight sensation, and when my hands are shaking it feels like a tickle. In the beginning I preferred the blade to be newly sharpened, licked against a stone until sparks flew, white and blue. Now I know that such delicacy would only deny me that part that I savor most, the throbbing of flesh compromised, meeting and mending. And sometimes when it is deep enough, there is an ache that fools my heart. Tricks it into a false memory of love lost to a wide, open sea. I say to myself, "Ah, this reminds me of you."

CHAPTER 8

Twenty-four figs, so ripe that their skins are split.
A bottle of dry port wine.
One duck.
Twelve hours.

I make a mental list of the ingredients for the dinner that I will cook and that you and someone else will eat. I was expecting a much larger party. Your French, though, was clear, and even I could see that your garret would not hold more than two or three comfortably for a seated dinner. I had pictured at least six or eight in total, all of them young, all of them male, a smaller cross section, perhaps, of those who congregate around GertrudeStein during the Saturday teas. Tall saplings crowding around an earthy patch, they always seem to me. Of course, I *notice* them. They are my weekly bonus, after all. If I had known, I would have agreed to work for these Mesdames for free. Money, I know, is not everything. Lust is an entirely different story. Thankfully, my Mesdames provide me with a steady supply. GertrudeStein and Miss Toklas prefer each other first and second, and then they prefer their Messieurs, young and American. I would have never guessed that these two ladies, so uncompromisingly past their prime, could surround themselves with such glory. Some are broad-shouldered, the angularity of youth barely contained by a well-tailored suit. Their hands appear to crush all that they grasp, but in place of the expected coarseness is a fluted plate, a shivery disk of eggshell white, bearing tender sweets. Some have lips that have yet to lose their childish pouts, pink and demanding, lush as they kiss with open mouths the rims of china teacups.

The figs and the port I will place in an earthenware jug "to get to know each other," as my oldest brother would say. Anh Minh, though, did not teach me this recipe. He has never even seen fresh figs. He has never walked the markets of Marseilles and counted the last centimes in his pockets. He has never had to learn that in that city figs, oranges, and dates are cheaper than bread. That hunger is magnified by a steady diet of sour and sweet. That a man can thirst for a bit of meat, a stomach-calming slab of savory. He has never dipped a handful of orange peels into the sea and licked away a soothing slick of salt. He has never met a stranger's glance dead-on, followed him to his hotel room, worked there in the dark. Anh Minh has also never dined on a meal costing twenty whole francs, exorbitant even if the menu boasted in a curvaceous hand of roast duck with figs and port wine, exorbitant and foolish even if I did eat my weight in bread, sopping up flavors that the dishes did not know that they had to offer. The remaining five francs, all that was left of my night's labor, sat in my hands and bemoaned the loss. I had emptied my pockets to line my stomach, relinquished my body to keep it alive, nourished my hunger, famished my soul.

"Robbing Peter to pay Paul," the Old Man clucks, like an old biddy, an old Catholic biddy at that. As he aged, the Old Man became more womanish or rather just less of a man. His skin came loose. It hung from his bones, giving him a deflated, soft look. He wore his thinning white hair in a small bun at the nape of his neck. He was prone to sudden attacks, which made him clutch his chest as if he were a breathless girl. He wore his rosary there like freshly cut blooms on a silken cord. "You are still the same idiot that your mother gave birth to! Your oldest brother would have taken that twenty-five francs and bought himself a decent suit, a place to sleep for the night, *and* he would have gotten himself a real job by now," the Old Man reminds me. Age and now the afterlife have had, regrettably, no effect on his feelings toward me.

"Robbing?" That is not the word, Old Man, that I would use to describe what I did that night with Peter or Paul or whatever his name was. Shall I describe it to you in detail, from the café where we met, to the money that he stuffed in the pocket of my pants before shoving me out of his hotel room? That, Old Man, should return you to your grave, the only safe place for you now, the only place where my shame cannot find you.

Twelve hours will be sufficient for a long and productive meeting. By then the figs will be plump with wine, and the wine will be glistening with the honey flowing from the fruit. The port is then ready to be poured onto the duck, which should sit in a clay dish, the insides of which have darkened from years of sustained use, preferably for the sole purpose of roasting ducks in port wine. Such a vessel, I have heard, requires no soap in its washing. Only water is needed. The residues have to be removed but not the flavors, forged as they are by heat and habit. The duck is then placed in a hot oven for one hour and basted, every ten minutes or so, with spoonfuls of port that have grown heavy with drippings and concentrated sugars. Before the wine reduces to nothingness, the figs are added, and just enough stock to evaporate and moisten the heat in the final moments of cooking.

Rice, coated with butter, threaded through with silver-green sage, will serve as a fine accompaniment. "Indeed, a fine accompaniment," Anh Minh would surely concur, offering as he always does reinforcement and congratulations for a lesson well learned. Anh Minh had taught me that rice, for the French, is never worthy of a solo. "Remember, it is never served alone and rarely is it plain," he had cautioned. Butter sauces, saffron and peas, onions, truffles and creams, all deserving, deem the French, to share in their occasional bed of rice. All are meddlers and aggressors, and, yet, the French are surprised by the spoilage and ruin that so quickly ensue. Prepared with only water, first as liquid and then steam, rice will keep for days, a lesson I never had to learn. Rice left from dinner becomes breakfast. Rice left from breakfast, though rare, as hunger is sparked by the rising sun, becomes lunch. As Anh Minh would say, "No reason to repeat after me, just open up your mouth and learn." Rice never remains the same. If I leave the pot uncovered, there is a conversion of textures, a layer of chewiness and a crunch, insulating a pocket of softness, hidden inside like an endearing character flaw or a sentimental heart. But if I cover it with a plate right after it cools, if the night air sags with moisture and rain, if there is not enough left to call a meal, then its fate is sealed. A pot of water is added the next day, and the rice is cooked again in its own starchy soup until each kernel expands, splitting itself in half, generously expanding its volume. What begins as a small bowl can now easily fill at least four. The spectacle fools the eyes but rarely the stomach, as the latter is always the more perceptive of the two.

I have learned my lesson well. A clear consommé, braced with laurel leaves and lemons, will begin, and an almond soufflé, spiked with orange-flower water, will end the meal. No, a tart is better. Apricots, maybe, though at this time of the year they would have to be dried. Pears, perhaps, would be best. You did say to keep the menu "simple," especially the dessert. That, in fact, was about all that you said before hiring me. You handed me an envelope of what I assumed was money and two keys from the inside of your desk drawer. You informed me that you would not be here on Sunday morning to let me in and that dinner should begin no later than eight. "Please plan accordingly" then ushered me back onto the stairway. If I had your voice, I would never be so terse. I would never stop talking. Why would I if I had a voice like a warm fire, not at the crackling and popping early stages but at the moment when all becomes quiet and the embers glow, when heat appears to melt the wood? If I had your voice, I would call out your name from the street, let it pound like a heartbeat at your door, offer it to you as a song. I would never cease.

"Simple?" What an odd request, especially of a dessert. What sort of man does not hunger for richness and sweet at the end of a meal? A dessert should never be just a farewell, no matter how simple the sendoff. A dessert, if I may borrow from Bão, should deliver the same message that Serena the Soloist does at the end of all her shows.

While the curtains slowly descend, the action on stage continues nonstop. Serena continues to amaze and to satisfy.

The curtains slowly descend.

Those in attendance are mesmerized and are desperate for more.

The curtains slowly descend.

110

Suddenly, Serena is no more. But like temptation, she has not bid the audience farewell. Rather, she has alluded to what's in store in the event of an encore.

Those in attendance respond with a resounding request for more.

"Simple?" Maybe, you meant something that could be left unattended. Something that I could leave for you to serve, to apportion at just the right moment. A soufflé is most definitely out of the question. Too temperamental, a lover who dictates his own terms. A tart is better, uncomplicated, in the wrong hands even a bit rough. Like an American boy, I would imagine. I will leave it cooling in the kitchen with a small bowl of *crème fraîche* alongside. Then, once the duck has been served, I will leave your garret for the night, for a café and a glass or two of something strong, very strong, and you and your someone else will be alone at last. My departure will signal that intimacy has joined the party. Civility has called it a night. You two can now dispense with the forks, knives, and spoons. Your hands will tear at an animal whose joints will know no resistance. The sight of flesh surrendering, so willing a participant in its own transgression, will intoxicate you. Tiny seeds from heat-pregnant figs will insinuate themselves underneath your nails. You will be sure to notice and try to suck them out. You will begin with each other's fingers. You will end on your knees.

★   ★   ★

I lie to myself like no one else can. I always know what I need to hear. What else am I to do, revert to the truth and admit that I am a twenty-six-year-old man who still clings to the hope that someday his scholar-prince will come? Will hear my song floating over a misty lake, fall in love with my voice before ever laying eyes on my face. Will rescue me from my life of drudgery and labor and embrace me in the shadows of his teak pavilion. I am filled with these stories. My mother fed them to me as we worked side by side. From the time I was six until I turned twelve, banana leaves, raw sticky rice, overripe bananas that no one else would buy, and my mother's stories were the subjects of my everyday life. The leaves Má taught me to cut crosswise into three pieces. We would then soak them in water to keep them pliant. They had to drink in as much water as their veins could hold. They would need it later, when the heat would be merciless and full of rage. There was a steady rhythm to our movements that I still carry with me, a dream to lull me to sleep:

Her right hand dips into a basin of water, shaking from it a fragrant sheet of green. Her left hand skims a large bowl, where the raw rice has spent the night, cool underneath a blanket of water. She grabs a handful of grains, slowly spreading her fingers apart, letting the milky water drip and drain. She places what remains in her hand onto the middle of the leaf. I reach over and add thick slices of bananas, cut lengthwise in order to maximize the surface that is split and exposed from where their sweet juices will then flow. Each piece shows off two rows of black flecks, the distinctive markings of their tribe. "The darker the seeds," my mother says, "the riper the fruit." Her left hand returns to the bowl for a second handful of kernels, which then completely cover the bananas. Her hands join together for a brief moment and leave behind a packet of green. She slides it over to me, and I wrap it with a length of fibrous grass. The steamer will finish the task.

While my mother's hands followed a set routine, her stories never did. They were free to roam, to consider alternative routes, to invent their own ways home. Sometimes the "she" was a peasant girl bending over a bed of rice seedlings, which had yet to take root. "She" was occasionally a servant girl in the Imperial Palace, a noble face misplaced among the lowly rank and file. "She" was also a fishing village girl, who sat by the shore and darned the nets, who sang the same songs as her brothers but had never been allowed out to sea. "Home," though, was always the same, the teak pavilion and the scholar-prince, a man who was first and foremost wise and kind. His handsome looks, my mother always mentioned as something of an aside. As I got older, I thought her brief description was unsatisfactory, and I began pressing her for details about the scholar-prince. The first time I asked about him, I was eleven. My mother smiled in response and called me her "little scholar-prince." I stopped tying the packet in my hand.

"What? *I am* the scholar-prince?" I repeated, struggling to retain meaning in a fantasy turned upside down. As I sat wrapping and tying, I had never had a doubt. All this time, it was I who had the voice that would float over a misty lake, and it was always I who, in the end, got the scholar-prince, the teak pavilion, the shadow-graced embraces. I was, of course, the peasant, the servant, the fishing villager, except that in my version the "she" was undoubtedly a "he." The scholar-prince, I left as is, a man wise and kind. Though, in truth, in my version he was much more handsome than my mother could have ever imagined. My dear mother would have stopped the stories if she had known in whom I found solace and in whom I found love. So in order to hear her stories, to keep her voice in the room, I never told her that in my version I was a kitchen boy who skipped smooth shards of stone across a silent lake, that as they skimmed the water's surface they would sing. The stones landed one by one each day at the feet of a scholar-prince, who strolled the shore, contemplating the water and its relationship to the sky. At first the scholar-prince was too immersed in his own thoughts to notice, but then the stone shards began to amass, notice-ably altering, intruding upon his tranquil path. The scholar-prince interrupted his reverie and picked up a shard, and as he was about to fling it back into the lake, he noticed a single word cut into its surface. Intrigued, he examined the others and found that each bore the traces of a different word. He, being a scholar-prince, naturally recognized that they were the broken pieces of a poem. Love was the subject. He, being a man, thought it was a challenge and a game. The scholar-prince rearranged the stones and composed a response. He sent them skipping across the lake. Of course, the lake was "misty." Some things are classic and should never be changed. Mist, as I had learned from my mother's stories, allows unlikely lovers to meet and forbidden subjects to wander the land. In my stories, the lakes are in a perpetual state of mist or under heavy cover of ocean-borne fog. As the stones crossed and recrossed the lake, each one a fragment of a rippling, luminous poem, the scholar-prince fell deeply in love with the kitchen boy who was now a man, and in the end, well, the end for me is always the same.

Even with my eyes closed, I know. Emptiness lowers the temperature of any room. I breathe in deeply, searching for coffee burning inside a still warm pot, for soap or shaving lotion evaporating, a fragrant steam rising from the bare surface of skin. I roll over on my back and listen for water flowing from a tap—hot and cold each have their own rhythm—for the rustling pages of a newspaper, for the sound of steady breathing in an otherwise silent room. No, nothing but absence mouthing the same wordless tune. I open my eyes and look around me. The light of a December sun hangs, a faded gray curtain, from the windows. Bottles of wine lie on the table, tipsy from their own fumes. Russet-colored pears, half-eaten, bear the bite marks of distracted eaters. Nubs of candles sit in pools of melted wax.

I will forget that no one came to dinner last night. I will forget that we celebrated Sunday by drinking wine from each other's lips. I will forget the baptismal and the communion. Last night was freely given, I tell myself. Pleasure for pleasure is an even exchange. Lust for lust is a balanced scale.

Do not bother chiming in, Old Man. I do not have to listen to your god anymore. Sad, though, how I can always anticipate both of your condemnations, that they have become second nature to me.

In the end, I get dressed, feeling my toes sinking into the rug by the side of the bed. I put on my socks and tie the laces of my shoes. I comb my hair with my fingers and grab a pear for the walk back to my Mesdames. I put on my coat, and I feel something foreign. The breast pocket, the thing closest to my heart, is stuffed and distended.

"Well, well, well. It looks like I was right all along. Whores do become cooks on boats. You pathetic piece of shit. I knew you would amount to nothing, but I would have never guessed that you would amount to even less. For once, *you* have exceeded my expectation. My oldest son, the sous chef, and now you, the whore." The Old Man, being dead and thus clairvoyant, confirms my worst suspicions.

The stairwell is a shaft of dust and dying echoes. Monday, already half gone, has slept in it, has lost its memories in it. The rue de l'Odéon is a smudge of storefronts and cobblestones, a blind spot disappearing from the corners of my eyes. My pace is so quick that I am generating stares. Passersby are astonished by such a burst of speed, annoyed by such an extravagant display of energy. I am sorry, but I am late. I have no reason to linger here, I think. This street will never commit itself to me, and I will reciprocate in kind. December's overeager shadows may have already claimed the buildings on one side of the street. Those on the other side may appear to glow that much more with light. Attention to such details, though, would be wasted here. It is only a site of business, commercial and mercenary. There is nothing unusual here to see, So move along now, I think, there is nothing here to see. I head toward the direction of the Jardin du Luxembourg and toward my Mesdames, who are sure to be furious. Who made their breakfast for them this morning? A pot of coffee, a plate of corn-flour cakes, a golden tower of crumbling squares, an American recipe that Miss Toklas taught me and that she and GertrudeStein adore. Who packed the basket for their Monday-morning drive? Chicken sandwiches wrapped in wax paper packets, which immediately glow with grease, and puff pastry fritters, delicate shells for the molten apples within. Turning onto the boulevard Raspail, I slow down my gait, collect my racing heart, and reacquaint myself with the things that I know best.

CHAPTER 9

Before coming to 27 rue de Fleurus, I spent many of my Mondays here, especially when there were no help-wanteds to reply to, no interviews to be rejected from, no benches available in the sun-starved parks of this city. When the moon had risen, when a drink or two had gone down, I would often find myself here as well. I would measure the distance down with my eyes, scan the water's surface for rocky formations, sandbars, and other bothersome obstructions. No, nothing but the moon's reflection. "What keeps you here?" I would hear a man asking. Your question, just your desire to know my answer, is what keeps me, has always been my response. I would then see him smile. I would open my eyes, and I would leave this bridge for the night.

I met him, the man on this bridge, in 1927. I have no recollection of the month. It could have been sometime in the late spring or, maybe, in the first days of autumn. What I am certain of, though, is that we met on a day when this city had the foregone appearance of a memory, as if the present had refused to go to work that day and said that the past would have to do. There was a mist rising from the Seine, and as water in all of its forms is inclined to do it softened and curved the city's angles and lines. The woolen sky, hanging low, dampened all the colors that the Parisians had to offer, robbing them of their carefully coordinated defenses against the gloom. A bright red scarf around a man's neck became a rusty coil. A pink veil on a young girl's hat disappeared into a haze of exhaust and smoke. On a day like that, I know that my Madame and Madame would have requested a stew. No, an organ meat of some kind. Roast veal kidneys, braised sweetbreads, sautéed mutton livers, something from deep inside to warm up *their* insides would have been their rationale. On the day that I met the man on the bridge, though, I was still many days and two years away from finding my Madame and Madame. This is the first Monday since coming to the rue de Fleurus that I have been back here, hands on the railing, face turned to the river. My days, after all, now belong to two American ladies, and they keep me busy with the culinary bustle that is the foundation of a continually entertaining household. Rectangular folds of puff pastry dough, circles of *pâte brisée*, bowls of heavy cream whipped with and without sugar, fresh fruit purées, fondant flowers and chocolate leaves, these are the basic components of sweetness that fill my days and someone else's mouth. Believe me, I had every intention of returning to them today, of fulfilling these beginning-of-the-workweek functions for them. But on this Monday, half-wasted, the boulevard Raspail took me here instead. The streets of this city are alive, I have always thought. They know better than I where I need to be, or in this instance who I need to see.

"Do I know you, Monsieur?"

"Let's say yes, and that way we can immediately call each other *bạn*," said the man who took his eyes from the Seine to address mine. He had on a black suit, coarse in fabric, too large for his frame, and many years out of fashion, that is, if there was ever a time in this city when such a suit was considered *à la mode*. Even if his last word had not confirmed it, that suit of his would have. He was undeniably Vietnamese.

"*Bạn?* Yes, why not?" I said, switching into the language that I now knew we shared. "Well, friend, are you lost or are you thinking? In my experience, when a person stands on a bridge, it usually means one or the other."

"'Am I lost or am I thinking?' That, friend, is a question worthy of a philosopher," the man on the bridge replied. "I believe the answer is . . . I am thinking about being lost."

"An answer also worthy of a philosopher," I said.

When some men smile, the skin on their face tightens, stretches to cover their cheekbones. His gave him the appearance of flesh underneath the skin. It filled in the hollows of his cheeks, brought

121

out a face from some other time. Not that he appeared old otherwise. Rather the opposite. He appeared without age, I thought, when I first walked by him. Handsome too, I noted, as I turned around and headed back to where he stood.

"Are you a student?" I asked.

"No."

"Oh."

"Guess again," he said.

Ah, a game. Why am I always drawn, I thought, to men who play games?

"Friend, I would not even know where to begin," I said. "You do not have enough bulk on your body to be rich, I know that much."

"A fine start. Please go on."

"I would guess that you have not had cream or cheese for many years now. You may have had some meat but not fatty. No, definitely chewy with muscles. An animal who has worked for its life, if you know what I mean."

"A fine, fine start, friend. And if *I* were to guess, I would say that you are a cook."

I smiled.

"Cooks have a vocabulary all their own," he continued, "and I know it always comes from right here." He pointed to the place where his belly would be, if he had had one.

"You must be a cook as well, then?"

"Yes, once."

"Let me guess . . . pastries. Thin people always make good pastries."

"Remarkable," he said looking at me admiringly.
"Yes, I made 'pies.'"

"What?"

"'Pies.' It's the English word for *tartes*."

"Oh."

"Assistant cook in the 'pie' bakery of a five-star hotel, under the command of a five-star *chef de cuisine*," he added, mocking a military salute and stance.

"Here, in the city?"

"No, in another city."

"Oh, of course! Forgive me, friend, I am slow when it comes to such details. A city that eats 'pies' must be a city that speaks English. You must have gotten paid well," I said, looking at him in a somewhat refurbished light. A man with savings, I thought.

"Paid well? I was paid very well, if you think paper is an even exchange for the salt of your labor or that—"

"Friend," I interrupted, "I am afraid you are losing me." The truth, I know, saves time, and as I had no idea how much of it I would have with the man on the bridge I thought it best to speak plainly.

"Please excuse me," he said, "the philosopher in me is talkative today. All I mean to say is that the bakery was unbelievably hot, twenty-four hours a day. We all had to wear a cloth tied around our foreheads so that our sweat wouldn't turn the pies from sweet to savory. I lost so much weight there that I thought one day I would just disappear. I had the moment all pictured in my head like the final scene of a play. 'Where's Ba?' Chef Escoffier would ask. 'There he is!' the other assistants would answer, pointing in unison to a wet spot on the floor, as the stage lights dimmed."

"Well, Ba, that's—"

"'Ba' is not my name, friend," he corrected. "That's what *they* called me."

"Oh."

"And you, friend, where do you work?"

"Everywhere," I replied. When I am telling the truth, why does it so often sound like a lie?

"Yes, I have worked there too," he said.

"Where?"

"Everywhere."

"Oh, of course. I told you I am slow."

He laughed and I joined in.

"Everywhere, hmm . . . I am beginning to think that yours is a trick question," I teased. "You are not *just* a cook, are you? You should have told me that there would be more than one right answer. How unkind!"

"That's one way of looking at it. Another is that if my question has many possible answers, then you, friend, have a much greater chance of getting it right. A partial credit—"

"Aha! A teacher."

"Yes, once."

"Come on, friend, let us play Catholic and let you be the first to confess."

124

He laughed again.

A good sign, I thought.

"The list is long," he began. "My day belongs to this bridge and to the river. Doesn't your day belong to someone?"

"No, not right now. Usually a park bench in the Jardin du Luxembourg, but it is not jealous and it is always willing to share."

"Kitchen boy, sailor, dishwasher, snow shoveler, furnace stoker, gardener, pie maker, photograph retoucher, fake Chinese souvenir painter, your basic whatever-needs-to-be-done-that-day laborer, and, my favorite by far, letter writer."

"Where do you get paid for doing that?"

"On a freighter. It was a long time ago, and I didn't do it for money. So I suppose you can add 'charitable donation giver' to my list."

"Oh," I said.

I have heard this story before, I thought.

"I helped one of the sailors find the words to describe the color of the Indian Ocean sky, and he deemed it poetic. His favorable assessment made its way to the rest of the crew, and soon I was the official letter writer for the *Latouche Tréville*," said the man on the bridge.

"What?"

"I said soon I was the official—"

"No, no what did you say the name of the freighter was?"

"The *Latouche Grandeville*. But it's been so many years now, it's difficult to say for sure."

Why a lie so early on in our game, I wondered. "How many years could it have been, friend? You look no more than twenty-five," I said.

"And you have been among the French for much too long," he replied, shaking his head. "Your ability to tell a Vietnamese's age is no longer in working order."

"Let me try again," I said. "A sailor named Bão taught me a formula. Bão said that with the French you subtract. If a Frenchman looks twenty-five, then he is really fifteen. So with us, addition is the rule. That would make you no more than thirty-five."

"I'm thirty-seven," he said, "and if I were to guess, you are twenty-four."

When Bão was not telling stories about Serena the Soloist, he was telling stories about a young Vietnamese man who had worked as a kitchen boy aboard the *Latouche Tréville*, a shipping liner that Bão had been signed up with previous to the *Niobe*. The kitchen boy, according to Bão, was well known and well liked among the crew for three things. One, he wrote letters home for the other Vietnamese sailors on board because he, unlike them, could read and write more than just their names. "No fee, even!" Bão emphasized. Imagine all the profits lost to youth and a lack of business sense! was what Bão was trying to say. Two, the kitchen boy was vague about everything except his and other people's ages. He, according to Bão, could guess a man's exact age and on a dare he could even attempt his month of birth. Three, one night when the kitchen boy did not show up for his usual letter writing appointments, Bão went to the galley and there he found him sitting on the floor. On one side of the kitchen boy was a heap of green shavings and on the other an entire crate of asparagus that he had stripped white. "He even cut the tops off of them," Bão said. "I told him to throw them all overboard before the cook saw them or his hide was going to be in the water with them. You *know* how the French are about their asparagus."

The kitchen boy shook his head no.

"Yeah, it's clear that you don't know how the French are about their asparagus!" Bão laughed.

The kitchen boy looked up at Bão with tears in his eyes.

Bão's stories tend to have an easily discernible point. Obvious and blunt are other more unkind ways of putting it. The stories he told about the young Vietnamese man, who worked as a kitchen boy aboard the *Latouche Tréville*, were meant to be broadly comic. They often were not. Sometimes, even Bão would not laugh after telling them. The young man, according to Bão, was named "Ba." I know the man on the bridge said that *that* was not his real name. Of course not. Real names, I know, are never exchanged during such encounters, but I was hoping for one all the same. I remember watching his eyes as I said Bão's name. Not a

127

blink, a dart, a dive, nothing but the calmness that favors the eyes of old Buddhist monks or babies after they have been well fed. Only the babies have to be well fed, not the monks. With their lifetime vow of poverty and their begging bowls, old Buddhist monks have long ago grown immune to the effects of a truly good meal. Babies are just beginning their lifetime of addiction. When I think now about the man on the bridge, I waver. Most of the time I am certain, and there are times when I think, No, he was just a man like all the others.

"I left Vietnam when I was twenty-two," said the man whose eyes were again back on the Seine. "I haven't been back since." His voice trailed off, his words taking a quiet leap into the water below.

At a moment like this, silence was the only appropriate rejoinder I knew. Time, in deference to its reflection, to the spiraling sadness that accompanies its consideration, had stopped, taken a breath, and was slowly beginning its journey again, while we stood side by side, two men on a bridge that connected us to neither here nor there. Our hands rested on the railing. Our faces turned toward a river too cold to swim in. What a pity, I have always thought, water that you cannot immerse your body in, worse than a fruit that you cannot eat.

"I have always liked bridges," he suddenly resumed, as if he had heard my complaint about the

128

Seine and was offering the bridge as a consolation. "And you, friend, how about you?"

This time silence on my part told him that, even in this setting, *that* was an odd thing to say.

"Bridges belong to no one," he continued on anyway. "A bridge belongs to no one because a bridge has to belong to two parties, one on either side. There has to be an agreement, a mutual consent, otherwise it's a useless piece of wood, a wasted expanse of cement. Every bridge is, in this way," he explained, "a monument to an accord."

"You should really add 'philosopher' to your list of jobs, friend," I said.

"I apologize. It's been several years since I've been back here. I forget that this city can make me—"

"Sound like a scholar-prince," I said, finishing the sentence for him.

"What? A scholar-prince? Yes, I must sound like an old mandarin to you." He laughed.

"Something like that," I nodded.

"I want to know more about you, friend. What brought you here?" the man on the bridge asked.

"The same thing that brought you here."

"Really?" he asked, his eyes brightening.

Like firecrackers in the night, I thought.

"Yes, a boat," I said.

He laughed again.

That is a very good sign, I thought.

"A boat did bring us all here. How true. I suppose the better question is what keeps you here?"

129

"I have no family left in Vietnam," I lied.

"I see," he said, shaking his head, visibly moved by the idea of me alone.

"And you, what keeps you here?" I asked.

"You mean what kept me here. I'm just a visitor now, a tourist. And you know how this city can make a tourist feel . . . like he's a poor relation, tolerated but not necessarily welcomed."

"This city makes me feel like that, too," I said, "and I have been here for a year now."

Why, I thought, are they always visiting? Just once, a man with a Paris address, or, rather, a man with a Paris address who will invite me there afterward.

"A year is not so long, friend. I lived here for almost four," said the man on the bridge.

Wishes, believe me, are tricky things, sly even. Precise wording is required. Figurative speech should be avoided. Being specific about date, time, and location is of the utmost importance.

"Where?" I asked.

"In a room." He smiled.

"Tell me the name of the street, and I will tell you where it is located, Left Bank or Right, what arrondissement, even."

"You'll know the second street that I've lived on, but not the first one."

"Try me."

"Fine, I'll start with the easy one first. Rue des Gobelins."

"That is too easy. Thirteenth Arrondissement.

130

That is not too shabby of a neighborhood, friend."

"Wait until you hear where I first lived in this city."

"Shall we make it interesting, friend? How about a drink for the right answer? There is only one, right?"

"Friend, if you know where it's located, I'll not only buy you a drink but a dinner," he said.

Please, please if there is a god, let me know the street, I thought.

"Impasse Compoint."

"I know exactly where it is! Seventeenth Arrondissement. An alley with only three or four houses facing out onto it, right? Forgive me for saying, friend, but I did not know that anyone lived in those houses. Mostly storage places, I thought."

"Amazing, friend, amazing. Maybe, I shouldn't say anything more about myself and let *you* tell me the rest."

"I only know streets. The poorer they are, the easier, and I am sorry to say, but impasse Compoint is one of the worst off in this city."

"You definitely know it, then," he said.

The man on the bridge, true to his word, suggested a restaurant on the rue Descartes. "I know the chef there," he said.

"From where?"

"A city."

"An English one?"

"An American one."

An American restaurant. Bargelike slabs of beef and very tall glasses of cow's milk, I imagined. But when we got there, the red lantern hanging outside announced that this was no American restaurant. "Oh," I said, sighing, "I was not expecting a Chinese restaurant." Three kinds of vegetables, any three will do, just as long they are cheap and drowned in a cornstarch-thickened slurry, I thought.

"Friend, I promised you a dinner, and it will be a *good* one," he said, resting his left hand lightly on my shoulder. He opened the door with his right, and we walked in. The interior of the place immediately struck me as, well, un-Chinese. No red letterings, no gold-leaf flourishes, no spangled dragon, no shiny-bellied Buddha, all the things that the French look for in a good Chinese restaurant were here nonexistent. No wonder it is empty, I thought. How can they tell this place apart from Chez Jean, Jacques, or Jules? Look, there is even a pretty French cashier, seated just inside the front door, a strategic position that will allow her to ignore us from the very beginning, I thought.

"Mademoiselle, a table for two," said the man from the bridge, his French delivered with a pleasant touch of authority.

"Any table is fine," she responded with a short, quick sweep of her right hand.

"*Cám on*," he said, lapsing unexpectedly into Vietnamese to express his thanks.

The young woman lifted her eyes from the book

132

that she was reading and looked at us for the first time. Her eyes were brown with ripples of sand inside. Like Madame's secretary's, I thought. "You're welcome, Monsieur," she whispered, even though there was no one else in the restaurant.

We had our pick of twelve tables. Each was covered in white cloth and set with forks, knives, and porcelain soupspoons—basin-shaped and generous, they were the only things inside this restaurant that told me it was in the business of serving Chinese food. We sat down at a table, and we grinned at each other without saying a word. As if we shared a secret, I thought. On the contrary, our childlike behavior was an obvious sign, I am afraid, that neither one of us had been in a restaurant for quite a long time.

"The chef here is American?" I asked. "How did he learn how to cook Chinese food?"

"He's not American. I didn't say he was, did I? As for your second question, he learned how to cook from his mother, didn't you?"

"Oh."

"Listen, friend, the chef here tends to be shy. He may come out of the kitchen, but he won't come to the table and talk. Don't think him rude."

The cashier, who was now doubling as our waitress, handed us the menu. She said if there was anything that we wanted that was not listed, please let her know, as the chef was willing to accommodate requests. She looked at me as she said all this, but her attention, the whole of her body, I could tell was focused on him. I know the scholar-prince is handsome, Mademoiselle, but he is busy for the night, I thought.

"Please tell the chef that I'll have the salt-and-pepper shrimp with the shells still on, please, and my friend here will have the same," he ordered in a French that did not belong in the mouth of any kitchen boy.

The young woman said, "Of course," and walked toward the curtained-off entrance to the kitchen.

"Friend," I whispered, "that will be an expensive meal . . ."

"Good food is the only thing I'm willing to pay money for," he leaned in to assure me, "and, besides, the chef here won't charge us a centime." He relaxed his back into his chair. The tightness that was building up in between my shoulder blades, a reaction to impending moments of financial constraint, relaxed as well.

The curtain parted. The young woman, who was holding a tray that looked too large to fit through the narrow corridor, swung her body sideways, and she and the tray entered the room with ease. Grace, I would not call it, because such movements are not inborn, not a willowy gift bestowed upon the limbs on the day of her birth. No, movements like these are practiced daily and perfected via the occasional workplace mishaps. I looked back at the man on the bridge and saw him looking at her, well, admiringly. Surely, he is impressed by the tray and not by the body, I thought. The tray, believe me, was impressive. Most of it was taken up by a pink mound of shrimp, all with their shells and their heads still attached. A red sash at the base of their heads, their coral shining through, identified them as females, prized and very dear when available in the markets of this city. There was also a plate on either side. *Haricots verts* sautéed with garlic and ginger were in one, and watercress wilted by a flash of heat were in the other. A compote dish towered above them all, holding white rice, steam rising at topmast. A bottle balanced out the tray, its cork announcing that it was a decisive step up from the decanted bottles of house wine.

We then exchanged words, sparingly, between generous forkfuls of food. Chopsticks had not been offered, and we did not ask for them. Why waste time on the technicalities of tableware when a feast is before us? I thought.

"Morels?"

Yes, he nodded.

"Morels," I repeated. An unexpected addition, I thought. Rich with the must of forest decay, these mushrooms were hidden below the *haricots verts* until their aroma gave them away and we began searching for them with the tines of our forks.

"Butter?"

Yes, he nodded.

Salt-and-pepper shrimp finished in a glaze of browned butter! I marveled. Not out loud, of course, as my mouth was entirely too full. When melted butter is brought to the color just moments after gold, it inexplicably acquires, as Anh Minh had taught me, the taste of hazelnuts roasted over a wood-fed flame. A lesson I was now pleased to relearn.

"Watercress?"

He stopped in midbite and stared at me. Startled, I thought. My previous inquiries—they were more like requests for confirmation—may have been simply worded, but they indicated a palate that had spent time in a professional kitchen. This question, however, could have been asked by a simple kitchen boy. Watercress is unmistakable, bitter in the mouth, cooling in the body, greens that any Vietnamese could identify with his eyes closed. I know this dish well. That was not the question. The recipe is a deceptively simple one that calls for oil heated till it smokes, seasoned with nothing more than a generous sprinkling of salt and the blink of an eye. Any more contact with the heat, and the stalks turn themselves into ropes, tying themselves up in your mouth, making it impossible to swallow.

"The salt?" I asked, moving closer to the crux of my question.

Yes, he nodded. "The chef here," he said, "uses *fleur de sel* to make this dish."

I shook my head. I wanted to signal my unfamiliarity with that French phrase, but I did not want to open up my mouth, which was again too full.

"Salt flowers," he translated. "Think of it in

terms of a poem. A 'flower,' as in the first to bloom in the heat of the sun."

"Now you are a poet, too? Me, I am no good at poetry," I said, filling my mouth with another forkful of watercress. The salt petals opened themselves slowly against the roof of my mouth.

"It's sea salt . . ." he began to explain.

I threw him a look that clearly said, Do not patronize me, friend! Even if I do have half a bottle of wine and more food in me than my body has held in several months, that does not mean that I have lost all of my powers to think rationally. I knew it was not salt quarried from the earth. That would have had a more explosive reaction on the tongue, pushy, even abusive if there was but a grain past moderation.

The scholar-prince ignored my indignation and patiently resumed his explanation, taking us into a landscape of saltwater basins, rice-paddy-like when viewed from a distance. "Except that the only things growing within these watery grids are mounds of salt," he said. I closed my eyes, and I saw there snow-capped mountains in their infancy, peaks being born out of the sea. "When seawater is evaporated by the sun in this way, it leaves behind its salt, in the same way that we will leave behind our bones." I opened up my eyes and saw him a world away.

A gradual revelation of its true self, as I was beginning to learn, is the quality that sets *fleur de sel* apart from the common sea salt that waits for me

137

in most French kitchens. There is a development, a rise and fall, upon which its salinity becomes apparent, deepens, and then disappears. Think of it as a kiss in the mouth.

The young woman returned to our table and removed our empty dishes. I looked around the room for the first time since the food had arrived. Still empty but not forlorn, I thought. Empty as in private, a suitable place for a *tête-à-tête*. Though I have never understood what the head has to do with this sort of get-together. Hand to hand, mouth to mouth, maybe.

"That was not Chinese food," I said.

"I didn't say it was, did I?"

"No. But, that was not American either, and it was not—"

"Again, I made no such claims," he interrupted.

"What *do* you call it then?"

"First of all, friend, the chef here is Vietnamese. He, like me, thought that he would be a writer or a scholar someday, but after he traveled the world, life gave him something more practical to do. He now cooks here on the rue Descartes, but he will always be a traveler. He will always cook from all the places where he has been. It is his way of remembering the world."

A kiss in the mouth can become a kiss on the mouth. A hand on a shoulder can become a hand on the hips. A laugh on his lips can become a moan on mine. The moments in between these are often difficult to gauge, difficult to partition and subdivide. Time that refuses to be translated into a tangible thing, time without a number or an ordinal assigned to it, is often said to be "lost." In a city that always looks better in a memory, time lost can make the night seem eternal and full of stars. The trip from the rue Descartes to the Jardin du Luxembourg was slowed by the weight of our full bellies. Our feet shuffled underneath us, unaccustomed to the weight of a sated body. In my ear, anticipation sounded like a strong wind billowing against a taut sail, like a fire when its flames are drunk on a gust of air, less of a tone, more of a vibration that muffled his voice even though his body was only the span of one hand away from mine. When we opened our mouths to speak, the night air became scented with cinnamon. We both have been this way ever since the young woman walked over to our table and said to us, "Please, wait."

Oh no, the bill, I thought.

She disappeared behind the curtain and returned with a tart covered with a bumpy top crust. The aroma of cinnamon, unmistakable and insistent, especially when coupled with sugar and heat, surrounded us. An apple "pie," she said, placing the dessert down in the center of our table. "Compliments of the chef," she said. "He says that he's sorry that you"—her eyes addressed the scholar-prince—"must leave Paris tonight. *Bon appétit*, Messieurs."

I looked over at the curtain. It had closed. I looked over at the young woman. She was back at her post as the pretty cashier. I looked back at the man on the bridge. He was still there. But not even for the whole of the night, I thought. "There is a quiet place that I know in the Jardin du Luxembourg," I suggested, and the scholar-prince smiled.

Although we strap time to our wrists, stuff it into our pockets, hang it on our walls, a perpetually moving picture for every room of the house, it can still run away, elude and evade, and show itself again only when there are minutes remaining and there is nothing left to do except wait till there are none.

"I will walk you to the train station."

No, he shook his head. "Train stations are terrible places for good-byes."

I returned to the bridge alone.

I always do.

CHAPTER 10

"Drunk and asleep," I confess to my Mesdames. "He gave me a bottle of rum. A bonus. I drank it all and fell asleep in the park," I lie. Really, how else could I explain yesterday's absence? If I had been late by two or three hours, maybe, but my disappearance for the entire twenty-four hours of a Monday that my Madame and Madame had bought and paid for was too much even for them to ignore. They are furious but not at me. They are horrified that *you* had given me such temptations. My Mesdames both drink wine like the apostles but consider hard liquor medicinal or a cake flavoring. No other use would be respectable. GertrudeStein calls you a "cad," and Miss Toklas takes the opportunity to remind us all that a telephone, if only GertrudeStein would agree to one, could settle this matter easily. "I would ring him right now and tell him in no uncertain terms that he need not attend next Saturday's tea," Miss Toklas assures me. "Do not worry about tonight's dinner, Bin. An omelet. No. Fried eggs will be more than fine," she adds, expressing her amnesty, her charity toward me via a code that all French cooks understand and practice. A soufflé, she knows, would require the most effort. An omelet takes practice to perfect and therefore is second best. Poached is third. Fourth and least are eggs that are fried. The preparation can barely be called cooking. An insult, in fact, if there are guests expected at the table. A plate of fried eggs can inform a "guest" as no words can that an invitation to dinner has to be earned and not willed. The latter is a pet peeve of Miss Toklas, who has over the years grown to loathe those artists and writers who have had the bad manners to arrive at the studio door actually "starving." "Twenty-seven rue de Fleurus is not a canteen!" she informed GertrudeStein, after several young Hungarians with German appetites insisted on paying their respects, their visits scheduled suspiciously closer and closer to dinnertime. "GertrudeStein is not at home. In addition, she has asked me to inform you that she wants never to see you again," declared Miss Toklas, delivering the quick but cruel blow to their Hungarian pride and to their German stomachs. Sitting in the shadows of the studio, temporarily darkened in order to emphasize further the finality of the expulsion, GertrudeStein was somewhat sad to see them go. Tonight, though, there would be just my Mesdames, a meal *en famille*, as the French would say. A platter of fried eggs and a loaf of bread placed in the center of a family's table are never an insult. It is a ritual in intimacy. It is food that has no business with the outside world, food that no hired cook would ever dare serve. A family member, maybe a friend, but never a servant. I understand my Madame's gesture perfectly. With Miss Toklas on one arm and GertrudeStein on the other, I step into the circle that Miss Toklas has in that moment drawn. There is no visible trace of its outline, but I always know that it is there. I have sensed its presence in all of the households that I have been in. Sometimes it is wide and expansive, its center bulging with Monsieur, Madame, and their entire brood of *filles* and *fils*. Family pets, the Baskets and Pépés of the world, are often found sleeping inside. On occasion there is even a nanny. I have also seen garreted spaces that have room only enough for one. The Old Man's house comes to mind, and, I am afraid, there are others. I want to cry, to shed tears and preserve this moment inside their orb, but my conscience has other plans. In the face of such unexpected kindness, such undeserved clemency, guilt makes a surprise appearance, forcing open my mouth and declaring to my Mesdames that "I am the cad," even though I was unsure what a "cad" would be. "He did not do anything," I lie. "I bought the rum," I lie again.

"You are truly feeble-minded!" the Old Man is screaming in my ears. "The first fools in this city to show any faith in you, and you throw it back at them. Those hags will never trust you again. A lie to save yourself is one thing. A lie to save another is pathetic."

Shut up, Old Man! This has nothing to do with you. My Mesdames have nothing to do with you. *You* are not allowed here!

I am trying to protect the only territory I have. The battle, though, is being lost on both fronts. The sight of warmth fading from Miss Toklas's eyes is a glimpse of my own death. Suddenly, I am no longer there.

"Bin, never lie to us. GertrudeStein and I will not have such behavior in our home," Miss Toklas warns. My Madame's anger registers on her lips, a controlled tremble, which lets me know that, while I have been permitted to stay within the doors of 27 rue de Fleurus, I have been excommunicated yet again from that perfect circle that is at the center of every home.

I have no hope, so all I have are suspicions. A pocketful of money and an empty bed mean the same things everywhere. You are dismissed. Your services here are done. I cannot bear to touch my coat, even though the weather is biting and cold with a bone-aching damp that makes me wonder why humans live near water. I barely make it back to the rue de Fleurus from the butcher. Two glasses of cognac—thankfully, Miss Toklas insists on cooking with only the best—cannot take away the chill. Sleet is now streaking and smearing the city's already sullen face. I take one look outside the kitchen window, and I give in. I go to my room and take my coat off of its hanger. Warmth never ceases to tempt me. Immediately I feel the money. Rolled into a neat coil, not stacked, doubled-over, or stuffed into a rumpled glomming mass. No matter, the effect is still the same. Unsolicited, unwanted and, worse, it is ruining the otherwise clean lines of my coat. I keep it on anyway and prepare to fight off the chill. Vanity, though, always compels me to do things I would rather not. I may be a fool, I think, but there is no need for me to look like one as well. I come to my decision after repeated attempts to press down and to smooth over the awkward lump growing from the left side of my chest. A fool with an enlarged, persistent heart, I reach in and take it out, spiraled and holding its shape with the help of a short length of string. Red, an unexpected attention to detail, I think. I slip the string off and watch the money uncurl in my hand. A small piece of paper shows itself and floats to the floor. I am horrified. A receipt, a protest, a threat, a complaint, what blundering thing did I do to deserve this? I bend down, and I feel my knees popping in protest. I pick up the piece of paper, and the French is so simply written, so carefully chosen, that even I can understand it on the first read: "For next Sunday's dinner. You and I are the only guests."

I look up, instinctually, as if someone has called out my name.

I am at sea again. I am at sea again. Not the choppy, churning body that bashes open a ship's hull like a newborn's soft skull. Yes, a sapphire that a ship's bow skims and grooves. A calming blue expanse between now and Sunday.

Bão told me on two separate occasions—one was during our first night at sea and the second was during our last—that I should change my name the moment we reached French shores. He said that it was the perfect opportunity to adopt something new, something heroic, perhaps. He boasted that he had had at least seven, one for every time that he left Vietnam for the waters of the South China Sea. What kept you coming back? I wanted to know and never did ask. Bão's answers, I thought, would only make me sad, make me endure an enumerated list of all the things that I do not have. Ignorance, I have always felt, is best for a man like me. Well, not "always." I am afraid that I am beginning to remember myself in a sea of absolutes, "always, nothing, never, forever." That makes me think of the Old Man, and that makes me cringe in front of his mirrored image. I forget that I have not always felt this way. I forget that I have had to amass these words, like slivers of glass in the palm of a hand, caked blood underneath my nails. It is difficult to remain objective when I am alone in my memory. I place undue trust in my recollections of the past because there is no one here who cares to contradict me, to say in defiance, No, *that* is not true. The truth for me has become a mixture of declarations, conjectures, and allegations, which are all met by a stunning lack of opposition. (Except for the Old

Man, but, believe me, he is a liar.) In this void, I flatter myself, the truth lies. To contradict oneself is an uncomfortable posture to assume, but in this instance I am willing to retract and say, I did not *always* feel this way. In fact, I can still remember the day, the exact moment in time, when ignorance stepped forward and recommended itself to me:

My mother and I were taking the long way home. When I first began going to the marketplace with her, we would sometimes take a roundabout route back to the Old Man's house, especially when business was good and all the rice packets sold early in the day. "Shall we take The-Long-Way-Home?" she would ask, renaming the two streets that we would then add to our walk. These streets were lined with little shops, and my mother would walk by all of them with her head held high. I thought that she was proud that her money belt was filled and heavy with change, that she could walk through any doorway and buy what she wanted. So I too pulled my shoulders back and pushed my chin forward, exhibiting, mimicking, what I thought was pride. Cloth-draped tables crowded the front of each entryway, colorful come-ons for the pleasures within. I rarely wanted any of the things set out before us. I, after all, already believed that all of it could be ours, if only my mother would so please. Nothing was worth stopping for, I concluded. Otherwise why would my mother and I continue to walk on by?

It was bound to happen. I was a child and far

from a saint. One day as we passed by a display of brightly painted wooden statuettes, temptation nailed me to the ground, refused to let me go, and insisted that *this* was worth stopping for. "Look, Má! Hoàng, Tùng, and me," I shouted, pointing to the figures of three small monkeys, lined up in a row, and joined together at the base. I liked the expressions carved into their faces and, particularly, into the corners of their eyes. Anh Minh, my oldest brother was, of course, exempt from the assembly of Monkeys, or for that matter Idiots, Stupids, and Fools, all names that the Old Man saved for us, the three who followed. "I am the one with his hands over his mouth. Hoàng has his over his ears, and Tùng . . . Tùng is the one covering his eyes." I doubled over with laughter, impressed even then by my own winsome wit. "Which one are you, Má?" My mother let go of my hand and placed hers over her heart. I looked up and saw sorrow scarring her face, cratering her eyes, slashing at the grooves around her mouth, sparing nothing from the forehead that I kissed at night, not even her earlobes.

My mother had worn jade earrings when she first came to his house, but that was long ago. She remembered the gold needle heated over an open flame, the thrust, the burn, the coolness of blood and then of the jade, soothing the pain. Tender flesh. Tender flesh. She was given a matching pair for her ears. "Tenderness," she was told, would have other meanings as well, those relating to matters of the heart. But that was long ago. After she came to his house, "tenderness" would mean only her flesh tender with pain. Jade, she was told, is a living, breathing stone. It would grow old with her, chronicling the passage of time. Kept in a box, it would remain a cloudy green brew. Worn against the body, jade would gradually deepen in color, melting away its own whitish veins. Only in old age would jade reward her with its true character and hue. A thing she could look forward to, she was told. He took them from her on the day that I was born. "She will survive, but she will never give birth again," the midwife informed him. Jade in the palm of his hand cooled his rage, lessened his ire toward such shoddy goods. A slight dimple in each lobe is all that I, her lastborn, would ever see.

Sorrow preys on the unprotected openings, the eyes, ears, mouth, and heart. Do not speak, see, hear, or feel. Pain is allayed, and sadness will subside. Ignorance, I was beginning to learn, is best for someone like me.

"I, myself, prefer humor," Bão said on our first night together at sea.

"But, I like the name I have."

"I'm not talking about throwing away your name, you dumb ass. The new name isn't for you. It's for them. TôiNgườiĐiên, AnhĐẹpTrai, TôiYêuEm . . ." he began listing for me his chosen names. After the third one, we were laughing so hard he could get no further. We rolled on our bunks, him on the top and me on the bottom.

In between gasps of air, he told me that they *never* know which is the given name and which is the surname, so it usually comes out all at once. It made life worth living, Bão said, when he could hear, "Hey, IAmCrazy, if you're late again, I'm throwing your lazy butt right off this boat, and I don't mean when we reach shore! Do you understand me, IAmCrazy?" or "Come over here, GoodLookingBrother, you call this deck clean?" or, his personal favorite, "ILoveYou! Hurry up with those crates! ILoveYou, a trained monkey can do a better job!"

By then, laughter had performed a miracle, separating me from my body, allowing me to forget at least for a while that there was a storm raging inside and out. The sky and the water had turned the same shade of pitch, and seasickness had been taking me by the ankles and throwing me headfirst into the waves. Bão must have heard my groaning and feeble protests, which he knew were useless. My body had to first let go of land before it could survive at sea. It is the body's stubborn resistance and violent refusal that are solely at fault, producing sham symptoms, tricking the mind into believing that the culprit is the ocean. It was unusual for Bão, actually it was unheard of for him as I would later learn, but that night he never stopped talking. He knew that the sickness would have to pass on its own, that sometimes the sound of a human voice is a steady raft on a lurching sea.

He usually worked, he told me, on large shipping liners, which carried more than seven hundred passengers and crew. Most recently Bảo had crewed on a liner called the *Latouche Tréville*, which, like the *Niobe*, made its primary run between Saigon and Marseilles. He would have never considered a freighter as bare-bones as the *Niobe*, he said, but he was broke, and having no money at sea, he had learned, is better than having no money on land. All meals are taken care of, and there is nothing on board to buy except, maybe, cigarettes or a bottle of gin. There are also no women on board or none who are for sale. "A great money saver," Bảo assured me. It was only my first night at sea, and the *Niobe*, despite everything, did not seem so shabby to me. So I asked him why the *Latouche Tréville* was that much better. "Even the ship's cooks had cooks!" Bảo replied, jumping off his bunk, leaning his upper body into mine.

Even the ship's cooks had cooks? How in hell does that affect you? I wanted to know but did not ask. The slight shift in the air temperature, a sudden warming as his body came closer to mine, was making it difficult for me to speak. AnhĐẹpTrai is definitely a fitting name for you, I thought. GoodLookingBrother, indeed.

By the time we left the *Niobe*, I had a long list of questions that I had never asked Bảo. I learned early on that his answers were unhelpful at best and at worst entirely uncommunicative. A ruse to deny me the full depth of his feelings, I told

151

myself. If I had questions, lingering and persistent, I was better off answering them for myself. For instance, the *Latouche Tréville* was better because Bão, I imagined, liked being so close to luxury, so intimate with its smells, the rumpled linens loaded in his arms, lavender-scented still by the fresh-bathed bodies of women whom he would never meet, the perfume and cigar smoke still dancing in the air as he mopped the decks clean at three in the morning. He walked on water, but he was a servant, after all. And like all servants he *had* to take solace from wealth and pleasure, even if they were not his own.

CHAPTER 11

The garret is cold this morning. You must have been out late last night, coming home shoulder to shoulder with the rising sun. I throw another piece of wood into the stove, a funny iron Buddha, presiding in the middle of the room. You prefer the steam heat, which rumbles through the coiled pipes, an innovation that you pay extra for with each month's rent. Odd that this modern contraption produces such ancient sounds. A trapped animal, it sounds like to me. I prefer the wood-burning stove. If I am to feel the warmth, I insist on seeing the flames. I kiss you hello, your cheeks, eyes, temples, saving your lips for last. I press my body against you to say that my lips have longed for you, have begged to touch your skin. I say your name, "Macus Laat-ti-moe," a greeting that makes you laugh. I try again, "MARcus Lat-timore." You award my effort with a kiss, one that does not end until we are on the floor, fumbling for buttons, flaps of fabric, until we are skin on skin, a prayer for the Buddha with the fire in his heart. You tell me that on Friday I was at the flower market on the Île de la Cité, that I had a small white blossom drooping from my lapel, that I looked lost. As I begin to understand what you are saying to me, I become acutely aware of my skin. I detect the existence of a forgotten terrain. I believe that my relationship to this city has now changed. I have been witnessed. You have testified to my appearance and demeanor. I have been sighted. You possess a memory of my body in this city, ink on a piece of paper, and you, a magician and a seer, could do it again. How can I carry my body through the streets of this city in the same way again?

"Sweet Sunday," I say into your ear, repeating the first English words that you have taught me. On the *Niobe*, Bão had impressed upon me the need to learn a few English phrases. The usual list of the usefuls, he said. Bão claimed that he knew of others but that these should get me through most situations: "please, thank you, hello, good-bye, beer, whiskey, rum, *that*-man-took-your-money, *I*-did-not-sleep-with-your-girl, I quit." You, Sweet Sunday Man, have yet to teach me a practical word. Your lessons are about their lush interiors, the secrets that words can keep. I have learned from you that the English word "please" can be a question, "May I?" and a response, "You may." "Please" can also be a verb, an effortless act that accompanies you into every room. Sweet Sunday, indeed. It is the only day of the week that I see you. Two months have passed, but together we have had only eight days. We, though, have already established a routine. I am at your garret by seven o'clock in the morning on Sunday. I stay till three or four the following morning, and then I return to 27 rue de Fleurus. At first it was just a precaution. I could not risk angering my Mesdames by oversleeping again. The arrangement must suit you, as you have yet to ask me to stay the whole of the night, to pick which side of your bed would be solely mine. We, yes, now have a routine, and this is the part of our day when you and I lie like children in our mother's womb, curled into each other for warmth and the feeling of skin. You are always the first to speak. I know you feel compelled to shoo silence away with your words. You speak to me in a childlike French, phrases truncated and far from complete. Your efforts are charitable, noble deeds that are taking you by the throat and strangling you. You open your mouth only to close it again, knowing that your words would weigh me down, keep me from touching shore, deepen the distance between us.

We will lie side by side, devising our own language. As in Sundays past we will push and pull at the only one we have in common. Yours is a languid French, a vestige of your south-ern America and its rich cadences, an English so different-sounding from my Mesdames'. My French is clipped and jagged, an awkward careless collection, a blind man's home, a drunk man's stumbled steps. We will throw all our words onto the table and find those saturated with meaning. Like the nights that we have had together, there

155

will be few. We will attempt to tell stories to each other with just one word. We will end up telling them on our bodies. We always do. You, like my Madame and Madame, have already given up on saying my name. You say instead what sounds to me like the letter "B." But you do not say "bé" like the French, but like they do in America, you tell me. You draw me a picture of a hive, and you draw a honeybee nearby. You point to it and then to me and say that I am your "Bee." Better than "Thin Bin," I think, but still no closer to my name.

The thought comes to me gradually, creeps into the room. I struggle six days a week and on Sweet Sunday I struggle no more. I tell you to speak to me in the language of your birth. I free myself from the direct translation of your words into understandable feelings and recognizable acts. I leave your words raw, allow myself to experience your language as a medium of songs, improvising and in flux. I imagine your language as water in my hands, reflective and clear. You reply that if you return to the place where moss hangs, wavy-haired from the trees, where mosquitoes bloody the nights, you will not want to stop. You will talk for hours, unearthing words whose origins lie deep within the shades of magnolia trees, whose roots have grown strong from blood-rich soil. You will tell me that you are southern but that you are *not* a southern gentleman, that your father owns land, which you will never inherit, that you are a son in blood only. Even before you were born,

156

your mother had forfeited your father's name for a lifetime income. A lover who, unlike your father, would always be constant, she thought. Your mother, you explain, is a woman whose legitimacy had also been compromised from the moment of her conception. Her legacy to you is that drop of blood, which made her an exile in the land of her birth. But you are not like her, you say, touching the tips of my eyelashes. The blood is your key, not your lock. A southern man without his father's surname is a man freed, you tell me, dispensing irony like a hard, uncrushed peppercorn. A man with a healthy income from his mother is also a freed man, you add, with a laugh that falls to the ground, exhausted and sad. Your mother's money has paved your way to this city. It first sent you to the north of your America for college. It knew that there the texture of your hair, the midnight underneath the gauze of your skin, were more readily lost to untrained eyes, you say, tracing the line of my collarbone as it rises to meet your shoulders. You are tempted to call it *his* money, but, when you think about it, it is hers now. She has earned it, fair and square. Squarely on her back, that is, you say, closing my eyes with a lock of your hair. Sweet Sunday Man, go ahead and talk, and I will get up and prepare our evening meal. For your benefit as much as mine, you can pause and say "Bee," your name for me, insert it where a breath would be, and I will look over at you, letting you know that I am listening.

157

When you first arrived in Paris, the Emperor of Vietnam *and* the Crown Prince of Cambodia were both here, you tell me, amazed by your luck, your lot in life. You have seen them both, you boast.

"Bee, they both speak French beautifully."

Like the Governor-General's chauffeur, I think.

The Emperor of Vietnam and Prince Norodom of Cambodia are very competitive. You are sure that every shopkeeper who has ever sold a trinket to one of these fellows knows that by the end of the day the other will come running in to ask for two or three of the same. Prince Norodom was the first to contact you. The Emperor of Vietnam is first only when women or gambling are involved. Only nineteen, and yet the Emperor keeps a notebook with the names of all the women whom he has bedded. He likes to name his racing horses after them. He gets a kick out of naming fast horses after fast women.

"Not a subtle man, this Emperor of yours, Bee."

Not a scholar-prince, I think.

Prince Norodom is a choirboy by comparison. He spent his first year in Paris composing music for the piano, exploring the consequences of removing all the sharps from his musical vocabulary. As for your work, he heard about it from his cousin, a medical school man. The Prince said that he was curious but skeptical. He, however, thought that it was very fortuitous, auspicious even, that you two

158

were practically neighbors. "'The rue de l'Odéon is not a street for a Crown Prince or for a man of science, but here we are,' said Prince Norodom, 'which means that we were destined to meet.'

"His logic, not mine. Impeccable nonetheless, Bee."

A scholar-prince, I think.

First, Prince Norodom wanted to see your maps. He closed the lid of his grand piano, and you spread them out on top of its inlaid surface. "These are an exact copy of the ones used by Dr. J. Haskel Kritzer," you explained to him. "His groundbreaking book on the subject was published in 1924." You were very fortunate to have studied with him, as so many had already been turned away. In your very first interview with Dr. Kritzer, he asked you to sit in a chair next to a sunlit window. The doctor looked into your eyes and after a short while asked, "Lattimore, do you believe that skin and bones can lie?"

"And *that*," you told the Prince, "is the first principle of this science." The second is that any quack can diagnose a fracture, but it takes a true doctor to diagnose the potential for breakage, the invisible fault lines, the predisposed weaknesses. Prince Norodom touched the outer corner of his right eye, an instinctual reaction that you have observed in many of your new patients. There is always a moment during the initial consultation when they realize that you may have already begun the examination, may have already recognized all the maladies that will inhabit their bodies in the years to come, may have already foreseen their aches and pains. You can assure them only by taking out the magnifying glass. The instrument allays their fears. It says to them that, No, the doctor has not yet begun.

"Prince Norodom was no different, Bee."

A man like any other, I think.

The Prince saw the circle of glass distorting the patterns of his Persian rug, and he relaxed and lowered his hand. Prince Norodom then leaned toward the piano, and you led him through the triangular sections of your maps one by one, until you had gone full circle, twice. Every organ, gland, and tissue in the human body is here, you told him, bouncing your index finger between the right and the left maps. Some organs are reflected in both. The thyroid gland, for instance, is represented on the right at about two o'clock and on the left at about nine. The theory is simple. Flecks, streaks, spots, or discolorations within a particular section of the iris indicate that there is a trouble spot, a weakness in a corresponding area of the body. As a diagnostic tool, it far exceeds the reaches of conventional medicine.

"Iridology is a science that can see the future, Bee."

A soothsayer, I think.

It is also an economical science, you assured the Prince. There is no equipment to speak of except for the maps and a magnifying glass. "Imagine if your fellow Cambodians were trained in this science," you said to the Prince. Equipped with their instruments, these men could easily canvass the countryside. "Imagine how the health and well-being of your people could be bettered and improved with this Western science," you advocated.

"The Prince looked up and said the oddest thing, Bee."

Prince Norodom said, "Dr. Lattimore, if even a quack can recognize fractures, then quacks are all that Cambodia needs right now."

He sounds like the man on the bridge, I think.

The Prince agreed to an examination nevertheless. You sat him down near a bright lamp and asked him to look straight ahead and past your face. You told him that every iris is unique, which made him smile. You had never seen royal irides before, you tell me. Now, you have seen four.

"Competition is a marvelous thing, Bee."

Sweet Sunday Man is an American, after all, I think.

You saw it immediately. There was a cluster of tiny spots in the right iris at about five o'clock. Unmistakable, but you continued with the examination without showing your agitation. You needed time. You needed to find the right words. You thought about leading up to it with a series of questions, but then you thought that if this was you, you would want it clearly and succinctly.

"Impotence, Prince Norodom."

The Emperor of Vietnam telephoned you the very next day. He wanted an appointment for later that same afternoon. He said that he would send over his automobile. The Emperor knew that Prince Norodom would see the vehicle, with its telltale curtains, cruising down the rue de l'Odéon. The Emperor's chauffeur opened the car door, waited for you to climb in, and shut it with just the right amount of force, a good sign in a driver. It says that the chauffeur is unlikely to go over a cliff with you asleep in the back seat. Once inside, you looked around, touched the flocked cushions, pulled the velvet curtains open, and wondered how many women the Emperor had sent for in this very car. Every *bonne vivante* in this town has at least one story to tell about the young Emperor. The plot is appallingly similar. The Emperor of Vietnam spots a beautiful Mademoiselle or Madame. The Emperor has no particular age or marital status preferences, but she *must* have blond, blond hair. The color of wheat is even too dark for him. His Highness sends his car for her. She arrives at his abode and is given a tour, which ends in his bedroom. He points her toward an ornate armoire and opens the door. The armoire, depending on who tells the story, is filled with stacks of French francs, carved jade bracelets, loose diamonds sitting atop red velvet pouches, gold bars stacked like a display of foil-wrapped chocolates. The supposed contents are endless. They grow more and more extravagant with each telling. As the Mademoiselle or Madame is sucking in her breath, trying to keep her knees from shaking, the Emperor says, "Please, *ma chérie*, choose a little something for yourself." The act of choosing, of course, has its consequences. Many blond, blond Mesdemoiselles and Mesdames have strolled into the fashionable cafés of Paris, not to mention Nice and Monte Carlo, with very consequential bracelets and diamond rings.

"He's not a subtle man, Bee."

A "cad," I think.

"Are you a Negro, Lattimore?" the Emperor of Vietnam immediately asked upon your entrance into the room.

"No, Emperor, I am an iridologist."

He winked at you, and said, "Doctor, please drop the 'Emperor.' I obviously know who I am. I thought I may know who you are as well."

There was another wink. A nervous tic? you wondered.

"Doctor, I've seen your face before. I can smell the bleach in your hair, the touch of lye. I'm not a bigot, Doctor Lattimore, but I'm no fool. You and I, we understand each other now, and *that* is the beginning of a trusting relationship. *Vous comprenez?*"

"Not a subtle man, Bee."

An Old Man, I think.

You took out the maps and searched the room for an uncluttered surface.

"Skip the educational part, doctor. I've no head

for those things. Let's get straight to the part where you predict my future," said the Emperor.

"I am a scientist, your Highness. I do not 'predict.' I render a diagnosis."

"*Mais oui*, Lattimore. I'm making light of your profession, your science. I make light of everything, doctor. No offense was meant. I'll make it up to you. Before you go, we'll take a little visit to that armoire that I'm sure you have heard so much about." The Emperor smiled. "You may choose an item, a small item, as you don't render the usual services."

Yet another wink, you tell me.

Not a subtle man, I agree.

You seated the Emperor of Vietnam in a chair. As you raised the magnifying glass to his eyes, you felt a rush of intuition. You looked immediately into his right iris, and there it was—a cluster of small spots at about five o'clock, a twin of Prince Norodom's. This time you did not hesitate.

"Impotence, your Highness."

The young man across from you collapsed, you tell me, as did the one who had sought your services just a day before.

You ask me to do the same for you, to tell you a story of my life, to let you hear it in the language that urged me into this world, a language whose words now congest my head and flood my heart because they have nowhere else to go. Trapped as it is inside my mouth, my Vietnamese has taken

164

on the pallor of the dying, the faded colors of the abandoned. I comply with your request but within minutes, I can tell that the experiment is disastrous, a torture that your body is responding to with a noticeable curving of the spine and a heavy-headed plea for mercy. The pleasure that I take from your words, you cannot take from mine. You are unused to the darkness that surrounds you, stuffs itself into your ears, coats your tongue. You struggle instead of letting your body float. It is the first time that I see you cry. I swear I will never do it again. I have been expertly trained, I try to tell you, if not bred for such things. Your training is different.

My comprehension, Sweet Sunday Man, is based mostly on my ability to look for the signals and interpret the signs. Words, I will grant you, are convenient, a handy shortcut to meaning. But too often, words limit and deny. For those of us who are better trained, we need only one and we can piece together the rest. We look for blood in the whites of your eyes. Anger, sadness, all of the emotional extremes register there first, a red spider web, a tangle of red rivulets. They all start there and then wash down your face, coloring your cheeks, your neck, the valley above your collarbone. For the subtler details, we consult the dark, round pools, lighter at the shallow edges and darker in the centers' deep, where light collects and falls inside you. Lies, you should know, always float to the top, foreign objects that, for most people, cause considerable discomfort and pain. There are some who are able to still the shift from side to side, calm the spasms of the irritated lids. A skill, I am afraid that you are either born with or not. The origin of a liar is the same as that of a lie: from one breeds another. Shame is often mistaken for one and the same, but I know it is different. Shame is heavy-hearted and does not float. It prefers the deep, where it disrupts the steady balance, tilting the gaze, forward and down. The lids behave differently as well. They are slow to open, slow to let anything in. Shame often passes for a sudden bout of exhaustion, a sleep that will not be delayed. It affects the whole body, slowing down speech, bloating limbs, until paralysis is a constant threat. Shame, I can assure you, Sweet Sunday Man, is the more toxic of the two.

CHAPTER 12

The first to notice was the gardener's helper. This in itself was peculiar given his advanced age and his otherwise turtlelike existence. In what must have been a requirement of his profession, the helper always wore green, a cotton shirt tucked into a pair of slightly heavier-weight canvas pants, both faded, like dried-out grass. He had been with the household staff longer than any of us, and in all that time, through all of the gossip sessions, his wardrobe never caused a stir. We never thought of him apart from the garden that he watered and weeded. In that setting, in the only setting that we could ever imagine him, green seemed very natural to us. Ironically, Blériot was the first to point out this man's camouflage.

"Why green?" Blériot wanted to know.

"What?"

"I said, 'Why green?'" he repeated.

"I know what you said, but what do you mean?" I asked.

"Why does the gardener's helper always wear green?"

"Does he?"

"'Does he?' You sound as if this is new to you."

"It *is* new to me."

"I'm glad to hear that there are *some* things that are still *new* to you," Blériot said, as he turned around to look at me or, rather, to allow me to look at him. A man in love with his own face, Blériot was feeling generous and wanted to share. From the dip and the swivel of his voice alone, I could tell that he was no longer talking about the helper's penchant for the color green. No, he was talking about me, a *garde-manger* who had taught him, a *chef de cuisine*, a thing or two about heat, about sugar, about the point at which all things melt in the mouth. Cooking had nothing to do with it. We were returning at that moment to the Governor-General's house, and I was walking behind him as usual. Behind me were three young boys carrying the vegetables and fruits that Blériot had purchased earlier that morning from the central marketplace. Blériot always hired the same three boys. They came as a set. Even if there was only enough for one of them to carry, the other two would come along as well. Companionship, loneliness, or fear? It was difficult to say what drove these three.

The three boys made their living in the marketplace. At first they tried shining shoes, but the real shoeshine boys—the ones who had invested in platform boxes filled with polish and two kinds of rags, one coarse for rubbing off the mud and

168

the other soft for buffing what was left of the leather—had banded together and chased them away. After several weeks the three boys returned. This time they watched over the stalls for vendors who needed to relieve themselves in an alleyway or who wanted to check out a competitor's new display of goods. The payment that the three usually received for their services was the last slurp of broth from the vendor's lunchtime bowl of *phở*. Lukewarm, beefy, but with no beef left, just a flotilla of broken noodles, and, if they were lucky, at the bottom of the bowl a bit of gristle that had been bitten off and spat back into the broth. I have seen other children work for this sort of pay before. How many slurps does it take to fill a growing boy's stomach? This is a trick question. It assumes that there is a finite number, a threshold at which point there is no longer a need, a gnawing that defines poverty at any age but especially in the young. I have seen other children trying to answer this question before, but it was the sight of these three sharing the broth left at the bottom of one bowl, the careful passing from one small set of hands to another, the look of relief as each of their faces emerges from a feast more imagined than had, that forever sanctified that marketplace for me. No incense, no marble, no gold, but faith lives here, I thought. Faith that there will always be something left at the bottom of the bowl, that none of them will take more than his share, faith that there will always be three.

The first time Blériot hired these boys I translated for him their asking fee, which was admittedly laughable or larcenous, depending on the mood of your Monsieur. Fortunately, Blériot was too fresh off the boat to know that the quoted amount was the equivalent of three bowls of *phở*, hold the gristle, thank you. It was Blériot's first time to a Saigon market. The vendors had overpriced, and he had overbought. Blériot was existing in a monetary system created just for him. Worth *is* relative, after all. Blériot looked at my arms weighted to the ground by his purchases. He looked back at my face and agreed to the three. The boys followed us to the Governor-General's house, carrying sacks of onions, carrots, and celery, the trinity of a French kitchen, horizontal in their arms. Later that same week when we returned to the marketplace, the three boys ran up to Blériot and held out those same arms. Still skin and bones, I knew, was what they wanted to say. Three bowls of *phở* can do only so much. Blériot held out a single coin, exactly one-third of what he had agreed to before. How quickly they learn. Madame's secretary is a good teacher, I thought. The boys nodded their heads in unison, knowing that even with the steep devaluation, Blériot's offer was still more than what they were worth in this marketplace. To his credit, Blériot never reduced their pay further, not even after he saw how they were usually paid. The first time he witnessed it, he asked me whether the woman selling bitter melons was their mother. "No," I replied, "those three boys are not even related to one another."

Blériot's mistake was an easy one to make. Madame made it all the time. At first she even thought that the entire kitchen staff clambered out of the same womb because everyone called the sous chef "Brother" Minh. Madame's secretary had to explain to her that "Anh" was used by the staff here as an honorific and that only the *garde-manger* was a blood brother of the sous chef. Madame was wary of the explanation, suspicious that it was all merely a cover-up for rampant nepotism. As for Blériot, I could not in truth blame him. How could he *not* assume a familial relationship after witnessing the boys eating from the same bowl? Blériot had not lived in Saigon long enough to understand that poverty can turn an act of intimacy into one of degradation. That in this marketplace, eating from the same bowl was the equivalent of pissing in the same pot. It was fine, especially if you were the first to go.

As we walked through the back gate of the Governor-General's house, it slammed shut behind us with such a clash that the sparrows fled from the surrounding trees, a scrap of black lace lifting into the sky, that the butterflies rose from the gladiola spikes, their wings filtering for a moment the strong light of the Saigon sun. But in the end I am afraid that it was the three boys who really gave us away. Blériot, admittedly, was of no help either. He was behaving like a typical colonial official.

171

He walked several steps ahead, keeping enough distance between us to say, We are not one. Yet he was still close enough to relay his exclusive control over the four Indochinese who followed him. At first Blériot thought the streets of the city were like the pathways of the Governor-General's garden. He walked everywhere with his head held high, which meant his eyes caught nothing of what went on below his chest. Frenchmen like him are a boon for Saigon pickpockets. During Blériot's first week, we on the household staff overheard Madame's secretary comforting him with mothering sounds, peppered with an occasional insult for what she called the City of Thieves. In fact, it had to happen to him several more times before he finally chose to learn. For men like Blériot, pride is apparently worth more than money, an extravagance that thieves everywhere adore. Blériot then became overly concerned about the carriage of his body and the bodies of those around him, especially if they belonged to an Indochinese. The rules he set forth for me were simple. No touching. No smiling. The first I could understand, but the latter I thought absurd. A smile is like a sneeze, necessary and not within my control. Any effort to suppress it would only draw more attention to it. So I defied him and smiled anyway, and given the manner in which Blériot had us walking through the streets of that city, the pathways of that garden, he never saw. I smiled at the back of his head, at his hair streaked red in the morning light. Like threads of saffron, I thought. I smiled at his white shirt, at the loose weave of the cotton, at the muscles that only steady work in a kitchen can provide.

As careful as Blériot was by then with his body, he lacked all control when it came to his tongue. He placed great trust in the power of his language to elevate him from the fray, to keep his nose clean even when he was rooting in the dirt of someone else's land. At ease with its power to exclude, its gate-slamming pronouncements, he grew reckless, especially when we were in the company of these three boys. He assumed, and he was right, that they could not understand a French word that he was saying. He failed to comprehend, though, that the tonalities of sex are, like those of desperation, easily recognizable and instantly understood, no matter the language, no matter the age. Yes, as soon as Blériot said, ". . . there are *some* things that are still *new* to you," the three boys recognized it, and they laughed, skittish and cheerless, the same as if we had embraced in front of them and kissed each other with our mouths open, hungry.

From his bed of marigolds, the gardener's helper heard the laughter and the slamming gate. He snapped up his head of white hair and caught Blériot's face as it turned from mine back toward the direction of the Governor-General's house. The gardener's helper had seen that look before. Fires have been started by less, he thought. The laughter of the three boys was, to him, also not new. Memories of it bloomed in his stomach.

173

The gardener's helper lowered his head. He was already in a posture akin to prayer. The earth below him was warm. He dug his fingers into the soil and longed for the day when his limbs would take root.

When I left the Governor-General's household, the gardener's helper assured me that it was not he. "I would never tell," he said. "I, of all men, would never tell," he insisted. I looked at his face, a drought-scarred plain. I looked through his parting lips, cracked by the lack of touch, and I saw the nubs and shoots of all that he had swallowed in the fear that some day what was natural in him would grow. Yes, I thought, of all men, this one would have never told.

The chauffeur was a different story. He liked the sound of his own voice, especially when he was speaking French, and he and Madame's secretary always conversed in French. The chauffeur had returned from France like all the others. He had developed a passion for the leisurely game of tennis and had acquired an appreciation for the worst-smelling cheeses. The latter, we in the household staff assumed, explained his fascination for Madame's secretary. Given her French father, we in the household staff felt that Madame's secretary should have been more beautiful, but she was not. She was more robust than most, maybe, but otherwise not much improved, we thought. If you took the average Saigon girl and pumped her full of air, the result, I think, would be the same. I suspect that her beauty or what passed for it, at least for the chauffeur, was her father's French. She spoke it from birth and it showed. There were rumors that she wrote it beautifully as well, and that it was she who composed Madame's more delicate rejections and affecting apologies. Madame's secretary, according to the chauffeur, on occasion also wrote speeches for the Governor-General. We in the household staff did not know what to make of this boast, uncertain whether we were dealing with a French expression that had lost itself in translation. We thought that, maybe, "writing speeches" for the Governor-General was just another way of saying that Madame's secretary was graciously offering her services to him as well. What kind of services these were would depend on the kind of woman Madame's secretary wanted to be. None of us really knew the answer to this question because, with the exception of the chauffeur, Madame's secretary ignored us all, even Minh Still the Sous Chef. My brother's functional French and his long white apron were obviously still not enough to hoist him up to her line of sight. Madame's secretary was as tall as the chauffeur, and taller than he when she wore her heels. Those shoes must have broken the chauffeur's heart. Men, believe me, are fragile in unexpected ways. Weak is another way of putting it. Madame's secretary, unlike the chauffeur, was often invited to the larger receptions and dinner dances held at the Governor-General's. Nothing intimate but still very lavish affairs that called for a silk dress and dyed-to-match high heels. During these occasions, the chauffeur sat out back on the steps leading up to the kitchen door and smoked his cigarettes one after another. When he stomped out their lit tips, we all knew that he was thinking of her, of who was resting his hands on the silk of her dress, on the small of her back. At least it is not Blériot, thought the chauffeur, as he peered inside the doorway to make sure that the chef's toque was still leaning into the heat of the stove.

That morning, from where the chauffeur stood all he could see was Chef Blériot returning from the market with four lackeys in tow. A prince and his entourage, thought the chauffeur. Well, the chauffeur more likely thought, a prick and his entourage. No matter, either way his dislike for Blériot was at that point no more or less than that of the others in the household staff. That morning the chauffeur was, in fact, more intrigued by the gardener's helper and his sudden jolt to life. The chauffeur saw the spot of white in the marigold bed. He saw it moving with an alertness, an uncharacteristic determination not to miss the moment, and he followed it and the old helper's gaze like the tracks of an animal. What the chauffeur saw, he stored away. He came to no hasty conclusions. He preferred to gather more facts. But in all honesty, the chauffeur did not even know what he was looking at or for. As for Blériot

176

and me, we were that morning just two figures in the chauffeur's line of sight. Over the next few months, the chauffeur made it a point to see what the gardener's helper was seeing. He watched as the gardener's helper searched for the lopsided smile on my face. He watched as the gardener's helper correlated its appearance to that of Blériot's. He watched as the gardener's helper watered, at midnight, the jasmine vines that trailed up to the kitchen windows. He watched as the gardener's helper marked the end of the workday by the lights dimming one by one in the kitchen, by the bodies that departed, by the bodies that always stayed.

When I left the Governor-General's household, the chauffeur drove up behind me in Madame's automobile. Its approaching headlights bore two dust-filled holes into the Saigon night.

"Hey, hey, where are you going?"

"Home," I said. If I had bothered to look up, I knew that I would have seen the chauffeur's head bobbing, barely above the steering wheel. Struggling for air, he always seemed to me.

"No, no. I meant where are you going to work now?"

"Why do you care?"

"Look, I'm sorry. She made me do it . . . You, you don't know what it's like to hear her go on about that prick. It was as if she were holding a gun to my head, and each time she said 'Chef Blériot' she was pulling the trigger."

"A gun to *your* head?"

"I can't take it back. I want to, but I can't. You should have seen her. All powdered and rouged, and she smelled great. She smelled new. When was the last time you smelled something new? When was—"

"Are we done here?"

"No. Look, I'll get to the point. When I was in medical school—"

"What? When were *you* in medical school?"

"In Paris."

"Stop lying!"

"I'm not. When I was in medical school, I heard about treatments for your condition."

"Condition?"

"Yes, your condition. There are doctors . . . there's been extensive research done in England and in America. I . . . I can help you."

"Never mind my condition. What is *wrong* with you?" I demanded to know. None of us in the household staff, not even my brother, knew what the chauffeur had studied while he was in France. We assumed it was poetry, as that was the only thing that he could do, besides driving, that could be called a skill.

"What do you mean, 'wrong' with me?" the chauffeur asked.

"Well, there must be something. Otherwise, why would a doctor make his living as a chauffeur?"

"At least I get to work with people."

"What did you say?"

"Look, like I said, your condition has been

178

studied and is much better understood now. A cure is probably—"

"Never mind a cure. What is wrong with *you*?" I interrupted.

"Nothing, nothing. Look, if I tell you, will you hear me out?"

Yes, I nodded.

"It's simple. When I came back to Saigon, I applied for a staff doctor position in their Native Affairs Office. Basic stuff. Mostly physical examinations to be performed at the beginning and at the end of their commissions and the routine visits in between. Venereal diseases, tapeworms, diarrhea. Basic stuff. And so I was hired."

"So?"

"So those overgrown French schoolboys hired me as a staff veterinarian. They wanted me to travel from plantation to plantation, checking on hooves, snouts, and whatever else was ailing them. When they said that I had the job, they didn't even say a word to me about it. No explanation, no nothing."

"Oh."

"As I was saying, your condition has been studied and is much better understood now. A cure is . . ."

This time, I had to let him continue. All that training should not be wasted, I thought.

The chauffeur prided himself on being cosmopolitan, a man of the world via Saigon and Paris. So he began by telling me about all the cafés and dance halls in Paris that are filled, he said, with men like me. He never visited any of them, he said. He had only read about them in the writings of those doctors who were trying to find a cure. "Men with men. Men with men who behaved like women. Women who behaved like men with women who behaved like women, et cetera. The mutations of your condition are endless," the chauffeur explained. Endlessly fascinating, I thought. After his informative and in-depth lecture on the varietal nature of human attraction, the chauffeur, or "Dr. Chauffeur," as he in all fairness ought to be called, prescribed for me a regimen of rigorous physical exercise and a decreased intake of garlic, ginger, and other "hot" spices. No garlic? No ginger. What a quack! I thought. But I suppose the chauffeur was simply proving himself to be a poet, after all. His recommended course of action had little to do with science. It was based on something more intuited than learned. It identified him as a believer, a healer who places his faith in the body's ability to transform itself through the denial of what it naturally craves. I would hardly call *that* a skill, I thought.

But being both a poet and a doctor did help the chauffeur to see that whatever the gardener's helper was suffering from had afflicted him too long ago and was now only an aching, a bell ringing in his kneecaps when it rained. Painful, yes, but hardly worth a thorough examination, the chauffeur thought. As for Blériot and me, the chauffeur saw blood pumping through a nicked artery. Immediate attention was required, he decided. Though if I am to believe the chauffeur, it was in the end Madame's secretary who told. "A woman is always to blame," as the Old Man would say.

Madame's secretary, according to the chauffeur, had devised an elaborate plan to seduce Blériot. Madame's birthday dinner was to be the place and time. A new dress, a string of freshwater pearls to accentuate the pink in her skin, and her signature special-occasion heels, the whole thing was sordid, but the worst part of it, according to the chauffeur, was that Madame's secretary had to go and tell him all about it. "Like I was her sister!" he said, shaking his head from side to side, a pendulum swinging from embarrassment to disbelief. "Like I was her sister," the chauffeur repeated. As the anniversary of Madame's birth drew closer, the details became more elaborate, said the chauffeur. Lace for the dress, perfume for the skin, barrettes for the hair, but all he could think about were her high heels. How they would make her feet raw with pain, red even, he thought. How tender they would be by the night's end. How he could rub them with salt and water. How swollen they would be in his hands. Desire comes to us in many guises, and the chauffeur's were apparently shod in a punishing pair of heels. And he thinks I am the one with the condition, I thought.

"I held out for as long as I could," the chauffeur

insisted. "She's just talking nonsense, I told myself, but . . ."

"But what?" I asked.

"But then this morning, she . . . she brought them in to show me. To show *me*, of all people! She had them dyed to match her dress, and they were returned to her speckled like a robin's egg. "They're ruined!' she said, sobbing into my handkerchief."

"What's a 'robin'?"

"It's a kind of bird. Never mind, I forget that there aren't any here. Never mind, I just mean that her shoes were supposed to be blue."

"Oh."

"They were blue all right but not all over like she wanted them to be. They looked like someone shook a brush dipped in blue paint at them. I wanted her to stop crying, so I . . . I said that if she could get me more paint, I would help her fill in the spots. She just cried harder. I thought . . . I thought that if I told her about Blériot, it would cheer her up. I thought that if she knew that there was no prize at the end of the race, she wouldn't care so much about running in it."

"I don't need to hear any more," I told the chauffeur. "I know the rest."

The chauffeur drove away after I finally agreed to meet with him in a week to discuss "my condition." What a quack! I thought. No garlic? No ginger?

182

When I now think about the chauffeur, especially in the early morning hours when the streetlamps of this city are hanging above me, muted by the mist that rises from the Seine, I think about the two dust-filled holes that receded into the Saigon night. I think about his floating head. I think about the sadness of this man who crossed oceans, chasms blue with the broken eggshells of the birds who flew so far away from home only to return with nothing at all.

In Saigon when the rain falls, the sun remains white with heat and the earth below steams. Heat, there, attaches herself to my back and I carry her with me no matter where I go, outdoors or in. "Sultry" and "swelter" are, there, the names of the seasons, an uninterrupted interlocking sequence of months that feel like years. Flowers, there, learn to bloom at night. Festivals, there, celebrate the moon underneath her forgiving blue light. I had grown accustomed, there, to life moving slowly. I had taken it for granted that speech would be an act forever slowed and delayed because words were so reluctant to leave the shaft of coolness that is the speaker's throat. I assumed that sudden flashes of anger were something to be avoided, as they would only encourage and increase the production of sour sweat. Madame's secretary, though, belonged to a different school of thought. Heat was to her a Madame, demanding action. When the sun seared, she did not seek refuge like the rest of us. No afternoon naps, no shedding of clothes, no lying down in the pathway of a known breeze. Madame's secretary thought of heat as a competitor, a ruthless compromiser. She was particularly frustrated by how quickly her body gave in to it. Every day, she felt defeated by the wetness that collected in the folds beneath her breasts. Every day, the watermark that was left behind, a wavy line where sweat had saturated the fabric of her dress, reminded her that these folds were deepening. Every night, when she lifted her breasts up to wipe away the salt of her own body, she thought of Chef Blériot's hands. Her body responded by blistering, turning itself inside out. Heat was to her a thief and a harlot. Heat was to her the woman whom she wanted to be.

This is all to say that the sun beating down on that day, the day before the anniversary of Madame's birth, served only as a reminder to her secretary of all that needed to be done before the sun set and, like her, faded away. Madame's secretary started with a list, as the order of things was very important to her. First, she summoned Blériot, whose hands smelled that afternoon of caul fat and thyme. He had been preparing squabs since the early morning, wrapping each bird in a web of fat and holding it in place with a jab of thyme. The birds looked like babies swaddled in crocheted shawls. They looked like babies with a branch of tiny leaves stabbed into their hearts. As they roasted, the sticky weaves would sear into their skins and disappear, leaving behind a glossy slick that would make lips smack in anticipation. Without the benefit of the oven's cleansing heat, Blériot's hands reeked. "I, too, am shocked. You must believe me that there have been no such indiscretions. None whatsoever," whispered Blériot, as he searched the office for a place to sit down.

From behind her desk, Madame's secretary nodded her head compassionately, reached out her hands understandingly, and said, "Leave it to me, Chef Blériot. But, if I'm to help, you must leave it all to me. *All* to me, do you understand?"

"Yes."

I often wondered whether Blériot had waited, paused for just a second before the "yes" or whether it was immediate, a pit poised on the tip of his tongue, discarded as a matter of instinct.

Second, Madame's secretary cornered Madame, who was returning home from the club and was still dressed in her tennis whites. "Get rid of him. Immediately! I don't want such filthy lies in my home," Madame announced in a squeak even higher than usual. "I can get two of them for what I'm paying for that one. Family always breeds trouble. Unfortunately, these people are all related to one another. These people! If they're not thieves, then liars. Poor, poor Chef Blériot. The humiliation," said Madame, carefully placing the appropriate outrage upon the alleged falsehood and not upon the alleged acts. She is French, after all. Madame is a snob but not a prude. She did not care about the relations of two men, just as long as they were of the same social standing and, of course, race.

Third, Madame's secretary sent for my brother. "I don't believe it," Minh the Sous Chef lied. "I don't want to call the chauffeur a liar, but I just don't believe it. I don't believe—"

"Of course you don't," Madame's secretary interrupted. "You're not paid to believe. You're paid to cook. I'm telling you that there is no doubt. He's been spreading lies of an explicit nature about Chef Blériot. Madame does not want him in the house. Who knows what he's capable of next? He's to leave here at once."

All of that took less than an hour from beginning to end. But Madame's secretary was not done. "A woman with a knife never cuts, she plunges it in and digs" is another of the Old Man's sayings. It became clear to me that afternoon that *that* was not a reference to a cooking technique. For her final act, Madame's secretary sat down at her desk and took out a small mirror and smiled into it. She used a fingernail to fix the coral edges of her lipstick, smudged in the excitement of all that swift talking. She inspected the skin around her mouth. This was her nervous tic. We in the household staff have watched her becoming more and more "nervous" over the years. She could not walk past a mirror or a shiny surface without looking and searching. It was the inevitability of it, we believed, that made her so nervous. Someday, she knew, she would find it.

At first it would resemble the fine lines underneath the surface of old porcelain. Then it would deepen and set itself in, until the area around her mouth became a cracked riverbed from which the colored wax that she applied to her lips would run. In the end, she would be left with the appearance of coral radiating from her mouth.

In the end, Madame's secretary sent for me. Spite was not flowing through her veins that day, just a curiosity about desire, Chef Blériot's desire. A closer inspection, she thought, would reveal what attracted Blériot's body to mine. She wanted to see for herself, to examine anew this *garde-manger*, this willow branch, she thought, of a man. A movement, a temperament, a tilt of the head, a swing of the hips, a tint of the lips, a thing she could adopt so that she could call Blériot her own. After all, Madame's secretary knows that the Vietnamese call men like me *lai cái*. What they mean is that I am mixed with or am partially a female. If a female is what Chef Blériot wants, why not the real thing? she thought. It was a rhetorical question because even she knew that lust and longing are never that simple, never falling into even halves when cleaved. Curiosity, however, is a weak-willed thing easily subsumed by crueler impulses and emotions. That afternoon, it was self-preservation that stepped in and suggested to Madame's secretary that she should be more thorough and absolute in her approach. "I've told your father," she said to me in Vietnamese, then again in French for emphasis. I stood there, the doorknob to her office door still in my hand. A note to the Old Man, she claimed, was her fourth, and this meeting was her fifth and final step.

CHAPTER 13

When I applied for the position as live-in cook, I did not know about the house in Bilignin. I assumed that the lives of these two American ladies and therefore mine would be centered in Paris on the rue de Fleurus. They did not inform me during the interview about their seasonal migration. Not that it would have made a difference to me then. Before joining their household, I thought that a home was a home, a Madame was a Madame, a city was ... well, even then I knew that Paris was a city and that many other places were not. So I suppose it might have made a difference if I had known. I might have asked for more money, hazard pay, months-in-the-middle-of-nowhere pay, you-cannot-pay-me-enough-to-live-here pay. It is only February and I know it is early to think about the summer in Bilignin, but Sweet Sunday Man has been asking. He wants to know whether my Mesdames are going there this year and, if yes, when. Of course, they are going. My Mesdames are very regular, Sweet Sunday Man. They like routines and schedules. They do not like to deviate

189

from the chosen paths of their lives. GertrudeStein, after all, burned sixty candles on her birthday cake this month, and Miss Toklas will burn fifty-seven in April. She has a French document, though, that lists her as being born on a day in June. There have been years when my Madame waits until then to grow older. I do not know what she has planned for 1934. I suppose it depends on how she is feeling about her age, advancing. I would wager, though, that Miss Toklas will celebrate in June again this year because June means that my Mesdames will be in Bilignin. When I began working for them back in the autumn of 1929, they had just finished their first summer in their country house. My Mesdames' routine there was just beginning.

When summer comes to Paris, my Madame and Madame pack their clothes and their dogs into their automobile, and they drive themselves and their cargo down to the Rhône Valley to the tiny farming village of Bilignin. I am left behind to lock up the apartment and to hand the keys over to the concierge, whom I have always suspected of being overly glad to see these two American ladies go. I have seen him in his first-floor window watching the young men who come to court GertrudeStein, and I have seen him shaking his head unable to comprehend the source of the attraction. With my Mesdames already on the road for over a day, I pack up whatever warm-weather garments I have that year, and I go and splurge on a hat for the hot summer sun. If I find a bargain, then I also treat myself to lunch at an establishment with cloth on the table and an attentive waiter who is obliged to call me "Monsieur." I then take what is left of the money that my Mesdames gave me for a second-class train ticket, and I buy a third-class one instead. I sleep all the way down to Bilignin, where I open up the house and wait several more days—as my Mesdames drive at a speed that varies somewhere between leisurely and meandering—before I hear the honking of their automobile and the barking of two weary dogs. I wait for them on the terrace. I have plates of sautéed livers for Basket and Pépé and for their Mesdames bowls of thick cream, dolloped with last summer's strawberry preserves. There are smiles all around, except for Basket and Pépé, who greet me with the usual disdain. My Mesdames admire my new hat, which signals that the summer in Bilignin has officially commenced.

I have the hat because the house there, while spacious enough to be called a *petit château*, has no running water, and I am often outside in the gardens, where there is a pump. I also have the hat because in Bilignin as in Paris I have Sundays off. The farmers in the village are gracious enough and at first simply curious enough to invite me, the first *asiatique* they have ever seen, into their homes. And their sons, I have to admit, are handsome enough to make me accept each and every time. All the families in this area make their own wine, so drinking is never a problem, and generosity fills my glass till I thirst for just a bit of water. I have found that water at the end of these nights eases my entry back into Monday. Though sometimes there is not enough water in the sea for me. I awake the next morning to the sound of Miss Toklas slamming pots and pans in the kitchen. These are pots and pans that she and no one else would need for the preparation of the simple breakfast of fruit and fresh sheep's-milk cheese that she and Gertrude Stein prefer when they are in Bilingnin. I climb down the narrow staircase that leads from my room to the kitchen, and I do the only thing that I know how when I am faced with an angry Madame.

"It is my health—" I lie.

"But I am improving as we speak," Miss Toklas finishes my usual speech for me.

I had overheard a *femme de ménage* from Brittany use those exact words in the home of a previous Monsieur and Madame, and I had her teach them to me. They are vague enough to cover most household mishaps and oversights and also have the assurance of in-progress improvement tacked on at the end. When she asked me why I wanted her to repeat it, I told her I thought the sentence clever and useful. The *femme de ménage* agreed, but she said that she could not take credit for it, as she herself had overheard an Italian nanny employ the same words in another household some years back. We servants, in this way, speak the same language learned in the back rooms of houses and spoken in the front rooms on occasions such as these. Miss Toklas and GertrudeStein have also developed an apparent appreciation for this sentence. On subsequent Mondays when my head is again too heavy with wine, my Mesdames' breakfast conversation floats up to my bedroom window, like pieces of burnt paper, from the terrace down below. Amongst their otherwise incomprehensible English words, I recognize the phrase "it is my health" spoken in a fair approximation of a laborer's heavily accented French. Laughter usually ensues. No matter, I think, as I turn over on my side. Laughter in this case is a good or, at least, a nonthreatening sign. Of course, I try not to indulge in this sort of behavior very often, not more than two or three times during the season. It is just that drink is cheaper in Bilignin. In fact, it is free. The farmers there ask very little of me, and when they do they seem to enjoy, unlike their Parisian cousins, the sounds of the French language faltering on my tongue. Sometimes they even ask to hear a bit of Vietnamese. They close their eyes, trusting and sincere, and they imagine the birds of the tropics singing. When they are like this, I remember what the man on the bridge had told me: "The French are all right in France." What he meant, he explained, was that when the French are in their colonies they lose their natural inclination toward fraternity, equality, and liberty. They leave those ideals behind in Mother France, leaving them free to treat us like bastards in the land of our birth. The man on the bridge, I know, would have liked these farmers whose sons never leave Bilignin.

In the summer, my Mesdames kindly overlook my Monday-morning absences. Halfway through the season, Miss Toklas even suggests that I take Mondays off for "my health." Of course, she also reduces my pay by one day. But life in Bilignin does not require a full wallet, so I gladly accept the change in the terms of my employment. I also gladly accept the additional glasses of wine and whatever else comes my way every Sunday and Monday night. The farmers in Bilignin work and drink like horses. The two activities do not seem to affect each other in any significant way. I, however, begin losing my appetite and my body weight right along with it. By the end of the summer, GertrudeStein, when greeting me, finds it necessary to repeat herself: "Well, hello, Thin Thin Bin."

A cook who has no desire to eat is a lost soul. Worse, he is a questionable cook. Even when I can no longer take a sip, a bite, a morsel of any of the dishes that I am preparing for my Mesdames, I never forget that tasting is an indispensable part of cooking. The candlelight flicker of flavors, the marriage of bright acidity with profound savoriness, aromatics sparked with the suggestion of spice, all these things can change within seconds, and only a vigilant tongue can find

194

that precise moment when there is nothing left to do but eat. For a less experienced cook, such a turn of events, the sudden absence of appetite, would be disastrous. Imagine a portrait painter who attempts to practice his art with his eyes sealed shut. I, thankfully, am able to maintain the quality of my cooking with the help of my keen memory. My hands are able to recreate their movements from earlier times. My loss in body weight, however, I cannot hide. It shows itself as a forlorn expression on my face, one that my Madame and Madame have yet to notice.

When we are in Bilignin, Miss Toklas loses all interest in matters of the kitchen. She leaves that all to me. From May through September, Miss Toklas's heart lies in the gardens, where she too may be found from the early morning till the hour just before the setting sun. I have heard her cooing from the vegetable plots. She does not know that she emits the sounds of lovemaking when she is among the tomatoes. I have heard her weep with the juices of the first strawberry full in her mouth. And I have seen her pray. GertrudeStein has seen her too, but she thinks that my Madame is on her knees pulling out weeds. The god that Miss Toklas prays to is the Catholic one. I have seen the rosary wrapped around her wrist, the beads trickling one by one through her fingertips. From the second-story windows of the house, GertrudeStein sees her lover toiling in a garden, vines twisted around

195

her hands, seeds falling in a steady rhythm from her palms.

Miss Toklas is in a garden, GertrudeStein, but it is divine. The Holy Spirit is in her when she pulls tiny beets, radishes, and turnips from the ground. When she places their limp bodies in her basket, she believes that she knows the joys and anguishes of the Virgin Mother. And along with her raptures, she is ashamed, GertrudeStein. Because my Madame has begun to think of life without you, to plan for it in incriminating ways. Miss Toklas knows that *she* will never be the first to go. She can never leave her Lovey so alone in this world. A genius, she believes, needs constant care. She is resolved to the fact that you, GertrudeStein, will be first, and then what will she do, so alone in this world without you? And, those, GertrudeStein, are the words that end all of her prayers.

Last year was my Mesdames' fifth and my fourth summer in Bilignin. About a week before we were scheduled to close up the house for the season, Miss Toklas came into the kitchen loaded down with baskets of squash, new potatoes, and the last of the summer tomatoes. As she sorted through the bounty, making it ready to be packed for the journey home, she looked over at me plucking a chicken for that night's supper. Even from behind an updraft of flying feathers, I could see that she was studying my face. Madame, do not worry, a few weeks back in Paris and I will be my old self again, I thought. After a short while, Miss Toklas cleared her throat and suggested that this year, maybe, I should ride back to Paris with GertrudeStein, herself, and the dogs. She could just as easily send the crates of vegetables back to the city by rail, she told me. I accepted the offer without hesitation. I have often watched with envy as Basket and Pépé ride away, Basket's ears flapping and Pépé's twitching in the wind, to take, as Má would say, The-Long-Way-Home. Along with their Mesdames, these two dogs take in the sights and stop, I imagined, for impromptu meals whenever GertrudeStein's stomach begins to flutter with the moths of hunger.

For the farmers of Bilignin, the end of the summer season is marked by two events, the departure of the two Americans and their *asiatique* cook and the gathering of the grapes. The gathering is a festival at which the younger farmers of Bilignin meet their future wives or lovers, but then again they do not do that sort of thing there. The wine casks and jugs from the past vintage have to be emptied to make way for the new. That requires almost as much work as the actual removal of the fruits from the vine. But that is why the farmers of Bilignin work *and* drink like horses. I drink like the Old Man. I am fine after the first bottle, but then I turn red. As these farmers and others have pointed out, I look as if I have been burnt by the sun. My cheeks, I am embarrassed to admit, are crimson. I cannot pass it off as a blush because the color is too intense. But beyond this red cast, I remain remarkably unaffected. Well, that is until I pass out. The line between being awake and not is easy for me to overstep, as I never see it coming. One moment I am sitting at one of the long tables set outside under the harvest moon for the occasion, and the next I am being slapped and doused with water. I take *that* as my signal to begin my walk back to my Mesdames' house. There, I am greeted by Basket and Pépé, who delight in the task. They begin to bark as soon as I open the iron gate to the gardens. They continue to bark as I unlock the door to the kitchen, where they are sitting in wait. These two act very undoglike at moments like these. They never jump on me, sniffing and nipping. They are obviously not happy to see me. His Highness and the Pretender to the throne do not have a drop of fear or protective instinct directed toward me either. These two sit by the stove and bark, obligated by a pact with each other to call attention to the time and the state of my arrival. When they are in Bilignin, Miss Toklas and GertrudeStein must sleep like dogs—well-mannered ones, that is. I never see their bedroom light turn on when I enter the gate, and I never hear them rustling about upstairs when I am in the dark kitchen below. Basket and Pépé, despite their mean-spirited efforts, always fail to rouse my Mesdames from their bed to come and see their cook, red, wet, and bleary-eyed.

Well, except for last summer when His Highness

and the Pretender scored a great victory. Granted I did help their cause by throwing up and then passing out before I could reach the stairway to my room. Their noses must have been offended by the strong smell of alcohol that my vomit released into the kitchen. I can imagine that their barking then reached a particularly persuasive pitch. Pépé does have a tendency to emit a eunuch-worthy howl when he is in pain or when there have been too many days of rain. I remember groping for the stairs one moment, and then the next I am being doused with water for the second time that night or, maybe, it was already morning. I looked over at the pool of vomit on the floor and then at a nearby pair of sandals standing slightly apart. "Bin, you will take the train tomorrow. GertrudeStein and I will take the vegetables with us in the automobile," said a voice that, I am afraid, like the sandals, belonged to Miss Toklas. The sandals then padded away, gently slapping the tile floors of the dark house.

The next day, I walked around the house, somber and silent, closing the shutters and putting cloth over the furniture. The last of the summer vegetables caught a ride back to Paris with my Mesdames. Basket's ears were flapping. Pépé's were twitching. The usual traveling circus took off in puffs of dust as GertrudeStein waved and said, "Good-bye, Thin Thin Bin." Miss Toklas was in no mood for pleasantries and kept her hands on her lap.

Good-bye, GertrudeStein.

Really, Madame, what was I supposed to do in Bilignin? It was never part of our original bargain. I spend my months there and never, never see a face that looks like mine, except for the one that grows gaunt in the mirror. In Paris, GertrudeStein, the constant traffic of people at least includes my fellow *asiatiques*. And while we may never nod at one another, tip our hats in polite fashion, or even exchange empathy in quick glances, we breathe a little easier with each face that we see. It is the recognition that in the darkest streets of the city there is another body like mine, and that it means me no harm. If we do not acknowledge each other, it is not out of a lack of kindness. The opposite, GertrudeStein. To walk by without blinking an eye is to say to each other that we are human, whole, a man or a woman like any other, two lungfuls of air, a heart pumping blood, a stomach hungry for home-cooked food, a body in constant search for the warmth of the sun. Before I came to the rue de Fleurus, GertrudeStein, the only way I knew how to hold onto that moment of dispensation, that without-blinking-an-eye exchange, to keep it warm in my hands, was by threading silver through them. Blood makes me a man. No one can take that away from me, I thought. But as you know, GertrudeStein, in order for me to stay at the rue de Fleurus, I have had to give up the habit that has sustained me. Miss Toklas inspects my hands every day. First she checks my nails to see if they are cut and clean—I assume her previous cooks had to submit to this examination as well—and then she turns my hands palms up, a step she has added just for me, her "Little Indochinese." I know, GertrudeStein, that that is what Miss Toklas calls me when her anger gets the better of her. *Her* Little Indochinese? Madame, we Indochinese belong to the French. You two may live in France, but you are still Americans, after all. Little Indochinese, indeed.

What you probably do not know, GertrudeStein, is that in Bilignin you and Miss Toklas are the only circus act in town. And me, I am the *asiatique*, the sideshow freak. The farmers there are childlike in their fascination and in their unadorned cruelty. Because of your short-cropped hair and your, well, masculine demeanor, they call you "Caesar." Miss Toklas, they dub "Cleopatra" in an ironic tribute to her looks and her companionship role in your life. As for your guests who motor into Bilignin all summer long, they are an added attraction. Last summer, the farmers especially enjoyed the painter who hiked through their fields with clumps of blue paint stuck in his uncombed hair. There was also a bit of commotion over the young writer who wore a pair of lederhosen to walk Basket up and down the one street of that village. As for me, the farmers are used to me by now. Only when they are very drunk do they forget themselves. At the grape gathering this year, one of them asked, "Did you know how to use a fork and a knife before coming to France?" I certainly knew how to use a knife, I thought. That was followed by "Will you marry three or four *asiatique* wives?" None, thank you. Then a usually quiet farmer, a widower who lives alone with his dog, which he claims is more sweet-tempered than his now departed wife, asked, "Are you circumcised?" I looked around at my hosts and then up at the harvest moon. Why do they always ask *this* question? I wondered. I could only assume that their curiosity about my male member is a by-product of their close association with animal husbandry. Castrating too many sheep could make a man clinical and somewhat abrupt about such things, I thought. The morning after, they never recall asking me this question. In a matter of a few short hours, everyone in that village loses his memory. Everyone except me. Believe me, I have tried. But no matter how much I drink, I am still left with their voices, thick with alcohol, and their faces burnt raw by the sun.

CHAPTER 14

Fame, you tell me, appears in the irides as a circle of flames.

"Bee, those two are going to bask in it."

"Why?"

Your eyes race toward the door, responding to a knock that is not there. A spasm of shame, I think. You, Sweet Sunday Man, are ashamed of yourself, not me. Ashamed that you chose me, a man who may as well be blind, you think. This October will mark my fifth year with my Mesdames. How could Bee *not* know? you must think. Sweet Sunday Man, I know. I know when my Madame and Madame wake up in the morning. I know the sounds that come from behind their bedroom door when they think that I am not around. I know the cigars that they smoke. I know the postcards that they collect and the women who recline naked on them. I know the old-woman gases that escape from them, and the foods that aggravate them. Brussels sprouts, if *you* must know. I know the faces of those who are invited often to dinner. I know the backs of those who are asked never to return. I know the devotion that my Mesdames have for each other. I know the faith that they both have in GertrudeStein.

"Why?" I ask again.

"Stein's books."

"Books?"

"Stein writes books, but they are . . . unusual, almost not books at all," you try to explain.

I am impressed anyway. Miss Toklas has a scholar-prince, I think.

"Here," you say, crossing the front room of your garret. You point to a row of books sitting by themselves on a shelf, and you say "Here" again.

I see a spine covered in flowers, one in the yellow of banana peels before they are freckled by the sun, one in the gray of my mother's best *áo dài*. I pick up a book wrapped in the blue of a Bilignin summer sky, and I leaf through its pages. Like rice paper, I think.

"It's vellum," you say, as you try to take the book from my hands.

"Vellum?" I repeat.

Paper resembling the skin of a calf, you explain with hand gestures and playful caresses against my own. I gladly give the book back to you. "Only five," you tell me with the outstretched fingers of your right hand, "deluxe copies were printed." Words printed on skin, I am still thinking. You carefully place the book back on the shelf and exchange it for another: "Here, this one, this is Stein's latest." I take the book from your hands, balancing its top and bottom edges between the tips of my fingers, mimicking how you held it in your own. Last year, you tell me, was a very good one for GertrudeStein. Not only was GertrudeStein published in 1933, but in 1933 GertrudeStein was also read. This is a minor miracle that you hope, by fixing your eyes on mine, that I can understand. "*The Autobiography of Alice B. Toklas*," you read to me from the book's cover. Hearing the title only in English, I am still able to understand. My Madame wrote a book about my other Madame. How convenient, I think. GertrudeStein would never have to travel far for her stories. They, I suspect, chase her down and beg to be told. You have stayed in Paris to wait for the French translation of *The Autobiography*, you tell me. A collector, I think. "I've also stayed here," you whisper, "waiting for you."

And am I but one within a long line of others? Are there wounded trophies who have preceded me? But why ask questions, I tell myself, when you are here with me now. Some men take off their eyeglasses, some lower their eyelids. You lower your voice. Desire humbles us in different ways. Your body comes close, and the scent of lime and bay is all around us. You tilt your head. You kiss my lips, lopsided by a smile. Your breath is warmth spreading across the closed lids of my eyes. Your tongue finds the tips of my lashes, flicking them aside. My Madame's books are set down for the night.

★   ★   ★

So that we are clear, Sweet Sunday Man, I have known from the very beginning that GertrudeStein is a writer. I just did not know that it was her vocation, her *métier*, as the French would say. From my first day at 27 rue de Fleurus, I have seen my Madame writing, but then again I have seen other Mesdames busying themselves with the task as well. I assumed it was all the same: letters, lists, invitations extended and withdrawn, thank-yous and no-thank-yous. Every afternoon, Sweet Sunday Man, I see GertrudeStein sit down at her writing table, also known as the dining table at other times of the day. After about a quarter of an hour, as if on cue, she rises, searches for her walking stick, and heads out with Basket for their daily neighborhood chat and stroll. When the studio door clicks shut, Miss Toklas appears, not like an apparition but like a floor lamp or a footstool suddenly coming to life. Sudden, yes, but there all along. Miss Toklas may be practical in nature, even staid in appearance, but she is a sorceress all the same.

First, my Madame pushes in GertrudeStein's chair and gathers the papers and notebooks knocked off the table by her Lovey's hands. When I first saw them I thought of overgrown knobs of ginger or sage sausages pushing against their casings. Either way, assertive and unmistakable, I thought. Next, Miss Toklas wipes away the ink from the fountain pen, replaces the tip that GertrudeStein has flattened like the top of a volcano, and returns the instrument to its red lacquer box. Opening up a nearby cupboard, Miss Toklas places the box inside and takes out a typewriting machine. She sits herself down at the dining table, not in GertrudeStein's chair but in the one to the right of it, and begins to type. The piece of paper, strapped to the machine, flails up and down as each key comes in for a slap or a kick and always looks to me as if it is resisting.

Before meeting you, Sweet Sunday Man, I never thought twice about Miss Toklas's typing. I thought of it as a typical act of overindulgence, like the careful cutting of meat into bite-sized pieces for a child who is no longer one in age, or a singular act of pampering, like the donning of a new pair of shoes in order to soften their leather for the tender feet of a lover. Miss Toklas is capable of doing both. After hearing your predictions about my Mesdames' purported fame, Sweet Sunday Man, I must admit that I am more curious about the cupboard with the heavy black typewriting machine and the red lacquer box lying inside, like the skeletal remains of a once heftier machine and its elongated heart. Who knows what else this cupboard may hold? I think. My curiosity, which is the term that we in the servant trade prefer, tends to peak on Mondays, and, conveniently, Mondays are also when my Mesdames are absent from the rue de Fleurus for the good part of the day.

At the beginning of everyone else's workweek,

my Madame and Madame take a leisurely drive around the city, often followed by a chorus of horns, to attend to their errands and occasionally to their friends. Today is no different. I watch from the kitchen window as GertrudeStein lugs a large satchel of books to their automobile. Miss Toklas follows with two *pâtés en croûte*, one perched in each hand. The "meat loaf," as Miss Toklas calls these pastry-wrapped beauties, are going to the homes of two of their friends. "One who is in poor health and another who is just poor," Miss Toklas said. "Skip the truffles in both," she told me. "It is the meat that they need, not the fuss." Miss Toklas has a judicious approach toward extravagances, culinary and otherwise. Waiting inside the kitchen for tonight's supper is a third *pâté en croûte* with three times the usual amount of "fuss." After all, Miss Toklas *is* a sorceress: an act of charity and self-indulgence combined into one. Lucky GertrudeStein is always the intended recipient of truffles and other reserved luxuries. Outside, GertrudeStein is sounding like a race car driver and she knows it. Miss Toklas knows it too and places her hands over her ears. The repeated revolutions of the motor, the sounds of petrol pushed into an unwilling machine, wake the concierge, and he leans out of his window and shakes his fist. "Crazy Americans!" he grumbles. GertrudeStein waves back and smiles, assuming that the concierge must have said something to the jovial tune of *"Bon voyage!"*

My Mesdames are too trusting. They never assume the worst about those around them. Though, sometimes, I think they are just careless about what they care about. Either way, it is an unusual trait in an employer of domestic servants. I once worked for a Monsieur and Madame who placed a chain around the icebox before they went to bed at night. You can keep the damn cold, I thought. I had another Madame who padlocked the door to the toilets before she left the house. The nearby café, as I was forced to discover, required the price of a drink with every flush. Madame, your kitchen sink will have to do when my bladder is too full and my pocket is too dry, she should have heard me thinking. The worst, though, was a Monsieur who locked up the kitchen knives at night and wore the key around his waist. They are the instruments of my trade, for goodness sake! You, Monsieur, do not trust me with your life, but you trust me with your meals? Absurd, *n'est-ce pas?* All of this is to say that I was anticipating a security measure or two with my Madame and Madame as well, but their cupboard opens quietly, easily.

I see table linens, bundles of tea-stained cloth tied with mustardy strings, a sort of graveyard for ruined tablecloths, napkins, and runners. I am not surprised that Miss Toklas would save such things. Odd, though, that she would store them in this cupboard, I think. But what was at first glance undeniably cloth turns into reams and reams of paper, as my eyes adjust to the sight, to the ivoried remains of what must be decades' worth of GertrudeStein's one-quarter of an hour. What *you* would have given to see this, I think. Opportunity presents itself to me so rarely. I am amazed that I still recognized it. Yes, I think, what would you give? Endless Sundays drenched in cathedral bells, the left side of your bed, a good-night kiss instead of a good-bye one, a drawer for my razor and comb, your eyes warm on my face when I am serving you tea in my Mesdames' studio, your desire for me worn there like a red bloom in your lapel.

Every Saturday, I wait. My presence, just inside the entrance to my Mesdames' kitchen, ensures that all the cups are steaming and that the tea table stays covered with marzipan and butter-cream-frosted cakes. Always discreet, almost invisible, I imagine that when the guests look my way they see, well, they see a floor lamp or a footstool. I have become just that.

"Hardly! You're not nearly as bright or useful."

Thank you, Old Man, for showing me the error of my ways.

At the edge of a crowded room, held in place by the weight of my shoes, thick-soled and cracked by the cold, I wait. The heat of so many bodies crowded together but not touching keeps the studio at a comfortable temperature, but the feeling of cold is, for me, a relative thing. Every Saturday, I search this gathering for Sweet Sunday Man's face and catch only glimpses of his back. But today, I tell myself not to be afraid. I will not be cast adrift. It is not only a matter of time. I do not need a reflection in a mirror, red on the blade of a knife, proofs that this body of mine harbors a life. I have my Madame and Madame. As long as I am with them, I have shelter. I am in the center of a hive, and it is Sweet Sunday Man who is the persistent bee. The honey that he craves is the story that he knows only I can tell. Last Sunday when I told him about the cupboard and what my Mesdames have stored inside, his breath left him. Sweet Sunday Man wanted to know the exact number of notebooks. He wanted to know the order of the typewritten pages. He wanted to know the exact words that GertrudeStein had written and that Miss Toklas had dutifully typed. I shook my head and shrugged my shoulders. In his excited state, Sweet Sunday Man forgot that the English language is to me a locked door. His breath left him again. He sat down at his desk, and I took that as a sign to begin preparing our evening meal. For the rest of the day, the usual rhythm of our routine prevailed. I cooked and he read. I caught him stealing glances, though. Admiringly, I thought. A sea change, I hoped.

But today's tea is like all the others. At 27 rue de Fleurus, even the furniture attracts more attention than I do. That cupboard is getting glances from all directions. Light from some unseen source is licking at its dark wood, sticking to it like wet varnish. Being at the center of attention can make anything glow, I think. Ah, I should have known. Sweet Sunday Man liked my story about the cupboard. He liked it so much that he repeated it. To everyone in the studio, from what I can see. Sweet Sunday Man, there is a fire at 27 rue de Fleurus. When you and the other guests show up for Saturday tea and see the flames, do you rush in to save my Mesdames, the contents of their cupboard, or their cook? The correct answer is Basket and Pépé. My Madame and Madame, as everyone knows, can take care of themselves. The cupboard also needs no assistance because Miss Toklas would run back into the burning apartment until every sheet of paper touched by GertrudeStein was safe in her arms. As for the cook, the assembled guests would scratch their heads and ask, "The Steins have a cook?"

Sweet Sunday Man, I did not consider my stories about my Mesdames then or now in terms of a barter and trade but as an added allure, a bit of assurance. With my continued "curiosity," I knew that I could offer you something no other man could. With my eyes opened, sensitive to these Mesdames of mine, my value to you I thought would surely increase, double and sustain itself. Value, I have heard, is how it all begins. From there, it can deepen into worth, flow into affection, and artery its way toward the muscles of the heart. My mistake, always my mistake, is believing that someone like you will, for me, open up red, the color of a revelation, of a steady flame. I long for the red of your lips, the red of your life laid bare in my mouth. But I forget that you, Sweet Sunday Man, are flawed like me. You are a dubious construction, delicate but not in a fine-boned way. Delicate in the way that poor craftsmanship and the uncertainty resulting from it can render a house or a body uninhabitable. Dubious, indeed. I hide my body in the back rooms of every house that I have ever been in. You hide away inside your own. Yours is a near replica of your father's, and you are grateful for what it allows you to do, unmolested, for where it allows you to go, undetected. This you tell yourself is the definition of freedom. As for your mother's blood, you are careful not to let it show. You live a life in which you have severed the links between blood and body, scraped away at what binds the two together. As a doctor, you should know, blood keeps a body alive.

Sweet Sunday Man, I marvel at the way that you can change from room to room. I envy the way that you carry yourself when you are in the studio, surrounded by the men who think of you as one of their own. The looseness of your limbs speaks of physical exertion for sport and not for labor. Your movements, large and deliberate, signal a life that has never known inhibition. You, Sweet Sunday Man, take full advantage of the blank sheet of paper that is your skin. You introduce yourself as a writer. You tell stories about a family that you do not have, a city in which you have never lived, a life that you have never fully led. You think yourself clever,

213

resourceful, for always using the swift lines of a pencil and never the considered stroke of the pen. You shy from the permanence of ink, a darkness that would linger on the surface of the page and the skin. You are in the end a gray sketch of a life. When you are in the studio, I see your stance, its mimicked ease and its adopted entitlements. When we are together in your garret, I recognize it as an assumption that you try to rid yourself of, shaking it free from where it clings to your body. In there, in the only rooms in this city that we in truth can share, your body becomes more like mine. And as you know, mine marks me, announces my weakness, displays it as yellow skin. It flagrantly tells my story, or a compacted, distorted version of it, to passersby curious enough to cast their eyes my way. It stunts their creativity, dictates to them the limited list of whom I could be. Foreigner, *asiatique*, and, this being Mother France, I must be Indochinese. They do not care to discern any further, ignoring the question of whether I hail from Vietnam, Cambodia, or Laos. Indochina, indeed. We all belong to the same owner, the same Monsieur and Madame. That must explain the failure to distinguish, the lapse in curiosity. To them, my body offers an exacting, predetermined life story. It cripples their imagination as it does mine. It tells them, they believe, all that they need to know about my past and, of lesser import, about the life that I now live within their present. My eyes, the passersby are quick to notice, do not shine with the brilliance of a foreign student. I have all of my limbs so I am not one of the soldiers imported from their colonies to fight in their Grande Guerre. No gamblers and whores joined to me at the hip so I am not the young Emperor or Prince of an old and mortified land. Within the few seconds that they have left to consider me before they stroll on by, they conclude that I am a laborer, the only real option left. Every day when I walk the streets of this city, I am just that. I am an Indochinese laborer, generalized and indiscriminate, easily spotted and readily identifiable all the same. It is this curious mixture of careless disregard and notoriety that makes me long to take my body into a busy Saigon marketplace and lose it in the crush. There, I tell myself, I was just a man, anonymous, and, at a passing glance, a student, a gardener, a poet, a chef, a prince, a porter, a doctor, a scholar. But in Vietnam, I tell myself, I was above all just a man.

CHAPTER 15

Gertrudestein is up early this morning, a rare and for me an unwelcome occurrence. "She wants an omelet," says Miss Toklas, who busies herself with the plates, silverware, and tray.

Six eggs beaten with a generous pinch of salt until the mixture is thick with air, until the color lightens to the bare yellow of chamomile centers. Two large soupspoons of butter, the first melted in the pan until it sizzles, a harmonic of anticipation. The second is tucked under the puffy skin that has formed in less than a minute, if the heat is just right. A simple dish that reveals the master, exposes the novice. My omelets are well regarded and held in high esteem by all those who have partaken. Like children, gullible and full of wonder, they always ask, "What is your secret?"

Do I look like a fool? I ask myself each time. Please, Madame, do not equate my lack of speech with a lack of thought. If there is a secret, Madame, I would take it with me to my unmarked grave, hide it in my bony jaw, the place where my tongue would be if it had not rotted away. Dare I say it

216

is your ignorance, Madame, that lines my pocket, gives me entry into the lesser rooms of your house, allows my touch to enter you in the most intimate of ways. Madame, please do not forget that every morsel that slides down your dewy white throat has first rested in my two hands, coddled in the warmth of my ten fingers. What clings to them clings to you. If there is a secret, Madame, it is this—I pause for effect, a silent tribute to Bão. Nutmeg! I lie. An important disclosure, they always think. They all believe in a "secret" ingredient, a balm for their Gallic pride, a magic elixir that anyone can employ to duplicate my success. Its existence downplays my skills, cheapens my worth. Its very existence threatens my own. Madame, if you add a sprinkle of freshly grated nutmeg to your beaten eggs, you will have an omelet laced with the taste of hand soaps and the smell of certain bugs whose crushed bodies emit a warning odor to the others. Nutmeg is villainous when it is not sugared and creamed. Used alone in an omelet, it will not kill you, Madame, but it will certainly choke you. If there is a "secret," Madame, it is this: Repetition and routine. Servitude and subservience. Beck and call.

While you have been waking up to the aroma of coffee brewing, dressing to the hushed rhythm of other people's labor, I have been in the kitchen since I was six and in your kitchen since six this morning. In my life as a minor domestic, a bit character in your daily dramas, I have prepared thousands of omelets. You have attempted three, each effort wasted, a discarded half-moon with burnt-butter craters, a simple dish that in a stark and economical way separates you and me.

From the very beginning, I knew. Miss Toklas would never be one to ask because she is a Madame who has secrets of her own. Miss Toklas places the omelet, the curved edges still humming heat, before GertrudeStein, a song of temptation falling on tone-deaf ears. GertrudeStein will not touch the food until it has dropped to the temperature of the dining room. Tepid, my Madame thinks, is best. Hot and cold are too easily discernible. Tepid is a worthy scientific investigation, a result that requires calibration and calculation. Tepid is also, for GertrudeStein, a delectable dose of revenge. Because Miss Toklas is happiest when her meals are consumed while hot, with thick tendrils of steam reaching up, catching her hair and dangling earrings. She insists on nothing less for those who sit at her table. She demands even more for GertrudeStein. When what is brought to the table simmers with passion and pride, its appearance, Miss Toklas believes, should quell all conversation, send hands reaching for forks and knives, incite lips to part in anticipation. Miss Toklas believes that with every meal she serves a part of herself, an exquisite metaphor garnishing every plate. GertrudeStein knows that for every minute that she indulges, entertains like an unwanted guest at the table, Miss Toklas suffers a little death.

Worse, rejection enters the room and threatens to steal Miss Toklas's chair. GertrudeStein in this way extracts satisfaction for every indignity that she has suffered at the hands of Miss Toklas. Most recently there was the banishment of cream and lard from their diet for six miserable months. Miss Toklas's resolve ensured that the sight of GertrudeStein struggling, clumsy and oafish, to rise from her chintz-covered armchair would remain a secret only we three would share. The exile of salt, the expatriation of alcohol, the expulsion of cigarettes, these were the other brutal regimes that came and went, trampling mercilessly on my Madame's will. Retribution comes to GertrudeStein in a form so passive, potent, and cruel that it could subsist only between two lovers, between GertrudeStein and her "Sweetie," her "Queen," her "Cake," her "Cherubim," her "Baby," her "Wifie," her "Pussy."

I have heard them all. I do not have a favorite. I do not know what they mean. Though "Cake" sounds to my ears like the English name "Kate." A "Kate" who is good enough for GertrudeStein to eat is a "Cake," I say to myself and smile. Bão would be proud. "Slip your own meanings into their words," he said, a bit of advice that has saved me. Language is a house with a host of doors, and I am too often uninvited and without the keys. But when I infiltrate their words, take a stab at their meanings, I create the trapdoors that will allow me in when the night outside is too cold and dark. When I move unnoticed through the rooms of 27 rue de Fleurus, when I float in a current swift and unending, and I hear Miss Toklas offering to GertrudeStein, "Another piece of Cake?" I can catch my breath and smile.

This morning, like all others, I am expected to prepare a plate of sautéed chicken livers for Basket and Pépé, after I have fully attended to their Mesdames, of course. At 27 rue de Fleurus as elsewhere, the order of things is very important. "Pink on the inside and moist, but no blood should run when they are pressed with a fork" were Miss Toklas's precise instructions. A splash of cognac, Madame? I was tempted to but did not ask. I prepare one plate for each dog. These two are absolutely unwilling to share. I have to agree with Pépé on this point. Basket is a chronic drooler who contributes his own broth to each and every dish. A plate of liver, a pretty girl, another dog's pungent anus, it is all the same to Basket. His Highness responds to all objects of excitement with uncontrolled, uninhibited wetness, which signals that he is pleased. At first Pépé responded to the sight of his breakfast drowning by backing away and skulking onto Miss Toklas's lap. I can say one thing for these dogs. They know who favors them. Because not long after that pathetic display, I received orders to prepare for Pépé his very own plate. "My liver-stuffed dogs" is what I call Basket and Pépé when their Mesdames are not around.

220

I say it in Vietnamese. I always speak to Basket and Pépé in Vietnamese. Believe me, "liver-stuffed dogs" sounds much lovelier in Vietnamese than in French. Anyhow, why should I disadvantage myself with a language that these dogs are more familiar with than I? "Fatten up, fatten up" is what I whisper to Basket and Pépé when I serve them their morning meals. Tasty, I always think. No wonder Basket and Pépé abhor me. They know that I would rather serve them than serve them. Basket and Pépé know what I mean, and they also know how best to punish me. Every morning Basket insists on breaking his fast underneath the very center of the dining table as opposed to his favored position by GertrudeStein's feet. He does it so that I will have to get on my knees and crawl toward him with my livers in one hand and my dignity in the other. As I emerge from beneath the table, as I stop this morning as always to marvel at the size of GertrudeStein's feet, my Madame pokes her head down and inquires, "Thin Bin, is Lattimore a Negro?"

No, GertrudeStein, he is an iridologist, I want to say, but I cannot remember the word for the science that you practice. You had warned me that the questions would come. They always do, you told me. Did her spine stiffen just by a degree, did her hand retreat after only a touch of your own, did her eyes linger a moment too long on your face? But GertrudeStein is different, you assured me. She has a democratic stare. Everyone is submitted to the

221

same close examination. She looks and looks until she sees. Once her eyes have completed their task, she possesses you. Or so you think. Her weakness, Sweet Sunday Man, lies in the sheer force of her suppositions, swiftly forming hurricanes. They make her vulnerable in unexpected ways. My Madame bellows and those around her swoon like sails. She is fortunate that she has not drowned. She believes that her ideas come into the world as edicts. It is an act accompanied by the ringing of bells, cast-iron beauties announcing their presence from darkened towers. A hallmark of genius, Miss Toklas believes. She heard them, sonorous and solemn, when she first met GertrudeStein, her "King," her "Fattuski," her "Mount Fattie," her "Hubbie," her "Lovey."

A draft is seeping through the dining room windows. Pépé trembles in Miss Toklas's lap. A knife blade of winter air is making my Madame lonely and making her long for the touch of GertrudeStein's hands on the small of her back. This morning even the width of the table, she thinks, is too great a distance between them. Was there life before I met her? Miss Toklas wonders, even though she knows that the answer would only make her jealous and wistful. Why ask whether there were other hearts fluttering, racing, at 27 rue de Fleurus before she walked through the door, before she slid through the vivid red, the scarlet-curtained walls of her second birth canal? "What a silly question," GertrudeStein would surely say dismissively. That is why, for Miss Toklas, there are some things that she would never share, not even with GertrudeStein. Now that, I have learned, is Miss Toklas's most elaborate and eloquent of secrets. She appears to the world to be profoundly giving, wholly selfless, graciously volunteering. She appears to the world an empty page inviting a narrative, even if it is not her own. Miss Toklas fools the world because it is populated with fools who do not bother to look at the light in her eyes, the crisscrossing lines of steel.

There was life before GertrudeStein, but Miss Toklas had not lived it. She was thirty, and she had never heard the bells of genius, never felt their vibrations against the walls of her veins and arteries. Worse, she was beginning to forget that they could sound for her. She had to travel thousands of miles from home to escape the setting sun. She thought she was giving in to her instinct to flee, a fear so animal-like that she submitted willingly. Now she remembers it as a homing instinct, a flight toward as opposed to away. Thirty years in San Francisco, and she was beginning to fear dusk. Each day she looked up at the purple clouds and the ruby skies and saw blood vessels broken and spilling colors. She equated the setting sun with a woman's bruised face, a face that she had once glimpsed from aboard a slow-moving streetcar.

Never before had she seen such a vision of violence and such a vision of open desire. She could not comprehend why the two had come together, joining forces, in that one body for her to see. Miss Toklas pressed her face against the window. She always stood this way even when there was plenty of room in the streetcar. Being near a window made her feel alert. The streetcar pulled up to a scheduled stop, and there on the sidewalk was a woman with her shirt unbuttoned, revealing the line between her breasts like a soft velvet string. A policeman had his hands around her arms. Her face was a riot of colors. As the streetcar pulled away with Miss Toklas still safely inside, she continued to look until all she could see was the back of the woman's head. She continued to look until she saw the moment when the pins gave way, when the woman's hair rivered down the back of her shirt, a sweeping stain absorbing into the fabric. Miss Toklas fainted. She fell into the arms of a stranger and had to be revived by the conductor. It was an astonishing occurrence on an otherwise routine trip from her father's house to the butcher, greengrocer, baker, fishman, and poulterer. It was a scene that should have faded long ago and would not. Miss Toklas held onto it, the broken face, the soft velvet string, as a talisman and a lure until she came to 27 rue de Fleurus.

★ ★ ★

Alice Babette Toklas arrived in Paris with a trunk filled with brocade jackets, Chinatown red; one fur coat, silver fox; a corset, cherry bright; and armloads of batik and silk dresses in colors that brought out the evergreen in her eyes. Tucked into her purse was a handkerchief trimmed with lace, one of the thirty-one she kept inside a balsam box, one for each day of even the longest months. She arrived with fingernails freshly manicured, each rose-watered digit topped with an arching white bower. She arrived wearing the scent of freesias and honey on her bare skin. The latter, GertrudeStein could not help but notice.

The earth underneath Miss Toklas's feet had lost its steady composure, had collapsed in a fit of hysteria, and she took it as a sign. An earthquake had transformed San Francisco into a biblical city. Floods emerged from the swollen tributaries of burst water mains. Fires lapped at the open wounds of cracked gas pipes. Unseasonable blooms flowered in the wake of the fires' insistent heat. Sections of the city were suddenly deserted, the inhabitants forced out in their nightgowns and bathrobes to face the strange calm of a cloudless sky. Miss Toklas's father slept through the quake. Five-thirteen in the morning was too early for him to rise. Miss Toklas walked into the garden, dug a hole, and filled it with the family's silver, an act she afterward could not remember performing, a preservation instinct that would always serve her well. In the days after

225

the quake, she craved cigarettes, a hot bath, and a host of other things, which she could not yet identify. She took it all as a sign. A year later, as September was disappearing into October, Miss Toklas knocked on the door of 27 rue de Fleurus. As she stood outside the studio waiting for an answer, she heard the sounds of leaves batting against the autumn winds. She thought she was hearing GertrudeStein's laughter. Many years later, standing outside the same door, I thought I was hearing my father's voice. She had left hers behind. I had unfortunately overpacked.

When Miss Toklas first met GertrudeStein, her countenance was steady. Calm, though, would be overstating it. Miss Toklas's expression, I imagine, was the same as the one that she wears now in all of her photographs: her eyes looking up, partially veiled by their heavy lids; her lips, fuller than one would expect, pressing together to ask silently, Well? Why must you stare? This is her expression in all of her photographs except for one. Taken in the year of the earthquake, a year before she would leave her father's house with no intention of returning, it is the only one displayed at 27 rue de Fleurus that shows Miss Toklas alone. Miss Toklas does not like to be photographed without GertrudeStein. The vice versa she knows is not true. The photograph shows her head and the upper part of her torso. Her head is turned sideways, and her gaze is directed down toward the lower, left-hand corner

226

of the photograph. For those who do not know her, the pose says that she is shy, averting her eyes, modest even. She is standing in front of a fabric backdrop, which is slightly blurred. A ripple is running through it, as if someone had just left the room, closing the door firmly behind her, displacing a current of air, an invisible thing that animates for an instant the unfinished piece of cloth tacked to the wall. The sudden movement, caught by the camera's lens, is now an interloper, an unknown face in the background of an otherwise carefully composed tableau. Miss Toklas is wearing a Chinese long robe with soft rounded shoulders, silk with a heavily detailed border. She feels seduced, or so she imagines that seduction would feel this way, every time she slips it over her skin and lets its loose shape, its generous cut, cover her. The garment is pure theater, with long sleeves ending in bell-shaped openings that could make even the portliest of arms appear spindly. Hers are slender, glowing with youth, accentuated by the photographer's lights. Her face and arms shine white, hot. Her arms are crossed in front of her, the hands holding onto their opposing forearms. Settling just inside the sleeves, her hands are barely visible. The camera is curious and follows them into the shadows. I suspect that this is why she chose the robe, wanted to memorialize herself in it. Its sleeves, ample and suggestive, serve as a proxy for an open neckline, bared shoulders, nipples arched against the swirling patterns embedded in the silk. A proxy, I imagine, for her desire to expose her body to light, a compulsion to wake it. This we have in common, I know.

CHAPTER 16

Madame's secretary, like most Vietnamese Catholics in Saigon, had heard of the Old Man. A proselytizer of the city's poor, they were calling him. A holy man even, except for the fact that he had a wife. They had heard, though, that after his fourth son was born, he took a vow of chastity. He is now fully devoted to God, they say. He is our next Father Augustine, they say. And among them, who had not heard the story of Father Augustine, a simple country priest who was handpicked by the Bishop of Saigon for the journey that is the closest that any of them will come to the doors of heaven while still standing on this unflinching earth? Father Augustine, they say, stood underneath the soaring dome of St. Peter's and marveled at the softness of marble, at the way that his God had allowed His servants to drape it, clothe His Son's image in it. Father Augustine kissed the papal ring but died before he could reach his final destination, the one that he believed would make his pilgrimage complete. He died on a cargo ship that was taking him to the south of France to the town of Avignon, the birthplace of the Jesuit Alexandre de Rhodes. Father Augustine was compelled, as the story goes, to see all that this Jesuit had left behind him, all that this missionary had relegated to a memory that would fail him, all that this man had sacrificed in order to bring Catholicism to the land that Father Augustine would never again see. His life for His faith, they say. A worthy trade, they say. The Old Man is cut from the same cloth as Father Augustine. That is his destiny. But now, he has the unseemly distinction of having a sodomite for a son. The wife is easy to overlook, but the sodomite is a sin against God. How could such a blasphemous fruit fall from such a holy tree? they will ask. Maybe the tree itself is corrupted, its wood pocked with grubs, is what they will think.

As all of this was playing itself out in the Old Man's spirits-soaked brain, he stood waiting for me at the front door of his house. From the look on his face, I could tell that no part of that structure belonged to me now. From the stance of his body, I could tell that he was beyond drunk, one shot glass away from kissing the floor. When I was younger, I used to think that if I shoved a lit match into his ear canal, his entire head would ignite into flames, burning away the alcohol that clogged it in a single flash. Now, well, now it was too late. As I walked toward him, I could see my mother's straw hat hanging in its usual place at the entrance to the kitchen. The kitchen was an addition, an afterthought that jutted out from the back of the house. It had its own entrance but no door. A piece of cloth the color of honey hung in the opening. My mother said that the color soothed her. She saved our tea leaves for a month before she had enough to dye the piece of muslin, which she had carefully ripped from a larger bolt. "Why not leave it white?" I asked, anxious for something to stand between us and the flies.

"White is the color of mourning," she said.

I know that she saved the rest of that muslin, rolled-up and hidden away. Did she take it out after I was gone? Did she take down the sheet of honey, kiss it as she would my cheeks, wrap it up to keep it safe?

"Don't come any closer!" the Old Man shouted. He lowered his voice and greeted me in this manner: "I have three sons. A chef. A porter. A printer."

Is that it? I thought. I was expecting something more violent. It began long ago with his thumb pressed into the soft spot of my skull. Then a stick of wood thicker than my arm splintered into my shin. Lately, a chair leg shoved into my Adam's apple. Though it was true that as I grew older, the Old Man had become less reliant on physical violence to get his points across, or maybe I had grown more adept at dodging his blows. Either way, the same damage had been done. In the end, words were easier for him. They took less of his time, and they tore through the same skin.

"Did you hear me? I said that I have *three* sons."

231

He sounds as if he is practicing for a speech, I thought. "I am a Catholic Holy Man, and I have three sons . . ." I imagined him refining his opening remarks.

"I've always had only three. You are your mother's. As for your father, you'll have to ask her. Because I'm a charitable man, I kept you both anyway, and this is how you repay me?"

A question is sometimes best answered with another: "Charity that has to be *repaid?* Wouldn't that make it a loan?" I thought and then uncharacteristically said aloud to him.

The Old Man, who was no longer my father, looked at me, spat in my face, and walked back inside his house.

I stand there still. A line of fire ants crawls up the frame of the doorway. Tiny orange marigolds, their petals bunched together, twisted inside themselves, crowd around the dirt path on which I stand. Out of the corner of my eye, I see the fraying chin strap of my mother's hat moving listlessly in the sun. I stand there still.

The story of Father Augustine, as I remember it, also included a journal that he left behind filled with ecstasies, raptures, and a dying wish. Death, they say, was kind to the Father and gave him prior notice. Father Augustine, according to his own entries, took that opportunity to secure a promise from the ship captain that if he were to die before they reached shore, his body would be delivered to Avignon and interred in a Catholic cemetery. In exchange for the promise, the captain was to receive all that Father Augustine carried with him, which—to the captain's subsequent surprise and to Father Augustine's as well, if only he had been alive to see—was a small fortune in gold chalices, a papal gift for the Bishop of Saigon. This is where their story usually ends. Death is the most moving conclusion, they say.

Far from finding it inspirational, my mother and I thought Father Augustine's story was a tragedy. To die so far away from home, we thought, is the worst possible ending. Overall, though, we liked the story. Not for its tears but for its gold chalices and the Father's unknowing transportation of them. We thought that these two details were both loose threads in an otherwise satisfactory tale. They were, for us, not quite inconsistencies but paths that should have been further explored. We used to tell each other different endings, taking up the matter of the gold chalices and their transport, and seeing where they would take us. My mother and I felt free to improvise because we did not attach to Father Augustine's story the religious significance that Vietnamese Catholics did. For them, he was a simple country priest who was chosen to travel to the Vatican as an envoy for the faithful of Vietnam. He was a simple country priest who was granted a papal audience because he had baptized his entire village, starting with his father and mother. He was a simple country priest who, when confronted by the praise of His Holiness, confessed that he had sinned. His motives, Father Augustine admitted, were selfish. He had been afraid of being alone in heaven. He was a simple country priest who kissed the papal ring, whose only sins were his fidelity and devotion to the Catholic Church. The lessons to be learned, the deeds to be emulated, were numerous and growing. For those who told it, Father Augustine's story became, like the chalices that he had unknowingly traded away, a vessel from which they, the truly devoted, could taste heaven, sweet and redemptive. For my mother and me, the story of Father Augustine was like any other, a thing to be repeated and retold. A story, after all, is best when shared, a gift in the truest sense of the word.

Father Augustine's god was, for my mother, not as compelling as the others in her life. She was born a Buddhist. She, in addition, was taught from birth to worship her ancestors. She never saw the faces of her grandparents, so that left her with only her father and mother, a god and something of a demigod in the order of honor at her family altar. It was not until the morning when she was wed that she was baptized a Catholic. Her head was draped in a white cloth, trimmed with two blue bands. When she walked into Father Vincente's church, she saw the statue of the "Virgin Mother," whose head was similarly covered, and she recognized the woman whom this religion wanted her to be. "Virgin Mother? But how do they have babies?"

the girl, who would grow up to be my mother, naturally wanted to know. The answer came to her that night and so did the pain between her legs. He is trying to push through to the other side, she thought. She had just begun her monthly bleedings, so when she saw the blood caked to the inside of her legs the next morning she thought it was one and the same. She took out the strips of cotton that her mother had given her and folded one into a narrow wad. She placed it in between her legs, wrapped either end of it around a second strip that she had already tied around her waist. Then she cooked for her new husband his morning rice. Her mother had given her ten cotton strips and a pair of earrings, two small jade hoops taken from her own lobes.

Long, fleshy Buddha lobes are a sign of good luck, the girl's mother had been told, but she frankly had suffered only bad. Her husband had passed away, and he had left her with nothing. Just a young daughter and no sons. That is the worst kind of luck, she had been told. By the time that her daughter turned twelve, the mother was tired of living off the meager, spiteful charity of her brother-in-law. She wanted to see her husband again. Desperately. She saw him in her dreams, and he told her what to do. Marry off their daughter and join him in the afterlife. "It is the only noble thing to do," he told her. His family could not afford to feed both of them forever, she agreed. She went to a matchmaker the next day and said, "I have a pair of jade earrings." She tucked her hair behind her ears and showed them to him. "Here," she said, "and I have a daughter and that is all."

"Don't worry," said the matchmaker, though his wrinkled face said, You should worry! Those earrings are hardly enough for a dowry.

She returned to her brother-in-law's house and wept. Her daughter slept beside her as she had done since her father was wrapped in a sheet of white. Their life continued in this way for another two years. Every few months or so, the mother would hear of another matchmaker who was passing through their village in search of a good deal on a bride. "I want to see my husband again," she finally told one of them. "Desperately," she added as she locked onto the man's eyes, forcing him to see what she wanted to do. "Desperately," she repeated. The matchmaker, a man with a heart, rare for someone of his profession, said that he would see what he could do. He returned a month later and reported the good news. A young man, a Catholic educated by the holy fathers, was willing to take her daughter for a bride. But first, the young man wanted to know three things. One, has the girl started to bleed? Two, is there a history of infertility in the family? Three, when was the mother planning to "see" her husband? The mother immediately answered, "Yes, no, and right after the wedding." The matter was then settled as the matchmaker had been instructed to accept the deal, if those were the exact responses.

"Worship" is a strong word. Especially when spoken as a command, worship should not to be used carelessly or lightly. My mother was taught the meaning of this word, the unblinking force of it, even before she could say "Má" and "Cha." Before she even knew what to call them, what their blood relationship to her was, she knew that their word was absolute, above law, equal to religion. She was told that in their death she would worship them, and in their life she must obey them. From the very beginning, "worship" was for my mother synonymous with "obey," and so she never thought to run, to stand up and let her bare feet carry her beyond the marshes surrounding her uncle's house. She sat still while her mother heated the needle and bled her earlobes. She sat still while her mother took the jade from her stretched lobes and placed them in hers. She sat still and received from her mother a rare gift of tenderness, which for the girl would always mean pain. This was her last memory of her mother. The next morning the girl awoke with no one by her side. She had been instructed by her mother the night before about what route to take, and how to send word through the matchmaker once the wedding had taken place. The girl touched her ears. She kissed the mat that they slept on because there was nothing else to bid good-bye.

The girl heard of her mother's death from the matchmaker. He always brings me bad news, she thought. The pounding through to the other side continued until she began to show. Her swollen belly brought with it a reprieve. The cycle continued two more times. Three boys. Her husband was lucky, indeed, she was told. After the first one, he was certainly flushed with pride. He built for her a larger kitchen at the back of his house. He wanted a room where she and the baby, who would not stop crying, could go when there was business to be done in the main part of the house. As she sat inside the addition, nursing his firstborn, she heard mumbled prayers and the clicking of coins coming from the central rooms. She heard strange men's voices, sometimes weeping and other times taut with ecstasy, all saying aloud "Amen." This "Amen" must be a powerful Catholic god, she thought.

In her second act of defiance—her first was her vow never to step back inside Father Vincente's church—she set up a small shrine at the back of the kitchen in honor of Buddha, in memory of her father, and in spite of her mother's lack of affection for her. The last, of course, troubled her but she dutifully tried to set it aside. Sometimes, though, during the nights when the rain would not stop and she was touched by something akin to the feeling of being cold, she would hold her baby boy in her arms and think about the love that her mother bore for her father. She wanted to know how love for a man could outweigh love for one's own child. How could love be so desperate that it would urge a mother to leave her only daughter behind to this man and his pounding to get through to the other side? At first she was afraid that her husband would find the altar, but soon it became clear that he would never go inside the kitchen, that that was hers. The dirt floor, the clay pots, the tin plates, the ladles made from coconut shells, the earthenware cistern kept out back for collecting the rain, she loved it all as she loved her child. At first, she was afraid that she loved it more because it belonged solely to her. The boy, after all, was also his.

A few months after his second son was born, she found at the back of the neighborhood schoolhouse an old discarded calendar. All the signs of the zodiac were illustrated on it in red ink. Red was the color of good luck, she had been told. So she hung the calendar on the wall of her kitchen, and every day she looked at her sign, that of the Dog, and wondered why her father and mother could not have waited another year so that she could have been born under the sign of the Pig. The Dog is watchful, loyal, a fierce defender of its own, she had been told. The Pig, though, is endowed with the gift of resignation and acceptance, the two things that would always ensure ease in a Pig's life. In this way, she had heard, a woman born in the Year of the Pig would always be lucky. But if luck was not her birthright, she thought, then she would have to look for it on her own. So from then on at the end of every week, the girl made it a point to return to the back of the schoolhouse to see if any other thing of value had made its way into the trash.

Why throw something so precious away? she thought, as she bent to pick up a tin box covered in a gaudy design. On its lid, a woman was flying up toward a full moon, and that reminded her of her mother. The Moon Festival had just ended, and she could still smell the cakes that the box had held for the occasion. She took the tin home and added it to the altar. Even without this offering, she knew that her father and mother were proud of her. She had just given birth to her husband's third son. Her belly was still distended, and she knew that her husband would not notice her again for several months. A blessing, she thought.

By the time of the Lunar New Year, her belly had collapsed, but she was too swept up in the festivities to worry about her husband's footsteps in the night. Like everyone else in Saigon, she wanted something new to welcome in the new year. A tiny bead of gold on a pink silk cord, an *áo dài* with a touch of embroidery around the neck, a straw hat with a cotton sateen chin strap—but she knew such luxuries were not in her future. So she went by the back of the schoolhouse to see what she could find. Lying there on the ground was another tin box. From the design on its lid, she could tell that it had held candied lotus seeds. She kneeled down to pick it up and was surprised to find that the box was unopened, a length of string wrapped tightly around it. She felt like a thief with

240

something so brand-new in her hands. She looked up to see if anyone was watching her. She looked up and she saw my father. He was watching her through the schoolhouse windows. He wore wire spectacles, small, oval, and almost invisible from where she was still stooped. They marked him as educated and of another class. A scholar-prince, she thought.

Their courtship began like that. Simple. A box of candied lotus seeds sweetened their first sighs of love. The schoolteacher loved her, and he loved her body. He loved it until it started to show. Her hair grew thick, shiny with oil, and smelled of the fresh orange peels that she used to mist her comb. Her face glowed, the color of sand, warm and clean. Her breasts grew tender, sore with milk. She was carrying her fourth and his first. The schoolteacher told her that he was going abroad for further studies. To France, he said. He gave her a small amount of money and no way to contact him. She could have sworn, though, that she saw him a few months later walking out of Saigon's Notre-Dame with a young woman by his side. It was Ash Wednesday, and they each had on their forehead a fingerprint the color of a monsoon sky. My mother took some of the money and bought a bolt of white muslin and an *áo dài* made of gray silk. For the future, she thought. She knew that it would have been impossible to keep the money in its paper form. If she had hidden it, the Old Man would have found it. He takes everything of value

241

from me, she thought. My mother was eighteen, about to turn nineteen when she gave birth to her last son. She was a young woman, and she had three boys by one man and one by another.

"Please, please, please," my mother begged. She had given what was left of the schoolteacher's money to the midwife, but she was afraid that the woman would renege on their deal.

"Are you sure?" the midwife repeated.

My mother nodded, yes, exhausted from my birth. The midwife stuck her hand inside her, and then there was an unfamiliar pain. When my mother woke up she heard: "She'll survive, but she'll never give birth again." My mother's husband was standing over the midwife as she washed her hands in a basin of water. His arms were folded across his chest. His rosary was caught in the crook of his bent arms, and the cross was pushed up and out. From across the room where my mother lay, she could see the man nailed onto it, the man who had given Himself for her sins, as Father Vincente had told her. For *my* sins? she had thought.

Her husband approached her, and she turned her head abruptly to one side because she thought he was going to hit her. He held out his right hand and said, "Give them to me."

She heard him say, "Give *him* to me." But I do not have the baby in my arms, she thought. The baby, she should have known, was of no interest to him. I was a boy and that was good, but otherwise he was through with her.

"I want the earrings," he said. "How am I supposed to pay the midwife?" he asked.

But I have already paid her, my mother thought, for different services, though. The midwife had asked for her payment many months in advance for performing an act of mercy. The midwife had promised to give her a reprieve for the rest of her life. "No more pounding, no more collapsing belly, no more breasts swollen with milk," my mother had begged.

My mother and I liked this ending best:

The night that Father Augustine died, the captain had the man's frail body wrapped in an old tablecloth and dumped into the Mediterranean Sea. Father Augustine's shoes went with him because no one else on board had such small feet. A day later when the ship docked in the harbor of Marseilles, the captain woke up, soaked in his own guilt. The Indochinese whom he had robbed was not just a man but a priest. The captain hastily arranged for Father Augustine's travel journal to make its own arduous journey back to Vietnam and to the Bishop of Saigon. A note from the captain accompanied the journal and declared in a shaky hand: "The Father's dying wish was, of course, respected."

My mother and I enjoyed this version because the last words did not belong to Father Augustine but to the man who took the gold chalices home with him. We wondered how they must have looked displayed on the windowsill of the captain's house. We imagined that they must have caught the glint of the sun and poured its light all over the room. Beautiful, we thought.

When I now think about the story of Father Augustine, I tell myself that the Bishop of Saigon must have known—not about my mother's blasphemous endings but about the gold chalices and Father Augustine's transport of them. This version I did not hear, however, until I had already left Vietnam. The man on the bridge told it to me in the Jardin du Luxembourg while the rest of Paris slept:

The Bishop of Saigon had been duly informed of the papal largesse and had sent Father Augustine to the Vatican to ensure the chalices' safe delivery. But when a year had gone by since Father Augustine was last seen kneeling in the apse of St. Peter's, his death at sea was assumed, and a Mass was celebrated in his memory by the Bishop himself. Meanwhile, Father Augustine's journal, with its black leather cover, the insides lined with marbled paper, a tribute to the only stone that Father Augustine believed was virtuous enough for Him, traveled the open seas and found its way home and into the hands of the Bishop of Saigon. The Bishop admired its Italian craftsmanship and thought the marbleized pattern tastefully done, a palette of plums and sea foam greens. The Bishop turned to the final entry. Father Augustine's last page, like those before it,

244

was written in Vietnamese, a language that had centuries ago been cast into a neat Romanized script, chased with tildes, circumflexes, breves, acute and grave accents, an oblation from the Jesuit Alexandre de Rhodes. The Jesuit, like all missionaries after him, understood the power of literacy. The written word never stops proselytizing, never dies of malaria, and has an uncanny tendency to reproduce, an act that he as a man of God was not privy to. The Jesuit dismantled the ideographs of Vietnam and taught his converts their catechisms in a language reconfigured for the sake of simplicity. Easier to learn and easier to teach, thought the Jesuit. The Bishop of Saigon was a living testament to the success of the Jesuit's invention. The Bishop's blue eyes skimmed the last page of Father Augustine's journal and were enraged to learn that a simple country priest had traded away his gold chalices for a burial in Avignon. The Bishop ripped out all traces of Father Augustine and kept the journal, with its remaining blank pages, for his own. Father Augustine was a simple country priest, indeed. He was an errand boy in the guise of an emissary, or maybe he was an emissary in the guise of an errand boy. Either way, the man was robbed, said the man on the bridge. His worship and his obedience had landed him in the depth of a faraway sea.

My mother, like Father Augustine, had experienced passion, rapturous, transformative passion, which she continued to feel long after the school-teacher went away. My father may not have been constant, but he was brave. Brave enough to love even though he knew that his love, like his vision, was predisposed to weaken and fade. She herself braved more, I tell myself. And this is where her story ends. Bravery, for me, is always the culmination of the story. What more is there left to say? My mother would certainly have agreed, if she had been there to hear. Bão, though, was the only one present. "This is the story of my mother" was how I began. "It is about a life that she must have lived, if just for a while, with her scholar-prince. It is a story filled with misty lakes, shadow-graced embraces, exotic locales, travel on the open seas, family secrets, un-Christian vices."

"Go on," said Bão. In the end, Bão thought that my mother was admirable, like Serena the Soloist but in a different way.

"Yes," I agreed, as I closed my eyes. The *Niobe*, calmed by the light of the moon, rested in a valley between two waves, a mother's bosom in a distant sea. In the dark, where my thoughts traveled without a trace of fear, I longed for her touch, for the look in her eyes when I parted the sheet of honey and stood before her.

Inside her kitchen, my mother had waited for me on her sleeping mat. She had heard the Old Man's shouts. When I entered, she got up to pour us a cup of tea. I sat down on the dirt floor because my life was moving too quickly, and I thought being closer to the ground would slow it down. I rocked back and forth on my haunches, like the old woman who sells whatever she has in her garden that day. My mother walked over to me. She sat down and wrapped herself around me, pressing my stooped back into hers. The gesture stopped time.

I know, Má. I know. I have never left your womb, is how you want me to feel. I will always be protected, safe inside of you, is what you want me always to remember. Yes, Má, I know. Yes, Má, I am there still.

My mother took a red pouch from the inside of the money belt that she had worn around her waist since my birth. The one place where the Old Man will never look, she thought. She put the pouch in my hand and told me she had no real need or desire for that bit of extravagance anymore. I gave her back the pouch, but she pushed it back into my hand. "I have all that I need," she lied. I smiled because my mother, even at a time like this, could not manage to sound angry or harsh. I put the red pouch in my shirt pocket. I kissed her cheeks, taking the time to smell the oranges in her hair.

CHAPTER 17

Stein and Toklas are brazen, you tell me. Lovey and Pussy? My Lord, those two really have no shame, you say, laughing out loud. You, Sweet Sunday Man, want to know everything about them, from their pet names for each other to whether they have kissed in front of me. You refer to them both as "the Steins," which confuses me, but you assure me that all the boys who gather at their Saturday teas call them "the Steins" as well. Behind their backs, that is, you say, warning me never to say such a thing to their faces. The Steins? Of course not, Sweet Sunday Man, that would make them sound like some sort of a machine. My Mesdames, believe me, are many things, but they are definitely not mechanically inclined. GertrudeStein and Miss Toklas own an automobile, but only GertrudeStein drives. Miss Toklas navigates. GertrudeStein has a love of the open road, but only Miss Toklas has the maps. Both my Mesdames, however, are equally ill equipped when it comes to the sludgy oil drips, the sputtering engine, the familiar slow rolling motion before each unscheduled stop. An automobile, my Mesdames agree, is a machine and animal confused into one. Caught somewhere in between, it is, understandably, a bit temperamental. Experience, though, has taught them that breakdowns are just temporary. Automobiles, unlike humans, have many lives. My Mesdames simply have to be patient and wait for the next reincarnation. Actually, they just have to wait for the next car. The sight of two women sitting in a vehicle, unaccompanied by a man and therefore seen as "alone," always stops traffic of all kinds, though traffic, or what passes for it, is often scarce: a young man on a bicycle, a hay-filled cart pulled by a farm horse and his owner, another man, this time not so young, on a bicycle. All are eager to help, but all are slow to reach it because the actual help is often several towns away. In France, mechanics are not like bakers. One is not needed for each town.

When Miss Toklas knows that their drive will take them outside Paris, to places where a taxi cannot be hailed at a moment's notice for the return trip home, she packs along their "waiting kits." Hers contains a set of knitting needles and several balls of apple green yarn, the disheveled kind with wispy hairs tangled on its surface. She likes the color, so unripe it makes her pucker just to look at it. But most of all, she likes how the crispness of the color serves as a foil for the texture of the yarn, a melt-in-her-hand sensation. The eyes tell her one story, and the hands tell her another. Miss Toklas is particularly fond of this sort of interchange. She thinks it makes the difference between a well-knitted scarf and an intriguing, well-knitted scarf. "Fashionable, stylish, pretty" are too subjective, she thinks, accountable as they are to personal foibles and the mood of the time. "Intriguing," however, always calls for a second look, an irresistible glance back, a heightened desire to know and to have. Intrigue cannot be added at the very end. A sprinkling of sequins, a glazing of glass beads, a handful of store-bought fringes, all suggest a lack of forethought, like salting a roast after it has cooked as opposed to before. My Madame knows that intrigue, like salt, is best if it is there from the beginning.

Miss Toklas's approach to knitting is the same as her approach to cooking. Take lamb à la Toklas, for instance. (This is my name for the dish, not hers. Too immodest a gesture, she would think.) In the early spring, American dinner guests at 27 rue de Fleurus are often served lamb. Only the Americans. Miss Toklas thinks that French lamb is wasted on the French. They have grown up with it, have come to expect it. But the Americans, they come to her table in ignorance, and it is they who will depart her table in bliss. On these occasions, Miss Toklas insists on *pré-salé* lamb, roasted simply in a disappearing swath of butter and served without sauce, condiment, or even a sprig of mint. Just a hunk of perfectly browned meat placed in the middle of an oval platter. The stark presentation is met with polite words of praise. Hypocrites, Miss Toklas thinks. She finds it most distressing that the world is so filled with people who flatter and eulogize before ever tasting. Miss Toklas would never waste her words in this way. Admire the china pattern, the crystal wine goblets, the hothouse blooms, but never compliment the food on sight alone. Wait until it has reached your tongue. After all, the tongue is an organ of truth. It cannot pretend to find flavors where there are none. Nor can it ignore the slip-slime of undercooked chicken, the aggressive tang of soured milk, burnt sugar's pervasive iron fumes. Miss Toklas is no fool. She knows and she expects that the lamb on sight alone will be sure to disappoint, raise invisible eyebrows about her supposed culinary skills. Ah, but then the lamb is carved and it is eaten and it is never forgotten.

Pré-salé lambs are named for the salt marshes along the northern coast of France where they graze. Saltwater overflows onto flat stretches of land and leaves behind a sweet mix of herbs and flora. Elemental and tender, *pré-salé* lambs are salted and seasoned from the raw beginning. Now *that*, Miss Toklas thinks, is forethought. The first bite is a revelation of flavors, infused and deep. The second bite is a reminder of why we kill and eat the young. The third allows the brain back into the fray to ask, But how is it possible? Not a visible grind of pepper, a milky grain of salt, not even the faintest traces of rosemary, wild fennel, or thyme, and yet the lamb gives all this and more.

251

Yes, intrigue is what my Madame aspires to in all of her creations.

GertrudeStein's waiting kit consists of a stack of blank notebooks, lined and margined for schoolchildren to use, and a box of sharpened pencils. Ink is absolutely out of the question. Even when she is sitting at a proper table, ink runs from her fingertips to her face and through her hair. Ink always finds her sleeves and too often the front of her shirt. Miss Toklas tells GertrudeStein that she should replace brown—the color that gives her Lovey's wardrobe its distinctly uniform-like quality—with the even more practical black. Not only would it hide dirt, which is the only reason Miss Toklas can imagine for wearing the color brown, but black would also hide the ink. GertrudeStein thinks it is an excellent idea until she sees the slyness, a green snake below the water's surface, in Miss Toklas's eyes. GertrudeStein rumbles and Miss Toklas smirks. And it is in this manner, with their waiting kits in hand, that my Mesdames are so often found by the side of the road. Miss Toklas never panics. Her heart keeps its steady beat. She understands that this tableau that she and GertrudeStein present to passersby is universally seen as a beacon for help. Miss Toklas knows from all the cowboy stories that GertrudeStein has insisted on reading aloud to her (whenever the detective stories are set aside) that there is nothing more foreboding within the landscape of rocky mountain ranges and a blue blanket sky than the sight of a saddled but riderless horse. In the French countryside, a manless car is a saddled but riderless horse, a sure sign that something has gone awry. Miss Toklas knows that their peaceful scene will, therefore, trigger an irritatingly similar albeit helpful response. GertrudeStein thinks that it is her winning American smile, an open-faced roast beef sandwich of a smile, and Miss Toklas's jaunty hats that flag down the many offers of help.

While GertrudeStein has little interest in how her automobile works or more often in how it does not, she believes that there exists between the two of them a bond, sinewy and organic. She feels that bond with motorized beasts of burden of all kinds, really. If it was up to her, she and Miss Toklas would be driving a truck. Every time she sits behind the wheel, she is certain that it helps her creativity to flow, that it encourages her words to find their otherwise reluctant mates. GertrudeStein thinks it is the rumbling motor, the bouncing seats, or maybe just the rolling promise of speed. Miss Toklas wonders whether it is the fumes. Petrol and motor oil may promote the release of genius, Miss Toklas thinks. GertrudeStein dismisses that as being highly unlikely. She refuses to assign such prowess to her sense of smell. Her nose, she thinks, is a dismal failure. She blames it for her inability to examine patients and her inability to cook. Miss Toklas thinks it is inappropriate and possibly grotesque for her Lovey to lump these two tasks together in this way. GertrudeStein reminds Miss Toklas that her first experience with a live patient in medical school was also her last. To be a good doctor, GertrudeStein has since concluded, one must possess a keen sense of smell in order to identify and, more importantly, to distinguish among the odors emitted from the body during its varying stages of decay. The breath, for example, unfortunately tells all. Honey could mean diabetes. Vinegar, an ulcerous stomach. The urine is also instructive. It can stink of turnips and cabbages, indicating a diet starved for meats. It can bloom with alcohol when the liver is drowning and has forgotten its function. There is also the oniony burn of unbathed sweat, the sweet sausage smell of a festering wound. Miss Toklas puts an end to GertrudeStein's line of comparison with a look that says, Proceed with caution! GertrudeStein heeds the warning but continues to claim that her nose had failed her because it could not bear the onslaught and retaliated by combining all of her patient's beastly odors into a solid wall of filth and stink, a wall that she was absolutely unwilling to breach. GertrudeStein's reluctant nose is, as she claims, also accountable for her absolute unwillingness to cook. Miss Toklas does not have to be reminded that an inquisitive sense of smell is of utmost importance in the domestic science, and that GertrudeStein would rather drink a glass of spoiled milk than bother to smell it beforehand.

GertrudeStein has to admit, though not to Miss Toklas, that in this instance she may be right. No place reeks of an automobile more than a garage, and she was in a garage the first time she became aware of the relationship between her creativity and her automobile. GertrudeStein was sitting inside someone else's equally temperamental vehicle, waiting for her own to be taken apart and reassembled with new spark plugs and a cigarette lighter for the dashboard, the latter a surprise for Miss Toklas. GertrudeStein was accompanied that afternoon only by a book, as Miss Toklas insisted that ladies do not frequent garages. The constant revving of the engines, the newly resuscitated automobiles tossing around their woolly balls of exhaust, were oddly riveting, GertrudeStein thought. The aggressive unmistakable smells of inanimate things coming to life, heat-blasted metals coming into contact with the musk of sweat, the smell of man ardently courting machine, were even more distracting. In the way that Miss Toklas in a corset is distracting, thought GertrudeStein. She looked down at the book on her lap, and she saw the printed words fighting for her attention, their confrontations disrupting order and meaning. To amuse her, to vie for her gaze, they allied themselves in provocative ways. They formed poems and plays, essays and the beginnings of very long short stories. They promised her the words to an opera and the history of everyone who has ever lived. GertrudeStein rummaged through the pockets of her jacket. Anything, a pin to prick some of her own red ink would be fine at a moment like this, she thought. Instead, her fingers found and pushed aside wrapped pieces of cinnamon candy that Miss Toklas had placed in her pockets in order to delay the faint fluttery feeling just prior to hunger, a feeling that she knew GertrudeStein deplores. Forethought is indeed Miss Toklas's hallmark, but forethought is never a match for a whim. This lapse in an otherwise spotless record of devoted anticipation left GertrudeStein in a rare predicament.

Recalling that it takes energy to fend for herself, GertrudeStein popped a red lozenge into her mouth and waited for the burn of cinnamon to wake her tongue. She then called out to the garage clerk and told him to hand her the pencil tucked behind his ear. For the next several hours, GertrudeStein steadily covered the book on her lap with her own writing. She found room inside the front cover, inside the back, in the margins, the cleansing expanses of white at the beginning of each chapter. The lines of text were printed too closely together, otherwise she would have written between them as well. When GertrudeStein returned to 27 rue de Fleurus, she presented the book to Miss Toklas, who promptly began to transcribe. Miss Toklas typed three complete copies and spent the remainder of the week carefully proofing each one. She then erased GertrudeStein's scribbles, turning the book pages gray. When she returned it to the lending library, both of their memberships were revoked. When Miss Toklas asked, GertrudeStein proudly identified their automobile as the mechanized muse. Every person and everything has its own throb and rhythm. The automobile, according to GertrudeStein, just helps to amplify them as it zooms on by. Now that she can so easily hear them, she told Miss Toklas, she would know exactly when to devote a sentence or a paragraph to any passing person or thing. Sentences can be hundreds of lines long. Paragraphs can be one word or two. Length has nothing to do with it. GertrudeStein does not eyeball a paragraph or a sentence. She hears it as her automobile zooms on by.

"Zooms on by?" Miss Toklas repeated, demanding to know how GertrudeStein could possibly drive and write at the same time.

"No, no," said GertrudeStein, "I was parked in a garage."

Miss Toklas wondered whether GertrudeStein's logic was, here, somewhat flawed. If Lovey was sitting inside a parked automobile, in a garage of all places, then it would suggest that movement and speed had little to do with Lovey's creative gush and flow. Miss Toklas concluded, despite GertrudeStein's assertions, that it must have been the garage and possibly the fumes.

Of course it was the garage. Sweet Sunday Man,

can you imagine any place more masculine, more exclusively male? Yes, there are the *pissotières*, but my Madame does not have what it takes to gain entrance there. GertrudeStein does have an automobile, and that is all she needs to be admitted into the meetinghouses of the fraternal order of mechanics, taxi drivers, freight deliverers, and chauffeurs, among whom there is rarely a lady present, except for my Madame. She enjoys the attention, the fizzy distinction of being the only one. Now, *that* is what this Madame strives for in her creations.

Miss Toklas notwithstanding, I have noticed that GertrudeStein tends to avoid the company of women. Tiresome, GertrudeStein thinks. During the Saturday teas, the door of 27 rue de Fleurus is opened to both men and women. Only the women, though, are taken for a tour of the apartment, a forced march that ends in the kitchen, Miss Tolkas's balmy lair. The same tea and cakes are served here as out in the studio, the same paper-thin china cups and saucers, the same bouquets of flowers, drooping, however, as they are unaccustomed to the oven's heat. Miss Toklas keeps the conversation rolling along. She compares and contrasts the latest trends in dresses and shoes, shares her opinions about the city's better milliners and seamstresses, and dispenses unsolicited culinary and gardening advice. The women—colleagues, collaborators, friends, and occasionally lovers of the young men who at that moment are all in the studio, oblivious to their absence—remain for the most part silent. From shock, I am sure. Sitting in the kitchen with Miss Toklas and her "Chinaman," as they inexplicably think that I am, is not where these American ladies have traveled all this way to be. Shanghaied, they must feel. Well, yes, my dear, but at least on Miss Toklas's barge, you have me to serve you tea and cake.

As the afternoon wears on, some of the women shift gears. Maybe if they amuse Miss Toklas, maybe then, they will be ushered into the glow and the hum of that other room. Their sleek heads lean into my Madame's voice and their shoulders cup her words. As they speak, they motion their heads toward the direction of the studio, their bodies yearning to follow.

No hope of that, my dear. Why fight my Madame so? Miss Toklas, believe me, is a package worth unwrapping. An artichoke, if you know what I mean. They never do.

Miss Toklas enjoys the attention, graciously answers all of their questions, and never forgets the task at hand. As the sun sinks, as the sounds coming from the studio rise, the women become resigned to the fact that the kitchen is their final destination. The more astute among them wonder whether they are confined here at the behest of Miss Toklas or GertrudeStein.

Both, really. But for different reasons.

GertrudeStein considers these women all merely "wives." Their actual marital status does not interest her, nor their sometimes obvious sexual interest in one another. Wives are never geniuses. Geniuses are never wives. GertrudeStein, therefore, has no use for them, especially at her Saturday tea. A social occasion, yes, but above all it is the first rite for the devoted. Those who amuse her, flatter her, hand over their beating hearts to her, are rewarded with an invitation for lunch, the second station toward intimacy. The third station can only be reached via an invitation for dinner. If there are wives involved, my Madame extends the dinner invitation to them as well, out of courtesy and rarely out of interest. For GertrudeStein, who already has one, thank you very much, wives are comforting, comfortable, and often someone to be comforted. They are amusing in small doses, distracting even, especially when their shapely legs arrive at the rue de Fleurus slipped into sheer stockings, a barely present mist that GertrudeStein knows can be made to disappear with several waves of her hands. Miss Toklas knows that GertrudeStein appreciates wives in her own ways. She sees GertrudeStein following the curves snaking up their skirts. Hell, blind men can even see GertrudeStein looking. Her appreciation for the female form is difficult to ignore. When Miss Toklas first visited the rue de Fleurus, she felt GertrudeStein's "appreciation" on her like a ribbon of steel. She felt her flesh rubbing against it, felt sweat dripping down her back, sliding down the inside of her thighs. She crossed her legs, and GertrudeStein looked at her as if she knew. Salt enhances the sweetness. Delicious, thought GertrudeStein.

Dangerous, Miss Toklas now knows. Gertrude-Stein, as usual, misreads Miss Toklas's motivation and privileges her own. "Selfless," my Madame sighs, and thanks her lucky star that Miss Toklas is always there to keep the wives at bay. Wives are so irksome when there is work to be done. Not Pussy, though. No, never Pussy. But those who make the rules reserve the right to carve out the exceptions to the rules. Behind the door of 27 rue de Fleurus, my Mesdames are always the exceptions. Miss Toklas, though, could never be a genius, as there can only be one, according to GertrudeStein, within any given family. Some rules are ironclad. Others have wings. The difficulty, for me, has always been in identifying which is which.

Take Basket and Pépé, for instance. Last month, Miss Toklas told me, "Only one meal a day." His Highness and the nervous little Pretender to his throne had gained too much weight. Actually, everyone at 27 rue de Fleurus, except Miss Toklas and I, had gained too much weight and was being placed on a restricted regime, everyone including GertrudeStein. No exceptions, I thought. By training, I am prone to respect absolutes. When I hear words like "only" and "one," I believe.

But as anyone can see from the bulging bellies of the guilty three, *that* rule is far from absolute. When GertrudeStein is not looking, Miss Toklas feeds Pépé. When Miss Toklas is not looking, GertrudeStein feeds Basket. And who feeds GertrudeStein? I do, of course. She pays half of my salary, after all. This rule, believe me, is ironclad.

Sweet Sunday Man, I see you watching my Mesdames. I see you looking when you think they are not, searching their irides for all the things that you are otherwise not privy to. They have been watching you too. About this I would not lie, Sweet Sunday Man. My Mesdames' curiosity is piqued by implausible things. They saw your hands and immediately knew that you are no writer. Too clean and well groomed, they thought. Writers rarely have clipped nails. They tend to use their teeth. Too smooth and callus-free, they noted. You are not a laborer either, they knew. Yes, I know that they could have concluded that just from hearing you speak, but my Mesdames are in this way like me. They never assume that words can tell them the whole story. But, Sweet Sunday Man, it was not your hands that first gave you away. It was your back. GertrudeStein saw it twice during your first visit to 27 rue de Fleurus. It was such an unexpected sight because those who gather around GertrudeStein never depart while she is in midsentence. Never. Believe me, "the boys," as you call them, rarely break away from the conversation circle, not even to relieve themselves. Miss Toklas is always amazed at how clean the toilet is after these crowded gatherings. GertrudeStein could see from the way you held your head that you were hanging onto her every word, even as you were walking away. Not listening but hearing. Hearing but not listening. You, Sweet Sunday Man, were by then a shiny new paradox to brighten my Madame's day. Later that evening, GertrudeStein reported your actions to Miss Toklas over a dish of my best Singapore ice cream. They both could taste the vanilla and the crystallized ginger, but only Miss Toklas could detect that there was something deeper, something that emerged as a lingering lace of a feeling on the tongue.

Peppercorns, Miss Toklas. Steep the milk from morning till night with ten coarsely crushed peppercorns. Strain and proceed as usual. The "bite" that the peppercorns leave behind will make the eater take notice, examine this dish of sweet anew. Think of it as an unexpected hint of irony in a familiar lover's voice.

GertrudeStein, too intrigued to be offended by your disregard, wanted to invite you immediately to dinner and examine you over some braised grouses. Miss Toklas knew that GertrudeStein's menu choice had little to do with the availability of game birds during the month of December. For GertrudeStein, it had more to do with the hunt.

263

Miss Toklas disagreed. She thought that such an uncharacteristic move would tip you off. Nothing can be gained from a subject who knows that he is being watched, a lesson that Miss Toklas had gleaned from all the detective stories that she has had to endure. Better than cowboys, she thought, but still she longed for those nights when GertrudeStein had read to her from the *Lives of Saints*. They had gotten only through the A's—St. Agatha with her amputated breasts, St. Agnes with her detached head, St. Appollonia with her bashed-in teeth—when GertrudeStein discovered the equally grim, though not as entertaining, detective stories populated with murderers and gamblers.

"Think of them as the *Lives of Sinners*," said GertrudeStein. "There are," she insisted, "similarities."

"Sinners lack passion," countered Miss Toklas.

Miss Toklas decided that they should not stray from their usual routine. They would invite you to the next Saturday tea but nothing more. Nothing should appear as if it had changed. Everything, of course, did once my Mesdames had their eyes on you, Sweet Sunday Man. Miss Toklas was delighted when you approached her that following Saturday with your inquiry for a cook. Such a convenient confluence of self-interest, she thought. That was when your hands unraveled your story. Miss Toklas noticed them immediately. A performer of some sort, she thought.

So expressive, the way his fingers bend, tracing the curving currents of air. An actor, maybe a puppeteer, in either case a man who makes his living by hiding himself away, she thought. Unlike me, Miss Toklas could not be absolutely sure. So she asked GertrudeStein that night whether your behavior had been the same as the week before.

"Yes," answered GertrudeStein, who then reported to Miss Toklas that you were much more discreet this time, but it was there all the same. Your erratic actions, your wayward bouts of disinterestedness, she announced, were rooted in an acute aversion to music or at the least any serious discussions of it. "A music critic, no doubt," GertrudeStein declared, her lips crackling into bits of much savored laughter. My Madame is always satiated by her own jokes. For Miss Toklas, I have noticed, the enjoyment is rarely the same.

"No, no, Lovey, he is not a writer," Miss Toklas insisted.

"I know he's not a writer, Pussy. I told you he's a critic."

"He is not a critic either, Lovey."

"Whatever Lattimore is, this afternoon he walked away right in the middle of my discussion with Robeson. A fascinating debate," GertrudeStein said, "for anyone with even the slightest interest in *music*."

"Robeson, the opera singer?"

265

"Yes, I asked him why he insisted on singing Negro spirituals when he could be performing requiems and oratorios. Do you know what that curiosity in a suit said? In that basso profundo voice of his, he replied, 'The spirituals, theys a belong to me, Missa Stein.'"

"Lovey, stop! You sound like a shoeshine boy. Have you considered that, maybe, for Lattimore your discussion with Robeson had nothing to do with *music*."

"No."

"Maybe it is Robeson who is the subject that Lattimore has no interest in, or maybe Lattimore has too much interest and does not want to let it show."

I suspect that Miss Toklas's intuition has always been above average, but after having to sit through the recitation of all those detective stories, it has sharpened into a bullet that never, never misses.

"Oh," said GertrudeStein.

"For goodness sake, Lovey, *music*? That is a bit of a stretch. When one looks at Mister Paul Robeson, the first thought that comes to mind is not music. Missa Stein, for a genius you ese a'ways plain wrong."

My Mesdames looked at each other, and their laughter rose up and consumed them. It climbed the walls, turned the corner, and followed me as I walked back into the kitchen. Malice, I was afraid. On second thought, that was not what I heard. Their laughter was not configured in that way. I know malice well, and it is a more meticulous, laboriously constructed thing. Theirs had a wormy center, a now-and-then upkeep. Unsettling to hear all the same. Unsettling because such things have no natural barriers, nothing that can contain their spread. Like my Mesdames, they can be born elsewhere and then taken abroad. That is how they seed. That is how they grow.

That was not what Robeson said, was it, Sweet Sunday Man? Tell me his response. Say it out loud.

"'Miss Stein, with spirituals I can sing. The others I have to perform.'"

GertrudeStein and Miss Toklas are brazen, indeed. Do you think, Sweet Sunday Man, that my Mesdames would have sent me out to just anyone? A good cook is a great commodity in this city. Any city, really. Ask yourself, "Where do they not eat?" and my point is made. Cooking is the answer to a universally placed classified ad. It allows me to live like a migrating bird, a fish in a barrierless sea. A blessing that is also a curse. Make no mistake, Sweet Sunday Man, Miss Toklas intended that I be an offering to you, a little mouse who could enter your kitchen, invited but otherwise unnoticed. From there, I could examine its cabinets and shelves and report their contents to the two curious Mesdames back at 27 rue de Fleurus. "Is Lattimore a Negro?" is what they, in the end, want to know. My Mesdames tell me that they just want to be absolutely sure.

267

All these years in France, you say, and Lovey and Pussy are still Americans, after all.

Of course, they are, Sweet Sunday Man. Of course, they are.

CHAPTER 18

Aboard the *Niobe*, I held the red pouch that my mother had so firmly pressed into my hand, and I thought about the days' worth of water between us. Then I thought about the weeks, months, years, decades of water to come. Time for me had always been measured in terms of the rising sun, its setting sister, and the dependable cycle of the moon. But at sea, I learned that time can also be measured in terms of water, in terms of the distance traveled while drifting on it. When measured in this way, nearer and farther are the path of time's movement, not continuously forward along a fast straight line. When measured in this way, time loops and curlicues, and at any given moment it can spiral me away and then bring me rushing home again.

I know, Má, the pouch is red because red is the color of luck, not the bad kind, just the good. The color of faith trumping fate, of hope growing ripe, of fruits on an endless vine. Red is the color of what travels through our hearts, an internal river that we never have to leave behind. When Monsieur and Madame see red, they think anger, death, a site of danger, a situation requiring extreme caution and care. Ridiculous, overblown, entirely misunderstood. Red on my fingertips, Má, means that I am still here. Red releases you thick from my body. Red is what keeps you near.

Má, I could use some good luck right about now, I thought, as I eyed the pouch nestled in my hands. Seasickness had been breaking my back four and five times a day, forcing me to stoop and bow before the commode, over the rails, into the dirty pots and pans. My paying of respect to the water and the wind was interrupted only by bouts of peeling potatoes, chopping onions, picking through the soaked-off husk of dried lentils and beans.

Yes, Old Man, those are not the chores of a cook, not even one on some leaky boat. But the *Niobe* is French, and I am Vietnamese, after all.

I was just the kitchen boy, a rank even lower than a *garde-manger*. At first I was not even allowed to touch the food, only the remnants of it on the cooking and serving vessels that were mine to wash and, to my misfortune, fill with whatever I had in my stomach that day. Once I was finally able to clean the dishes faster than I dirtied them, the *Niobe*'s cook, a Frenchman named Loubet, asked me where I had worked before. "The Governor-General's kitchen in Saigon," Loubet repeated after me. For the rest of the voyage, Loubet woke up late, smoked his cigarettes, and stared at the sea through the greasy portholes. I, in the meanwhile, demonstrated for him all that I had learned in the Governor-General's kitchen: Work without glory. Appreciation without praise. Pleasure without recognition.

When the captain's compliments came back to the galley along with his empty dishes, Loubet smiled and murmured, "The Governor-General's kitchen in Saigon."

I should have known better, I thought. Ignorance or a claim to it, as I had told Bão, was always better for a man like me.

But the wisdom of this rule I again ignored when I told Bão about the red pouch. I told him that I had no doubt about what was inside of it. The pouch had come from my mother's money belt. A couple of hundred *đồng*, I told him, in grimy bills that have been pressed against her body since who-knows-how-long. Probably money she had saved for her casket or, maybe, some white flowers for her grave, I thought. The Old Man, like the French, believed that black was the only appropriate color to display and wear in order to show grief.

I know Má, black is the color of our hair, the color of our irides with the coming of dusk, the color of a restful night's sleep, of coal rice, of tamarind pulp, of the unbroken shell of a thousand-year egg. How can this black be the color of sorrow? Underglazed with red river clay, deep water blue, high-in-the-tree-top green, black is luminous, the color that allows us to dream.

"Whew!" Bão whistled upon hearing about the red pouch. He said that I *had* to open it up because he, for one, was curious even if I was not. Well, he might not have said this in so many words. He might have just mumbled "stupid bastard." "Whew!" Bão whistled again after I undid the ties, and he saw what was sitting inside. "What are you doing down here?" Bão immediately wanted to know. "You can get your own room and a seat at the captain's table every night with that, you stupid bastard."

Yes, I thought, how true. I wrapped up the pouch and placed it back underneath my pillow.

Red is a firmly pressed hand. Red is a mother giving birth. Red is luck that she had somehow saved, stored, and squandered on her youngest son. Before I left home, my mother gave me a pouch filled with what I thought was money. As with all things about her, it would take time to understand, to find out what lay inside, protected as in a womb. When I close my eyes, I can see her in the kitchen still. The dirt floor, the clay pots, the tin plates, the coconut shell ladles, the rain-collecting cistern, all this my mother gave me and, in return, I left her. By no means an even trade, I know.

I did not learn until many days at sea that I had been resting my head on a pouch filled with gold leaf, one sunlit layer on top of another. Lighter and more valuable than its paper counterpart, gold is worth that is of the earth, my mother knows, and has to be honored anywhere upon its curving surface. Paper money gets its values from those who print it and therefore often suffers, finds itself totally degraded, when transported and removed from familiar surroundings. Perishable, like a fish out of water, or imagine a man on the open seas.

Every day, I hear the Old Man's voice shouting at me from beneath the earth, where, I tell myself, he now lies. The moment that he took his blood from mine, separated it as if his were the white and mine the yolk, I placed him there. "Where there is gambling, there is faith" is the tired aphorism that the Old Man clings to and continues even now to push through the soft center of the globe, coordinating its location with the longitude and latitude of wherever I happen to be. For a man who has never even seen the sea, he is a master navigator. His internal compass is where his heart should be. I had faith, Old Man. I had faith—

"I know all about your 'faith'! How dare you use the word of God to describe the things that you practice. Only a fool like you would believe that that French sodomite was going to save you. Out of love? Out of lust for your scrawny, worthless body? I've always told your mother that you are a pathetic loser, and here was the final proof. Yeah, you gambled and you *lost*—"

Is that what really upsets you, Old Man? That I *lost*? If that French 'sodomite' was still keeping me warm, if he was still keeping your bottles from going dry—

"Shut your mouth! It sickens me to think about what you do, shaming my name. After all that Minh the Sous Chef did for you. I told him he shouldn't have bothered with you, and I was right. 'But he needs to learn how to read and write,' he insisted. 'In this day and age, a *chef de cuisine* has to be versatile, adaptive, fluent . . .' he kept on saying. Now look at what you've done with it."

What are you talking about, Old Man? Anh Minh taught me how to read and write so that I could make a list of provisions, answer a help-wanted ad, follow the recipes that some French chef had committed to paper in anticipation of his death. But above all, Anh Minh wanted me to recognize the contours of our surname, a one-word epic that would one day be embroidered on the chef's toque of his dreams. White and tall, like a beautiful French girl, Anh Minh sighed in the middle of the night. Are you so pissed drunk, Old Man, that you think that I learned how to love, how to find passion in another man's body, from reading and writing? Do you think I learned it from a book? I am not like you, Old Man. I love my fellow man because of who I am, not because I was told to by the holy fathers and their holy gospel. In the name of your god, I commit your body to this earth where it . . .

But that, I am afraid, was my mistake from the very beginning, the fatal flaw in my design. I thought that I could suffocate the Old Man with shovelfuls of dirt and mud. But with his body in the soil, in the specific silt of this family's land, everything on it was bound to die. Rancor seeped from his eyelids, his mouth, his ears, his ass, where his head had been all the days of his life. I should have never made him one with the land. I should have thrown his body into the sea, expelled it and not me. My anger keeps me digging into the earth, pulling at its protective mantle, eager to see his body decaying deep inside. The Old Man has refused to cooperate. His body is wholly intact. Years of alcohol can do that to a person, make him dead but not departed, make him indelible to those who have had the misfortune of sharing his name. Pickled and preserved is another way of thinking about it. All the water that is normally found inside a body had been in his displaced by alcohol, of a proof strong enough to kill anything that comes into contact with it. The tiny animals, the grubs, the worms that help to bring about the decomposition of the body before it can be returned to the earth, had with him no hope of doing their work. So they left him alone, left his hate to poison the land, a process so gradual, so obedient to his still functioning will, that it would take my lifetime to complete. If I had a son, it might take his lifetime as well. This is as close to being immortal as the Old Man ever had the right to be, and I am the one, the only one who keeps him that way.

Yes, Old Man, I gambled. I gambled away my position as a *garde-manger*, a pitiful lifetime tenure that, contrary to what you thought, I was not lucky to have. I gambled away the long white apron, the coveted position as Sous Chef Someday, under the reign of Minh Finally the Chef de Cuisine. I gambled away a future—"better," I know, was presumed—that Anh Minh believed in like a benevolent god. Merit will be promoted. Service will be rewarded. Loyalty will beget loyalty. Anh Minh's faith sustained him but not me.

When Blériot came to the Governor-General's, I took one look at his face and one look around me, and I thought, Really, what do I have to lose? The answer to this question, believe me, depends on what the gambler believes is fixed and constant in his life. What will always be there? What will never change? Even if the gambler should lose is the implied condition tacked onto the end of these questions. Another way of thinking about it is: What does the gambler have faith in? Those who never wager, I imagine, do not have to ask themselves these questions, never have to acknowledge that the answers are few. The answer, or if he is truly lucky, the answers, define the gambler's notions of risk and restraint. If "nothing" is the gambler's answer, he is bound to lose because there is nothing to guide him back from the edge, nothing but the urge to jump. Risk encourages a gambler to be brave. Restraint advises a gambler to be prudent. It is the balance between the two that keeps him in the game.

I had faith, Old Man. You are the one who had

none. No faith in me whatsoever, if you thought that I was naive enough to look at Blériot and see salvation in his arms. He is a Frenchman, after all. Even in the throes of what I choose to remember as love, my body felt the lines stretched between us, razor-sharp when pressed against the flesh. I understood the limitations, the demarcations, the barbed-wire rules of such engagements. And contrary to what you still think, Old Man, in Blériot's blue eyes with the black bursting stars inside, I did not see a promotion, a pay raise for Anh Minh, not even cans of tinned peaches and pears for Má. I did not see a paid ticket to somewhere else—'better,' again, was presumed. In his blue eyes, I, unlike you, did not see my savior. I saw a man worth gambling for because I had faith—

"Stop using that word! I told you 'faith' belongs to God, belongs to the Church, to the Devout and the Saved. It belongs to me," says the Old Man, spitting dirt with every word.

Shut your mouth, Old Man, and let me finish. This is my story. I will tell it, and you will lie there mute.

I had faith. Faith that the Old Man had felt for my mother four moments of kindness, four tender touches, four pure reasons to sigh. That they, like four brief glimpses of the moon, softened the darkness of those nights during which my brothers and I were conceived. When I was a child, I could not look up at the stars or close my eyes to the sun and believe that it was not exactly the same time

277

all over the world. And, like all children, I also could not look up at the man whom everyone called my father and believe that he had brought me into this world in an act of scorn and contempt, which continues even now. Stupid, unquestioning faith that because my life came from his, my father, while cruel in action and brutal in speech, could never be so in heart. A tragic miscalculation on my part, if I am to believe the Old Man, a drunk and a gambler, a thief who took away my home.

"You fool! You *gave* it to me." The Old Man laughs with the satisfaction of knowing that what he has said is fact.

Yes, I thought, how true. I should have known better. I should have thrown his body into the open sea, I should have expelled it and not me.

After my mother gave birth to me, there were many things that she could no longer pray to her father and mother about. They would have disowned her. Then whom would she have left to worship, whose likeness would she have left to reconfigure from memory for her family altar? There is no forgiveness in ancestor worship, only retribution and eternal debt. Even in the afterlife, my mother was bound to see them, her father and mother and an entire clan of people whom she had never met but whose role it was to sit in judgment of her. What would they all say? she worried. The great sadness of her life was that she already knew. She had paid someone to take away the only worth that

278

her husband had found in her body. She had stolen from him who knows how many unborn sons. She had dared to exert sovereignty over her own body when she had been explicitly told that she had no rights. Thief, squanderer, and, worst of all, a disobedient wife, the epithets followed her every day as she went to the market, and they followed her home at night to pull her sheet away, curling her body up with guilt. She woke up and found herself at forty, the wife of a man who preferred the company of men, his tongue craving the body of a man named Christ—"a Holy Communion," the Old Man told her; a peddler who earned money just to see it taken away; a woman who gave birth to sons to see them learn how to walk, never toward and always away; a mother of four sons, one of whom believed that her love alone was not enough—"otherwise, why would he have left me?" she asked herself; a daughter whose father and mother had barred her from ever joining them in the afterlife. It is one thing to be alone in life, she thought, but to be alone in death would be unbearable.

My mother, believe me, is strong. Not in the ways of the chestnut trees of this city. These broad-leafed giants withstand the blasts of winter's winds with rigidity and years' worth of concentric armor. There are other ways to survive. When the monsoon winds were thrashing, tossing about plant life and small animals, my mother saw that the bamboos always escaped unscathed. She once saw those in the thicket at the back of her kitchen garden blown sideways during the height of a storm, their skinny bodies parallel with the ground and the sky. Today they would surely break, she thought. As she watched over them, waiting for the tragedy to unfold, the storm picked itself up and went away. By then, the rainwater cistern had fallen on its belly, and a sheet of water gushing through a crack along its side was washing over red and orange chili peppers scattered all over the ground. Some still had their green stems attached, others had been ripped away too suddenly from the neighbor's garden and had to leave their stems behind. Regret spilled out of them in the form of small, pale seeds. As if in grief, the bamboos were pressed to the ground. But within a matter of minutes, they nodded and waved. They shook off the rain and reoriented themselves toward the sky. My mother was impressed, indeed. Now *that*, she thought, is strength. Perseverance and flexibility are not opposites. Survival requires certain compromises. Endurance is defined by the last one standing. These were the lessons, I imagine, that she must have learned.

My mother resolved to be the last one standing. Unlike her own mother, she would never let a man take away her life. She wanted to watch her husband grow old, decrepit. She thought of how his body would look floating down the Mekong, out into the South China Sea. She, unlike me, would never allow him to claim the land that she calls home. She wanted to be there to welcome her youngest son back to her kitchen and back to her house. But in order to proceed with her plan, my mother first had to reconfigure the confines of her faith. She needed something to believe in that would offer her some way to escape the wrath of her ancestors, some place to go when she died where they would not be waiting for her. She, like the truly desperate before her, turned to Catholicism for refuge. I will not call it a conversion because that implies an abrupt shift, a reversal from one side of the leaf to another, a change of heart. She still kept her family altar and the Buddha that sat there smiling back at her. She is Vietnamese, after all. She hedges her bets.

When I left home, my mother had been in theory but never in practice a Catholic for twenty-five years. The drops of holy water touched her head on her wedding day, after which she was told to open up her mouth and receive the Host, dry and flavorless on her tongue. These Catholics are terrible cooks, she remembered thinking. By the time I left home, my mother had lived if not with Him, then in proximity to Him for over two decades. She had taken in, absorbed through the tiny pinpricks of her pores, more than any of us had realized. In Catholicism, she recognized a familiar trinity: the guilt, the denial, and the delay in happiness that defined her adult life. She found a Father and a Mother, though these two were here not married to each other.

She also found a Son to replace the one who went away. In Catholicism, my mother heard her voice lifted in prayers and in songs. The last time she sang out loud her boys were still her babies, and we had fallen asleep to the rise and fall of a young girl's voice, to the pleasing warmth of that girl's body enlivened by songs. In Catholicism, my mother found a place where she could one day go, ascend to in her gray *áo dài*, like smoke rising from the incense at her family altar. There was only a small part of her, only her earlobes, I imagine, that felt remorse, that regretted that her own mother and father would not be there to greet her. They would just leave me again anyway, she thought.

My mother never wavered, however, when it came to her vow never again to enter Father Vincente's church, the place where she was bought and sold. Every Sunday, after the Old Man washed his face, drank some strong tea to mask the sweet-sharp smell of liquor on his breath, he left for Father Vincente's church to assume his post at the frontmost pew. My mother would then put on a clean blouse, tie on her straw hat, and walk all the way to Saigon's Notre-Dame Cathedral. The first time she attended Mass there, she was given a string of beads, maybe not gold on a pink silk cord, she thought, but at least there was a choice: blue with the man on a cross or pink with the woman who kept her head covered, like a perpetual bride. That morning, Notre-Dame's tolling bells told my

282

mother that Mass was just ending and that she was still many boulevards away. She kept up her pace and arrived in time for the beginning of afternoon services. She slipped through the slowly closing doors and sat down in one of the polished pews. She gazed up at the chrysanthemums, gladioli, and Easter lilies that adorned the altar, stippled with gold. Beautiful, my mother thought. Even if Father Vincente's church could afford more than marigolds and cockscombs, she would never attend services there. To worship in the same house as the Old Man, she thought, would be sacrilege. That morning, my mother did not know that in the Catholic faith what she had done to her body after my birth was also a sin, mortal and irredeemable. By the time she found out, it was too late. Ignorance or a claim to it had already saved her.

Faith is the beginning of the story of my life. The Old Man believed in the Father, the Son, and the Holy Ghost. He believed that if one Son was good, an entire brood was even better. He believed in bringing to life men who would forever be indebted to him. Why should I not have servants of my own? he thought. In order to proceed with his plan, he had to procure for himself a wife. He, otherwise, would have never wanted, would have never desired, a woman. The only woman he had loved had given him away, placed him in front of God's doors and told him to close his eyes and pray. He prayed for her smile to come back to her face. He prayed for rice in her bowl and not only in his. He prayed for her chest to heave fewer sighs, especially when she thought that he had fallen asleep for the night. He opened up his eyes and found himself alone. His prayers for her had been answered. Those were the last selfless thoughts that he would ever have. By the time the girl who would be my mother was brought to him, he saw in the despair of those around him only the promise of a steady income. In his long life, the Old Man surrounded himself with gamblers, desperate for good luck in any form. These were the kind of men who already believed in wearing the same pair of pants over and over again. Others ate only beef, when they could afford it, before each game. Many refrained from having sex before an especially important hand. These were men who were susceptible from the very beginning. Faithful fools for the flock was what the Old Man dealt in. One man's superstition is another man's religion, he knew. There were also women with bulging money belts and a willingness to embrace whatever gods necessary, to repeat whatever prayers needed, in order to win, but the Old Man could not stand the sight of them, the smell of them. One in the house was already too many, he thought. But as he was a man who believed in the proliferation of sons, he had to touch this girl who smelled like the only woman he had ever loved. It sickened him each time. He committed the act quickly and without ever closing his eyes. No woman would play that trick on me again, he thought.

My mother kept her eyes closed. She squeezed them shut, sealed them with the tight weave of her lashes. He can make me open my legs but never my eyes, she thought. When she felt herself ripping, she swam away into the darkness in search of her mother. She wanted to know whether her mother was certain. Was her mother absolutely sure that this was the man? In the darkness, her mother and her father, who came along for added authority, told her, "Yes, *this* is the man!" How could both of them be wrong, the girl thought, and she opened her eyes. Her husband was finished, and she got up to clean herself. She squatted over a washbowl filled with rainwater. She lowered her backside slowly into it. She had added a spoonful of salt to the water to help cleanse the wound, just as her mother had taught her. The water bloomed pink. She looked down at the color and cried. The salt was causing her wound to sting. "Obey," like "worship," is a strong word. Her mother and father had told her so, and she believed them. They gave her life, they told her, so that she could give them grandsons. She had been prepared to perform that task from the very beginning. When her body took the first step, her mother found for her a husband. A scholar-prince, the girl had imagined. In the days that followed her mother's announcement, the girl was reminded again and again that she must obey this man. He must be wise, the girl thought. She must not displease him. He must be sensitive, the girl thought. She must not leave him. He must be kind, the girl thought. From the soft mouth of the woman who gave her life, my mother received the words that would keep her, still and unmoving, underneath the Old Man. The words swam with her in the dark and kept her from reaching up with a knife and cutting his neck like that of a chicken. Her mother told her to swallow her anger, and she gulped it down until her belly became distended with it. Worse, her mother knew that it would.

CHAPTER 19

"I had a brother, once . . ."

GertrudeStein is fond of throwing this non sequitur before the baffled faces of her newly formed acquaintances. It is a test for alertness, skill, and agility. Think of a martial arts master who suddenly, violently, turns on her disciple. If the disciple passes the test, he proceeds to the next level of instruction. If the disciple fails, he is left to die of his injuries. Whether the wound is fatal or merely an abrasion is left to the hapless youth to decide by his response. For GertrudeStein, if the young man switches the topic of conversation to the whereabouts or wherewithal of her brother, then it is a fatality. Too easily distracted, therefore not worth knowing, she thinks. A brother is not interesting, not interesting enough to displace her from the center of her own conversation. But if the young man does not venture down that shadowy lane, if he is able to resist the tantalizing reference to the brother Stein, then Miss Toklas and I are certain to see his face again at 27 rue de Fleurus.

"Actually, she has three and a sister," Miss

Toklas can often be heard amending from her corner of the studio.

"But, Pussy, for me there was only one," my Madame would then insist.

How true, I think. We all have only one, no matter the size of our family. The one for whom we would dive into an algae pond, drink in its muck, and sink into its silt to save. The one for whom we would claim, "It was all *my* fault," no matter the infraction or the crime. The one whom we worship and envy in tandem, until envy grows stronger and takes the lead.

GertrudeStein had a brother, once. She crossed the Atlantic Ocean for him. She had reached the age of twenty-nine in the land of her birth to find there nothing but a sharp, sloping hill. She could take graceful, mincing steps down it, or she could ask, "Can women have wishes?" and run down that same hill flinging her arms in the air in a series of "Yes! Yes! Yes!" Paris had two things to recommend it, her brother Leo and the new century. Already three years into the twentieth, and she still had the distinct impression that she was living inside a museum, under glass, properly shielded from the white glare of the sun. Oakland, Allegheny, Cambridge, Baltimore, all the cities that she had slept in, but never quite awoken in, had the nineteenth century written all over them, she thought. No greater insult could she ever imagine for a city or for herself. Certainly, life for her had been eventful. She had studied and she had loved. She preferred the former because there her talents for thinking and talking allowed her to excel. Thinking and talking, though, were never helpful to her when it came to loving. She, like many of her fellow medical school students, tended to suffer the symptoms of whatever illnesses they happened to be studying. The topic at hand was the heart, so she was certain that there was something terribly wrong with the circulation of her blood, a condition she thought chronic if not fatal. She could no longer take deep breaths. She woke up during the night to find the hair on her head, in the folds of her underarms, in the V that parts her thighs, all matted with sweat. The peculiar smells of her own odors rising, a steam coming off her, nauseated her and aroused her to the presence of her body. During those nights, she did not so much sleep but close her eyes and wish the night away. During those mornings after, she swore that there had been butterflies, that they had landed one by one on her eyelids and along the empty clotheslines of her lips. She thought it was surely a condition to be treated, if not conquered, by medical science.

Gertrude "Gertie" Stein, twenty-nine and almost two hundred pounds, was in love, and she mistook it for a disease. She, like the chauffeur, believed in the power of strenuous exercise and a modified diet. She stopped having afternoon teas at the home of her beloved and started boxing with a welter-weight, a man who no longer had any hope of glory and made up for it by making this fat young lady jab and swing. Lips red with strawberry jam, skin like slowly pouring cream, hair the color of properly brewed tea, all this was what she was giving up. She thought boxing would make her breathe again. She was wrong and that infuriated her. This loving thing is brutal, she thought, especially when there are three. Three is an unlucky number when it comes to love, especially when she was the third, the last to arrive upon the site of a fallen honey hive, still sweet but already claimed and jealously guarded. She wanted to be the only one. She would always want to be the only one.

"Obstetrics failed me," Gertrude wrote to her brother Leo. "Obstetrics has freed me, unlike my counterparts," she added. It was actually the other way around. She had failed Obstetrics. She had failed the class by such a great margin, with such fanfare, that everyone in the university had heard about it. "This young lady is taking and, worse, wasting valuable resources," declared the faculty of the school of medicine in one united, disapproving voice. A woman in medical school means one less man in medical school, these learned men reasoned. That, however, was what they had had to accept in exchange for a generous endowment from two phlegmatic spinster sisters, who had grown tired of disrobing before learned men whom they never, never intended to marry. The medical school took the spinsters' money and admitted women into their program of studies, but when Leo Stein's sister became the first among her sex to, well, show no interest whatsoever in female reproduction, she became a symbol, a very large living one at that, of how the natural order of things had been violated by the spinsters and their money. The repercussion was felt throughout the university. The male students smirked at her, and the female students shunned her for compounding their already heavy burden. In the end, there was for this young lady no other way except out. She could voluntarily take a leave of absence or she could stay on and suffer a formal expulsion. Without much hesitation, she dove into the Atlantic and backstroked her way toward the Old World, which her brother Leo had assured her was now really the New.

At 27 rue de Fleurus, Leo was the painter and his sister was the writer. His *métier* was a conscious decision, and hers was somewhat of a default. She had to do something with the pieces of her heart, a solidly built thing, dropped by the fluttering hands of a woman named for the fifth month of an unbearable year. She thought it best to set it down on paper, but there on the blankness that was hers to fill she placed her broken heart inside the body of a man. Unrequited love for a woman, the story that she found herself telling, remained otherwise unchanged. At 27 rue de Fleurus, she sought and found comfort in the tangle of her prose, in the thick nest of her hair, in the wraps and folds of her somber-colored kimonos. A trunkful of these

291

garments, souvenirs from Leo's travels without her, were waiting for her in the studio. She thanked her brother with a slap on the back and a hug that made his crushing lungs wheeze. She immediately discarded the kimonos embroidered with cranes, peonies, and cherry blossoms and began wearing the rest. Solid, impenetrable fields of blues, browns, and grays, these everyday kimonos were ideal, as they allowed her to dispense with a corset altogether. A string of prayer beads that she found at the bottom of the trunk completed her ensemble. The handsome necklace, each bead the size of an unripe plum, swung from Gertrude's neck down to where her waistline would be, if she had had one. She was then just "Gertrude," the sister, the younger, the follower in her brother's footsteps, and so Leo more appropriately bore their last name. *He* is the one, Gertrude thought. Their household at 27 rue de Fleurus was to be the beginning of a lifetime of cohabitation. No husbands and no wives here, she thought. No husbands and no wives needed in the twentieth century, she proposed and wholeheartedly accepted. She was, of course, wrong.

"*She* is always wrong when it comes to the practicality of daily life," as Miss Toklas can attest. This conclusion required the passage of time—the growing gray of my Mesdames' hair, the yellowing of their teeth, the blue veining of their calves—to be proven valid and true. Its corollary—"GertrudeStein is a genius"—did not, and Alice Babette Toklas, thirty years of age and fresh from her own ocean crossing, made it a point to proclaim it so. The moment these words were spoken, a spell that declared its intention never be broken, Gertrude, thirty-three and unabashedly corsetless, became "GertrudeStein." No longer a diminutive, as female names are doomed to be, but a powerful whopping declaration of her full self, each and every time. Not any Gertie but GertrudeStein, the older, the wiser, the writer. "*The* genius," Miss Toklas added, as she gently placed GertrudeStein's head down upon her lap.

"But, Pussy, there can be only one in any given family," GertrudeStein murmured, as she slipped her hands underneath the fabric waves of Miss Toklas's skirt.

"Then for the Steins, it is you, Lovey."

GertrudeStein was already inclined to agree. She, by then, had lived with her brother Leo for four years, and he in her opinion had grown increasingly pale. The reason was clear. Leo no longer painted, and that, thought GertrudeStein, was depriving him of the rush of creativity that kept her own cheeks pink. Worse, Leo had allowed his interest in other people's art to surpass *their* interest in his. Over the years, they together had distinguished themselves in this city precisely for the interest that they showed in other people's art. At 27 rue de Fleurus, they collected paintings, artists, and a society of people who were interested in all three. The relevant three were the paintings, the artists, and the Steins. The paintings, they hung on the walls of the studio. The artists, they sat on its settees and chairs. The people, they invited through the studio door to gaze up and around. It was the simultaneous existence of all three, as Miss Toklas had come to see, which formed the tricolor of advancing fame that flew high over 27 rue de Fleurus. But Leo, like his sister, thought that there could be only one in any given family, and Leo was certain that it was he. The older, the wiser, *the* genius, thought Leo. Worse, he made it a point to proclaim it so: "Certainly, Gertrude contributes to the cause, but it begins and ends at the cosigning of the check. My sister does have her opinions, but mine are informed. Of course, she has her favorites, but I prefer the artistic to the merely artful."

GertrudeStein loved her brother, her only one. She loved him enough not to hear a word of what he was saying. But after Miss Toklas began her daily visits to the rue de Fleurus, Leo added jealousy and cruelty to the list of his difficult-to-love attributes. He began to spend hours, the same ones that Miss Toklas was spending with his sister, at the cafés of this city, where he, with the assistance of a bottle or two, concluded for all to hear that Gertrude's writing was nothing more than babble, the mark of an undisciplined lazy mind: "She thinks it is an art to be read and not understood. She is playing an elaborate practical joke on herself. She claims to innovate, but she is just mimicking the insane."

294

"She," who was by then undeniably Gertrude-Stein, refused to be ridiculed by anyone, especially by Leo. The infidelity, the betrayal, the savagery of it, shrunk her love for him into a thing so small that one day it disappeared.

"Babble!" GertrudeStein complained to Miss Toklas.

"Lovey, there can be only one," Miss Toklas whispered, repeating the phrase that would absolutely, mercilessly sever GertrudeStein from her brother Leo, her only one. Miss Toklas knew that it would.

Choose something from the middle, you tell me. No one ever remembers what happens there.

"No."

"Bee, they'll never even notice."

"No."

"Bee, please . . . just for the week and then you can take it back with you the following Sunday."

What an odd request, I think. Or is it more of a plea, a childlike wish, which in the mouth of a man can quickly become an either-or command?

You want to see GertrudeStein's handwriting, her crossed-over words, the discarded ones. She *is* the twentieth century, you tell me. What she keeps and what she does not will tell you about the future, you insist. My Madame is not a soothsayer, I think.

"Ask me something else," I beg. The tips of my fingers are throbbing, picking up as they always do the electrical charge that is in the air, that precedes the appearance of any threat, lightning before a driving storm.

Sweet Sunday Man, please understand. My Madame and Madame sustain me. They pay my wage, house my body, and I feed them. That is the nature of our relationship. Simple, you may think. Replaceable, even. The morning meals, the afternoon repasts, the evening suppers, the day-to-day is what I share with them. You may think that that is just an unbroken string of meals, continuous but otherwise insignificant, but you would be wrong. Every day, my Mesdames and I dine, if not together, then back-to-back. Of course, there is always a wall between us, but when they dine on *filet de boeuf Adrienne*, I dine on *filet de boeuf Adrienne*. When they partake of *salade cancalaise*, I partake of *salade cancalaise*. When they conclude with *Crème renversée à la cévenole*, I conclude on the same sweet note. Do you understand, Sweet Sunday Man? These two, unlike all the others whom I have had the misfortune to call my Monsieur and Madame, extend to me the right to eat what they eat, a right that, as you know, is really more of a privilege when it is I who am doing the cooking. My Mesdames do not even demand that I wait until they have finished, that I scrape together my meals from what is left of theirs. When I place that first bite of *boeuf Adrienne* in my mouth and I am brought to my knees—figuratively speaking, of course, as I reserve that posture for

296

love and prayers—by the white wine, cognac, laurel, thyme, and red currants, that elusive final ingredient that ends all of their compliments with a question mark, I know that my Mesdames are on their knees as well, saying a word of thanks for two heady days of marinating and one hour of steady basting. With their meals of beef, my Mesdames insist on oysters as an accompaniment. These briny morsels are more of a juxtaposition, a counterpoint to the buttery aftertaste of cow's blood. *Salade cancalaise* provides my Mesdames with that and more. Inside the curl of a leaf of lettuce is a single poached oyster. Underneath this dollop of ocean fog is a soft pallet of potatoes. A shaving of black truffle covers all. The potatoes are there for heft and texture, but the truffle, ah, the truffle is a gift for the nose. Pleasure refined into a singular scent, almost animal, addictive, a lover's body coming toward yours on a moonless night. Even this my Mesdames have shared with me. Do you understand, Sweet Sunday Man? My Mesdames, like the French, prefer their salad after the main course, something tart and piquant to heighten the sweetness of what is to come. That, Sweet Sunday Man, is why Americans think French desserts are barely sweet enough when eaten on their own. Think of a dessert as an ensemble player who should never be forced to perform naked and alone. Speckled with the seeds of vanilla beans and ribboned through and through with chestnut purée, *crème renversée à la cévenole* elevates the humble baked custard to a state of grace. As Anh Minh would say, "If you don't believe in God, then how do you explain the chestnut?" GertrudeStein and Miss Toklas undoubtedly agree. When the first strong winds of winter blow, my Mesdames drive to the Bois de Boulogne and stand underneath the chestnut trees singing "Angel, angel!" When my Mesdames return home to the rue de Fleurus, *crème renversée à la cévenole* is what they hunger for.

"GertrudeStein judges a cook by his desserts, and I judge a cook by everything else," Miss Toklas had informed me during my interview. I have found this statement, like all of Miss Toklas's statements, to be unquestionably true. Believe me, it has not been easy for me to work for these two. Miss Toklas is a Madame who uses her palate to set the standard of perfection. In order to please her, her cook has to do the same, an extremely difficult feat. Her cook has to adopt her tongue, make room for it, which can only mean the removal of his own. That is what she demands from all of her cooks. Impossible, of course, and so eventually they have all had to go. I have stayed this long because I am experienced, qualified in such matters.

Once she became my Madame, the first thing Miss Toklas asked me was whether I had a recipe for gazpacho.

"Yes."

"Did you learn it in Spain?"

"No."

"Then it is best to forget it."

"Oh."

"Here at 27 rue de Fleurus," Miss Toklas began, "there are four kinds of gazpacho. We will begin with the gazpacho of Malaga. You will need four cups of veal broth, prepared the night before. Be sure to add two cloves of garlic and a large Spanish onion to the bones as they steep. A large ripe tomato, peeled and seeded, cut into cubes no larger than—let me see your hands—no larger than your thumbnail. One small cucumber no thicker than half the width of your wrist and . . ."

Our first lesson continued in this manner until my Madame declared, "Mix thoroughly and serve the soup ice-cold. Exquisite. Tomorrow," she promised, "the gazpacho of Segovia." Miss Toklas closed her eyes as she said "Segovia," which told me that it was exquisite as well.

I ran through the complete list of ingredients in my head: veal broth, tomato, cucumber, garlic, onion, sweet red pepper, cooked rice, olive oil. I opened up my mouth to ask, "What about the—"

"Salt is not essential here," Miss Toklas interrupted. "Consider it carefully, Bin, before using it." A pinch of salt, according to my Madame, should not be a primitive reflex, a nervous twitch on the part of any cook, especially one working at 27 rue de Fleurus. Salt is an ingredient to be considered and carefully weighed like all others. The true taste of salt—the whole of the sea on the tip of the tongue, sorrow's sting, labor's

299

smack—has been lost, according to my Madame, to centuries of culinary imprudence. It is a taste that Miss Toklas insists is sometimes unnecessary, as in the gazpacho of Malaga, and other times, as in the gazpacho of Segovia, it is the hinge that allows the flavors of the other ingredients to swing wide open. "In my kitchen, I will tell you when salt is necessary," my Madame said, concluding the real lesson for that day.

Working with this Madame, I could already tell, would not be easy. She is an attentive Madame, which frankly is the worst possible kind. What about the other one? I thought. Two attentive Mesdames, and I am out of here in a week, I remembered thinking.

I know, I know. It is this other Madame who interests you more, Sweet Sunday Man. But what you do not seem to understand is that they are one and the same, and what you ask of me, I cannot do to my Madame and Madame. The infidelity, the betrayal, the savagery of it, even I am not capable of it, Sweet Sunday Man.

"Bee, what about a photograph?"

Yes, I nod, acknowledging my childlike wish for an image of you and me.

"We'll do it. We'll go to Lené Studio and have our photograph taken, once you . . ."

An even exchange. A fair trade. A give for a take. I have played this game before, I think.

"Please, Bee. Just one week, Sunday to Sunday, and then you can . . ."

300

"Our photograph" is all that I want, and it is all that I hear. Sweet Sunday Man is a honey talker, and I am his Bee, after all. When I am with him, I am reminded that sweet is not just a taste on the tongue. Sweet is how my whole being can feel. He quickens my pulse, and I stay in that alert state, even when our bodies are no longer one. He inhabits a body that is free to soar through the continuous blue of this city's sky, and he takes me with him when he dreams. He fills my lungs with his breaths and his sighs. I cook for him, and he feeds me. That is the nature of our relationship.

Dressed in her kimono and her prayer beads, GertrudeStein is standing in front of the door of the studio, and she is waiting. For Miss Toklas, I imagine, when I look at this photograph. GertrudeStein's hair is abundant and continues to grow thick and lush inside this image. A half smile graces her face, deepening the dimples in her cheeks. It is a smile that says, Remember me. It is not so much a command but a sage bit of advice, a tip on a winning horse. My Madame is staring into the camera so intently that I imagine it was she who willed the shutter to close and open back up again, fixing her in that moment when she declared, *I am the one.* It is an important occasion that my Mesdames are for some reason reluctant to share. But then again, my Madame and Madame have always been somewhat erratic about what they make public and what they press, viselike, to their

301

bosoms. This photograph, for instance, they have chosen to keep inside the cupboard along with Miss Toklas's typewriting machine and GertrudeStein's notebooks and papers. Resting against the back panel of the cupboard, the photograph shows GertrudeStein with her hands clasped in front of her breasts, a knot waiting to be untied. By Miss Toklas, I imagine. The hem of GertrudeStein's kimono touches the ground and disappears into the white border of the photograph. I hold onto her there, at the hem of her garment, and I ask my Madame, "Would you do the same?" Miss Toklas, I know, would answer "Yes!" GertrudeStein is never faced with such dilemmas. She stands there and she waits, not patiently but confidently, for what she knows is rightfully hers. She is the recipient and never the procurer of love and affection. She has Miss Toklas for that.

I stand in front of the open cupboard, in the silence that takes over 27 rue de Fleurus when my Mesdames are locked arm in arm for the night. I take from the cupboard a thin notebook that to me says it is small, insignificant, forgettable even. The notebook is not from the middle of the stack as Sweet Sunday Man had advised, but it is not from the very top either. It is a safe distance away, I gauge, from where I have seen Miss Toklas running her thumb through the accumulated pages. Their edges sliding down the smooth hillock of her finger makes her ticklish with anticipation, leaves her with a sensation that she would later remember as inevitability. I close the cupboard, but not before I bid GertrudeStein, beatific in her kimono, good night. I return to my room, close the door, and open the notebook. I see inside an unbroken string of words. My eyes scan them for ones that I may know, that I may recognize, like the face of a brother in the blur of a passing crowd. No, nothing, I think. Then I see the word "please"—one of the few English words that Sweet Sunday Man has taught me—and I see it again. I turn the page and "please" is there as well.

"Please" can be a question: "May I?"

And a response: "You may."

"Please" can also be a verb, an effortless act that accompanies Sweet Sunday Man into every room.

"Please" is also a plea, a favor that he has asked of me.

My index finger jumps from "please" to "please." Here . . . it is a question. There . . . it is a response. Here . . . it is an act, and there . . . it is a plea. I am following a story line that I may be alone in finding, but for an instant I tell myself that I, like Sweet Sunday Man, am reading my Madame's writings. I turn the page, and I see there the word "Bin." I recognize it as the spelling of my Mesdames' name for me. I find my American name written again and again on the following pages as well. With each sighting, I am overwhelmed by the feeling that I am witnessing myself drowning. There . . . I am, I think. Here . . . I am again. I am

303

surrounded on all sides by strangers, strung along a continuously unraveling line that keeps them above the water's surface. It is a line that I cannot possibly hold onto. GertrudeStein knows it, and she has cast me in there anyway, I think.

I did not give you my permission, Madame, to treat me in this way. I am here to feed you, not to serve as your fodder. I demand more money for such services, Madame. You pay me only for my time. My story, Madame, is mine. I alone am qualified to tell it, to embelish, or to withhold.

Here, Sweet Sunday Man, here. This notebook may belong to my Madame, but the story, it belongs to me. Look, it has my name all over it. Here and here and here. Your eyes follow my finger as it skims the inked pages, and you smile. "Don't worry, Bee," you assure me. The story, *my* story, you tell me, could be affectionate, glowing, heroic, even. You place my Madame's notebook inside your desk. You lock the drawer with a key that you wear around your waist. "I'll tell you all about it next Sunday. Now, we should go or we'll be late for our appointment," you say, smiling again. A photograph of you with me, I think. The sound of the drawer shutting, the flat note of wood on wood, the sharp click of the lock, follow us down the rue de l'Odéon. The sun is shining, and I am lost in its glare. I close my eyes, and all I can see there is my Madame's face smiling back at me.

After this photograph of GertrudeStein in her

304

kimono was taken, Leo wrote a note to his sister, as they had chosen no longer to speak, accusing Miss Toklas of stealing her away from him. When Miss Toklas read this, she laughed, and wrote back: "Your sister gave herself to me."

How true, I think. A gift or a theft depends on who is holding the pen.

CHAPTER 20

A February sun is offering itself to this city, a rare commodity that Parisians snap up by the handful. They swarm the Jardin du Luxembourg, finding comfort in the puddles of light. Like melted pools of butter, I think. The chestnut trees have been bare for months now. I am still taken aback when I see them, so many in a row, turned upside down, their leaves deep in the earth, their roots waving with the wind. Contortionists, acrobats, a spectacle that, I am afraid, I alone see. I find myself searching the brambles for rose hips. I am moved that they have remained, stoic orbs of color in a city that has otherwise lost its palette. I trace the lines of low-lying branches. My fingers find the swelling just beneath the surface, the node that marks the persistence of life. A winter garden is a gift that this city has given me, honey in a hive, corals in a raging sea. To see it, I must endure. Children run past me. Their nannies follow, eyes on their charges, gossip on their lips. Young women walk by, arm in arm, their bell-shaped hats swing to the brisk rhythm of their feet. Students, I imagine. Eyes too kohl-rimmed for shopgirls. Tourists, Americans maybe, file past with their guide, a Frenchman wearing a beautiful blue overcoat and a crooked ivory smile. I am the only fool sitting still. There is no competition for the benches in February. Another benefit of this garden pruned by the cold.

Winter waited for me on the shores of this country like a vengeful dowager, incensed and cold-shouldered. She never lets me forget that I had ignored her existence for the first twenty some years of my life, never felt her in my bones, never longed for her on days when the sun was too high in the midday sky. At first, she was all patience and beauty, disguising herself in colors, hiding among autumn leaves. When she blew the first kiss, I welcomed her with arms opened wide, never suspecting that within days she would make me cry.

When I was born, heat licked her heavy lips and embraced me. Before my mother could take me into her arms, I smelled her. Before I could take in my mother's milk, I tasted the salt on her nipple. I tell this to myself, repeating it like a prayer to keep me safe, something warm to wrap around me. Overcoats are never thick enough for me. I would try wearing two, but I own only one. And wind would merely whip through the additional layers of wool, and then I would wish that I owned three. I get lost in this city only in winter. I am lost in this city today. Ice intensifies my lowest emotions, magnifies what I lack. Snow makes me want to sleep, not in my bed but on the corners of busy boulevards, in alleyways, underneath the awnings of crowded shops, wherever I happen to be when my body says, Please, no more. The desire is sometimes so strong that I return to my Mesdames' apartment exhausted from the struggle. It is not always a victory for me. Often I have lost the day on a park bench, sitting so still that pigeons were inspecting themselves in the shine of my shoes. How long I have been there, I can tell only by the stiffness of my limbs, the time it takes for blood to spike through my arms and legs.

Today I am watching a group of children playing on the stone steps leading up to where the cold has bolted me to this bench. I first notice them when a little girl with big eyes breaks from a circle of children and runs up the steps. She leaves the walkway and heads directly toward the trees. Once underneath, she begins to dig at the snow with her mittened hands. She dislodges a thin arm-length branch with one brown leaf still attached to it. She runs down the steps, and the ring of children splits open, their padded bodies forming the hemisphere in which the tragedy I had not anticipated would unfold.

The girl with the big eyes, now the only one obscuring my line of sight, breaks off the leaf and throws the branch to the side. She kneels down and begins to fan the leaf at something that I cannot see. My body leans forward, and my eyes focus on a sweep of gray, moving, barely. A pigeon, an ordinary, city-gray pigeon, stumbles between the girl's black boots and tries to spread its wings. The right one opens to its full span, a flourish of white. The left one collapses halfway, a crush of gray. The bird pitches forward and falls on this sloping left wing. It lies there while the children become excited. A boy is laughing and jutting his finger. The girl with the big eyes is still fanning but is no longer kneeling. Children passing by are now stopping. Their nannies pull them away, scolding them for looking at something dying. The little audience fluctuates in size, but all who join keep a wide ring of stone between themselves and the bird. There must be space enough for such things, an instinct that they all possess, except for the boy with the jutting finger and the girl with the big eyes. She continues to fan and is now on her knees again. Her face is down low, almost touching the pigeon's head, a head that picks itself up and drops itself down, a visible jarring each time it hits the cold surface of stone. The boy with the jutting finger remembers the discarded branch and runs toward it. He brings it back and pokes the pigeon on the back of its neck. The girl stands back, deferring to something violent, deferring to something in herself. The bird responds by rolling itself back onto its feet. Head wobbling to a quiet song, it hops down one step and attempts again to spread its wings.

A flourish of white, a crush of gray.

A flourish of white, a crush of gray.

Adults are now stopping. The spectacle has become a matter of public interest. Death, a private thing, is making a limited appearance, a February sun. Faces, creased and concerned, peer down at the children and the pigeon. Nearby, a man and a woman exchange whispers. I imagine that they are not speaking French. Her shoes, after all, are too practical. No Parisian woman would stand so unadorned and close to the earth. The woman touches the shoulders of those before her until there are none, except for the boy with the jutting finger, a finger made grotesque by the branch that has extended its natural reach. The woman bends down next to the bird that has lost all memory of flight. Sitting on its folded feet, it warms an egg that it can no longer understand is merely stone. The woman takes off her gloves. The gesture stops time. The world becomes small, and she and the bird are the only ones casting shadows on its spinning surface. I close my eyes but cannot keep them shut, another useless flutter on this winter's day.

The woman cups the pigeon in her hands, a washerwoman's mottled pink, and straightens her body. The expected resistance, the bird's fight for freedom, never comes. She walks down the steps, the pigeon before her, raised like an offering to the snow beds down below. She places the bird on a patch of ground where the snow had melted clean. Her hands continue to cup its body, steadying it for what is to come, warming it like no sun can ever again. The assembly has followed the woman down the steps, and, from where I am sitting, I can see their bodies speaking with uncertainty. Backs turn away and then turn back again. Heads form small circles only to unfurl in wavy lines. Uncertain, I can see, about whether the woman's cupped hands have delivered the last rites, whether they can now resume the day, reclaim the minutes lost to a little death. The girl with the big eyes still has the leaf in her hand, fanning the air before her. The boy with the jutting finger stands with two younger boys by his side. Lessons are being learned. Cruelty passes from one to the other, a not so secret handshake.

I see a sudden ripple of coats and hats. Children are being quickly led away, their small hands covering their mouths, larger hands covering their eyes. The ordinary, city-gray pigeon is again in my line of sight. It is attempting flight, creating a spectacle worse than death. With its breached left wing, it manages only to skim the snow. It flies toward a nearby hedge and hurls its body into a tangle of branches. Its feathers catch on thorns and other small curious growths and are lifted up, exposed in shameful ways. The pigeon flaps its wings with a force that shakes the hedge, makes it tremble, startles it with something akin to life. The bird falls back onto the snowy ground. Its refusal to die a soft, concerted death is an act thought willful and ungrateful by those assembled. They show their displeasure by pulling their attention away, a recoiling hand. The bird flies again into the branches, confused and exhausted.

I close my eyes, a useless flutter. I open them, and I see you half a world away. I hear fever parting your lips. I feel your shiverings, colorless geckos running down your spine. I smell the night sweat that has bathed you clean.

The woman with the pink mottled hands is the only one who has remained. No one wants to stand so close to desperation. It is too thick in the air. It is naturally invasive, has the dank odor of musty rooms and vacant houses, a distinct taste, tangy and burning on the tongue. The woman should know. She carries desperation with her, soiled into the seam of her skirt, sewn into the lining of her coat. She examines the bird and recognizes the signs, the secret markings of her tribe, and she knows that this will take time. She picks up the pigeon, again a swift wrapping of pink, and walks it up the steps. She walks it past me and lays the bird under the trees, near where the girl with the big eyes had dug up the branch. The woman looks over at me, and we exchange promises. Someone would do the same for me when my day comes, I imagine her saying. With no farewell words, she leaves me.

"*Ça suffit!*" I shout at the children who are regrouping on the top steps. "That's enough! That's enough! That's enough!" My barely comprehensible French makes them laugh, makes them consider my sanity. The deliberation is brief. I am crazy, they decide. They run off, leaving me on this bench at the edge of a garden that is trying to tether a retreating sun. I hear the pigeon thrashing its body against a mound of snow. With each attempt, its wings become heavier, ice crystals fastening themselves, unwanted jewels, winter's barnacles. The faint crunch of snow is making me cry. I will sit here until it stops.

I know you are in your best *áo dài*. You bought it when you were just eighteen. Gray is not a color for a young woman. Gray is the color you wanted because you were practical even then, knew that gray is a color you would grow into, still wear when your hair turned white. You snap yourself into this dress and cannot help but notice that it hangs from your body, nothing to cling to. Your breasts are smaller now than when he first saw them. Your belly bears the scars of your four sons and your one husband. You touch your face the way that no one else has since I have gone. You smile because you know that I am with you, understand your need to don this dress, a thing you can call your own. You know I am holding your hand, leading you out the front door of his house. You step out into the street, and you are a sudden crush of gray. Silk flows from your body, softness that he had taken

313

away. In the city of my birth, you keep the promise that we made to each other. We swore not to die on the kitchen floor. We swore not do die under the eaves of his house.

CHAPTER 21

"Bee, the Steins are making plans to go away."

Sweet Sunday Man, of course, I know where and why. I cannot believe, though, that you already know. My disappointment is a fish bone lodged in my throat. I have been saving that bit of news for over a month now. I have been saving it for later on tonight.

Yes, what you have heard is true. My Mesdames have received telegrams from the Algonquin Hotel in the city of New York. The telegrams confirmed that the Algonquin would have a steady supply of "oysters" and "honeydews." I have made it a point to remember these two English words, and as I repeat them now for you, you as usual smile. I have to say them again several more times, altering and flattening out my tones as best as I can, *AYster, aySTER, booNIdoo,* and so on, before you recognize them. The translation of "oyster" into French is easy enough for you, but you are having difficulty with "honeydew." You explain to me that a honeydew is a melon, but you are uncertain whether there is an exact equivalent in French. You will have to spend some time, you tell me, looking through your books and dictionaries. I look at you and shrug. I, frankly, do not understand the reason for your anticipated effort. Words, Sweet Sunday Man, do not have twins in every language. Sometimes they have only distant cousins, and sometimes they pretend that they are not even related. At least with this one, we know the family: melon. I, therefore, know that a honeydew is a fruit that smells like a flower, a fruit with a texture that hovers somewhere between solid and liquid, a fruit whose juices cool the lucky body that consumes it. As for the other characteristics of a honeydew, those I will just have to imagine.

My Mesdames had received the Algonquin's menu in the mail in January, soon after the preparation for the trip began. Actually, I believe it may be more accurate to say that the preparation for the trip did not begin until the hotel's menu arrived in the mail and was judged suitable. GertrudeStein read each item out loud while Miss Toklas offered occasional commentary. I myself was surprised to hear that a menu from an American hotel would include so many French dishes: *canapés, meunières, paupiettes, glacées.* The words were comforting for me to hear as I walked back and forth between the dining room and the kitchen, clearing away the remains of my Mesdames' supper. As to be expected, there were also some items, presumably American in origin, that I did not recognize. By the end of the recitation, Miss Toklas looked impressed, maybe even a bit proud. GertrudeStein looked simply relieved. She had located the two items, apparently the only two items on the menu that she had any interest in. In the month since, we at the rue de Fleurus have received more menus from hotels in cities all over America. The same reading aloud has occurred with each one. When oysters and honeydews were not read aloud or even when they were but the wording was vague or made references, I assumed, to seasonal availability, a frantic course of correspondence would then begin with Miss Toklas drafting telegrams and anxiously awaiting their replies. More often than not, though, GertrudeStein recited "oysters" and "honeydews" with a noticeable sigh of pleasure after each word, and the tension that accompanied these proceedings would then leave the room.

Oysters on the half shell and fresh honeydews both served on a bed of crushed ice, you tell me, are the only foods that GertrudeStein can eat before she gives a lecture.

"Lecture? But I thought my Madame writes books."

"She does. Then she lectures about them."

"Oh."

You had heard a rumor about GertrudeStein that, until now, seemed far-fetched. It had been whispered at the Saturday teas that she is nervous before she lectures, that this monument of a woman actually has to sit down to keep from fainting. Even though you are an iridologist and not particularly interested in the internal organs, you know that a jittery stomach is a sensitive one. So while you personally could not imagine keeping down a meal of raw oysters and cold honeydews even on the best of days, you could certainly understand how the delicate colors of these two foods could have a calming effect on GertrudeStein.

"Before she lectures," I say, trying to imagine GertrudeStein standing before an audience of people so formidable that they could cause my Madame's confidence to waver.

"That's why the Steins are returning to America in October."

"How do you know?" I ask.

"I read it in the newspapers."

My face expresses shock that the newspapers would know about my Madame's prelecture menu, and you smile.

"Oh, *that*. Don't worry, only you and I know about the oysters and honeydews," you assure me.

"Shh, Messieurs, please remain still and look straight ahead," the photographer Lené instructs.

We both take in a long deep breath and wait motionless for the flash of white light. In the middle of the ocean in the middle of the night, the stars, believe me, are never that bright.

"Come back next Sunday, Messieurs. I will be here, and so will your photograph," the photographer Lené says, as he hands you the receipt.

318

You fold the blue slip of paper in half and place it inside the pocket of your coat.

"Only seven days," I say to myself.

When we return to the rue de l'Odéon, the scent of narcissus, the sunlight undressing at the garret windows, the belly of the Buddha stove growing full and warm, all assure me that this was a gamble worth taking. A week's worth of anxiety for a week's worth of anticipation, a fair enough trade, I think. Anything for my scholar-prince, I think. Really, how can I not imagine you in that role? Your interest in my Madame's books is far from casual. Your desire to examine the writings in her notebooks is certainly academic in purpose. Your ability to gather facts about her and Miss Toklas has lately equaled even my own.

Powdered sugar, cracker crumbs, salt. A short walk out onto these city streets today, and I will be covered with them. I am no poet, so forgive my lack of appreciation, my nonaffection for the snow. Back at the Governor-General's, the chauffeur told us that it was like the softest down of the whitest dove, that it nestled like blossoms in the hats of all the pretty French girls. He told us that when snow touched his face it felt like a kiss. I know now that *that* was just memory talking, blatantly making things up because the chauffeur, like all of us, so wanted to believe. When the Saigon sun cracked our lips, splitting them open like some soft fruit, the promise of a kiss, even one so far

319

away, could get us through the endless procession of days. I, in truth, have always preferred the rain. It has little to do with my vocation. Cooks, unlike poets, are unmoved by the weather. From the very beginning, the best ones, according to Minh the Sous Chef, know how to use the extreme heat, the bitter cold, to their advantage. They take the sun and turn the flesh of fruits or animals into a mouth-savoring chew. They never forget, even as the skin underneath their fingernails turns blue, that the appearance of ice means the advent of meat without maggots or a crust of salt. As for the rain, it means that yeast may be slow to rise and that eggs may rot within days. My affinity for the rain really has little to do with its culinary consequences. I, like all my brothers, was conceived in a downpour. What else was there to do during the rainy season? Hell, I suspect everyone in Saigon was conceived amidst the sound of water, carousing on the rooftops, slinking down the drainpipes. In this city, well, anyone conceived in Paris today would be treated to the sound of automobile horns and church bells because a snowfall contributes nothing to the city's constant chatter. A snowfall in February, silent—sullen would not be overstating it—is for me the most unforgiving. There is no pretense of grace, no lofty swirling, no laceworked confetti. The sky just opens up and pours down powdered sugar, cracker crumbs, salt. These are my exact thoughts. Nothing poetic, nothing profound, nothing more worldly than the miserable weather and how I would have to be out in it before the markets closed for the day. Breakfast has been served. Basket and Pépé have been stuffed with livers. Lunch for their Mesdames is still hours away. GertrudeStein and Miss Toklas are staying in for the day because of the weather and because photographers are expected later for tea. The rhythm of a Monday at the rue de Fleurus punctuated by a gripe about the snow, a refrain about tropical rain. Fate, though, is listening in. Worse, it mistakes a melancholic aside for a bout of nostalgia. The latter honors the past. I am merely regretting it.

"Thin Bin, *this* is for you."

I turn my head from the ice-flocked window, and my heart stands still. So soon? I think. It has only been a day, Mesdames. Only one day.

Miss Toklas is standing just inside of the kitchen doorway, and next to her is GertrudeStein. GertrudeStein has one hand in the pocket of her skirt, and the other is pointing to a small silver tray in Miss Toklas's hands. "Thin Bin, *this* is for you," GertrudeStein repeats.

A one-way fare for the *métro?* Severance pay minus the cost of one notebook, used? A letter of recommendation for my next Monsieur and Madame: "Marvelous cook but clumsy when inebriated and has on occasion been known to pilfer. Yours truly, The Steins." No matter, whatever my Mesdames have for me on that tray, I can at least assume it is not a *canapé*. In all the years that I have been with them, I have never seen them together in quite this way. First of all, GertrudeStein rarely accompanies Miss Toklas into the kitchen. They have a division of labor, and GertrudeStein's half has nothing to do with this room. Second, Miss Toklas always does the talking when it comes to matters of domestic affairs. GertrudeStein does not even know how much I get paid. As for the silver tray, I can only assume that these two are a bit more formal about their dismissal practices than other Messieurs and Mesdames. The timing, after breakfast and before lunch, is classic. More cooks are discharged during these few fateful hours than any other. Most Messieurs and Mesdames require coffee and something sweet from me before they will let me go. Monday is also the preferred day of the week for such tasks. It leaves Monsieur and Madame with enough time to find a replacement. That is why most dinner parties are scheduled from Thursdays through Saturdays. The beginning of the week is set aside for the general flux of firings and hirings. And, of course, there is the snow. Inclement weather always seems to encourage Monsieur and Madame to show me the door and lock it. But for once, I have no intention of hastening the process, so I glumly stand my ground. Mesdames, you already have it on a silver tray. You might as well take those extra steps and serve it to me.

"Thief," I hear the Old Man hissing in my ear. Shut up. It was mine to give.

"Liar."

We have something in common, after all, Old Man.

GertrudeStein takes the tray out of Miss Toklas's hands and walks it over and places it into mine. I am, by now, sitting on their kitchen floor. My life is moving too quickly, and as always I believe that being closer to the ground will slow it down. My Mesdames have grown used to my occasional slipping away. At first they chalked it up to the gulf in languages, then to the stupor brought on by drink. Lately, they have attributed it to a degenerative hearing loss on my part, which would explain their raised tone of voice and their repetition of even the simplest of commands.

"No, no, his hearing is fine. He's not deaf, just dumb," the Old Man screams in my ear.

Thanks for the clarification, Old Man, but I am afraid my Madame and Madame cannot hear you. I am the only one present who suffers in this way.

"Thin Bin, we assume *this* is you?" GertrudeStein asks for the third time.

I look down at the envelope and nod out the rhythm of a universal "yes." GertrudeStein, I know my name looks very different there from how it sounds. Tonal languages often do. Imagine capturing the lilt of my mother's voice, the grace note of her sighs, with the letters of your alphabet. Do not bother, GertrudeStein, a French Jesuit already did it many centuries ago. He is responsible for the discrepancy that lies before us now. Though I can assure you that *that* is the name that my mother gave to me on the day of my birth. And that in the corner, that is the name of my oldest brother, the sous chef in the Governor-General's house in Saigon.

At the sight of Anh Minh's angular hand, I shiver with the cold that lives in the center of all of our bones, that is registered by the brain as the sensation of being very much alone. I have not thought about him for months, not since my Mesdames came home with chestnuts stuffed in their coat pockets and heaped onto the back seat of their automobile. Anh Minh believes that chestnuts are the dainty crumbs from the mouth of God. A French god, of course. Or maybe just a god with a French chef. Either way, no one would have enjoyed that bounty more than he, I thought. Anh Minh is the only one. I did not have to see his name on the envelope to know. No one else on that or any other side of the globe would have written to me but he. I had sent him a letter years ago, almost five to be exact. It was full of rambling observations, biased accountings, and drunken confessions written in the cigarette haze of a crowded café. I would have preferred someplace more quiet, but the bodies all around me kept that establishment heated and warm. Outside, the city that night was celebrating the birth of the son of their god. Inside, the celebration was, as the Old Man would say, godless.

Blame it on the chauffeur, Old Man. He was

324

the one who first told me about these places. The chauffeur's cautionary tales, a travelogue of all the establishments that he claims never to have visited, have been for me a necessary road map to this city. When there is change in my pocket, as there was on that Christmas Eve, I would buy a glass of something strong and sip it slowly. When there is nothing in my pockets but my hands, I would wait by the door for someone lonelier than I to walk by. That night I wrote to Anh Minh that I was sitting at a marble-topped table in a small but elegant *salon de thé*. I lied because I did not want him to throw my first letter home away. When months passed without a response, then years, I had to remind myself that Anh Minh is a man of few words. He would never waste them on things that have remained exactly the same. Why would he write? I said to myself, when nothing, absolutely nothing back home would ever change. He is Minh Still the Sous Chef. Anh Hoàng toils in second-class even now. Anh Tùng every day swallows the taste of printer's ink. The Old Man, well, he prefers communion wine with a chaser of rum.

"It is time for you to come home to Việt-Nam," Anh Minh writes. "No matter what he may have said to you, he is our father, and he is going to die."

My brother goes on to say that the Old Man has had a stroke, that he has lost all movement on his right side and is now confined to his bed. So it is true, I think, the Old Man's god can strike a man down. But from the sound of it, his god has yet to slay him. Yes, I am afraid, the Old Man is still very much alive. Forgive me if it has been easier for me to think of him as deceased. Since my first night on the *Niobe*, I can sleep only after I have eased his coffin into the sucking clay, after I have pushed Father Vincente aside to deliver my own version of the last rites. Otherwise, how could I leave her behind? Imagine brushing my lips along my mother's cheeks. Imagine her telling me to go if I must but for her sake "Don't look back." Then imagine him still breathing in the very next room. Forgive me if I am unable.

"He is our father," I read Anh Minh's words over again. Liar, I think. Whose version of this story should I believe? That my dear mother had a lover, who was her scholar-prince if only for a short while, who gave her shadow-graced embraces, who left her with me, her last son. Or that the Old Man is my father and that in spite of that fact he stood in front of his house, one that I will never again see, and he lied to me so that he could see me dead inside. As they say, Old Man, blood is thicker than water. But in our case, you have mired the seas with so much refuse and malice that no ship, Old Man, can navigate those waters and bring me back to you again. When your day comes and goes, believe me, I will not be wearing white.

The Old Man is breathing in air. He is breathing in dirt. It does not matter much to me anymore. My mother has finally had the courage to leave him. I did not have to read it in the body of my brother's letter to know. I have known for many days now. Anh Minh's letter only confirmed the reason for my mother's nightly visits. We said our good-byes in the Jardin du Luxembourg. The city, as it did today, had covered itself in a mantle of white. She was dressed in her gray *áo dài*, and I was bundled into two of my sweaters and my only winter coat. We sat on a park bench and chatted about nothing in particular, like two people who have spent their entire lives together. The snow around us was just beginning to melt, and she shivered with cold. I sat with her until the rising sun took her away. The visits continued until one day I saw her, but I was wide awake. In the hopes of easing my sorrow, she had taken the form of a pigeon, a city-worn bird who was passing away. Death, believe me, never comes to us first in words.

"God has given Má wings," Anh Minh writes. Succinct as always, I think. What he means is that our mother was no longer afraid. After years of saying her rosary, she went to sleep one moonless night and saw heaven vivid on the horizon. She stepped out from under the eaves of his house with a resolve that is the truest gift of faith. Her husband, a false prophet, could never follow her to where she was going. Her four sons, well, that is up to them. With that her final thought, her body became one with the earth, and her soul rose to heaven. A flourish of white.

"Amen," writes Anh Minh.

"Amen," I read aloud.

Startled by the sound of my own voice, I look up from my brother's letter. The kitchen is empty. My Mesdames must have left it long ago. I hear voices coming from the studio. In here, there is no one but the stove and the copper pans.

CHAPTER 22

As usual, I have to let myself in. What he does with his Saturday nights, he will never tell me. He is clean, freshly shaven, and has on a pressed shirt by the time he comes back to his garret on Sundays, so I do not ask. What does it matter, I tell myself, when he is here with me now. There is then the simple exchange of greetings, the swapping of our given names, what we have waited all week to say, the ways that our bodies make up for the lost time. Sweet Sunday, for me, then officially begins. My hands this morning are shaking, and the damn keys are sticking to their locks. I have not slept all week. Anxiety and anticipation have been playing their loud music all through the nights, and my heart has been keeping time to their jazz beats. Either that, or my Mesdames' next-door neighbors have purchased a phonograph and are choosing to believe that din and ruckus, like Basket and Pépé, do not travel. It is difficult for me to say for sure. About the source of the disturbance, of course, not the status of the dogs.

Basket and Pépé, believe me, are not going

anywhere soon. My Madame and Madame are attempting to lessen their guilt about it by acquiring for His Highness and the Pretender to his throne the accoutrements of travel. They bought them leather collars, two apiece, punched through with shiny metal studs, and, for Basket, a fitted coat. No trousers. Basket is a dog, after all. Dogs, even the overly pampered variety, do not seem to require coverage of their hindquarters. As for Pépé, he looks better unclothed, and my Mesdames and he know it. Luckily my Madame and Madame have been much too preoccupied with such preparations to notice my hands, trembling. They think I have been spilling their tea, breaking their china, cutting myself on the flowery shards because I am unused to and, therefore, unhinged by the persistent ringing of their telephone. We at 27 rue de Fleurus finally have a telephone of our very own. GertrudeStein never answers it. Miss Toklas is the house operator. At first she followed the French convention of responding to the rings with an *"Allô!"* shouted into the mouthpiece. Now she just picks it up and breathes. She waits for the voice on the other end to stumble forth a salutation and an identification. If she does not like what she hears, she hangs up. No explanations, no feigned excuses, nothing of the kind. She does the same thing with her eyes when she greets people face to face, so why would she behave any differently over the telephone line? GertrudeStein laughs out loud when she hears the dull thud of the mouthpiece hitting its cradle. She and I both know that Miss Toklas signals her distaste for the caller by how loudly she lets it drop. Such a useful machine, Miss Toklas thinks.

My Mesdames have been in a playful mood as of late. They are giddy. They have been telephoned. They have been telegrammed. Best of all, they have been photographed. GertrudeStein has not sat down to her writing table for weeks, and Miss Toklas has not once opened the cupboard to make use of the typewriting machine. I have been apprehensive all the same. Because photographers are even more curious than servants. The only difference is that photographers practice their invasive art while my Madame and Madame are still in the room. Midway through their visits, I often hear GertrudeStein sending Miss Toklas off to fetch some small souvenir of their years together in what, I imagine, must be an ongoing effort to sate the assembled crew. Miss Toklas is prouder than anyone of her life with GertrudeStein, but if it is a memento that she does not display in the studio, there is always a compelling reason why. Take "La Argentina," for instance. This past Monday, GertrudeStein sent Miss Toklas to retrieve her for the benefit of two Spanish photographers who had braved the snow to have tea with my Mesdames. La Argentina is a flamenco dancer, whose spinning skirts, red-tipped and full, wake my Mesdames up each morning and each night from where she dances high above their bed.

Despite her name, my Mesdames acquired her in Madrid. The label on the back of the poster says so. The front of the poster, well, the front of the poster is a fine example of how some women can look pornographic even when they are fully clothed. If I look at La Argentina for long enough, I can almost smell her. It is no coincidence that I can see up her skirts while lying on my Mesdames' bed. This last statement is, of course, only conjecture as I would never presume to test that angle for myself.

Miss Toklas is a Madame with refined taste. She has *bon goût*, as the French would say. The lining of her purse is in the same color family as the lining of her coat. Matching would be overdoing it. The fragrance that she wears on the nape of her neck compliments the fragrances rising from her dinner table. Competition would be a waste, Miss Toklas thinks. GertrudeStein is a Madame with appetite, unmediated animal appetite. That means that in addition to La Argentina, GertrudeStein has cabinets full of figurines of her favorite Catholic saints made from seashells and chicken feathers, the handiwork of an order of devout but, I can only assume, profoundly blind nuns. She has shelves full of miniature fountains with pastel doves perched upon their ruffled rims, which I have seen peddled at tourist stands throughout this city. She has walls covered with paintings of women with green faces, broken noses, misshapen eyes, who often are also nude but who, unlike the flamenco dancer, would look much better clothed.

Twenty-seven rue de Fleurus is filled with this and more, and it is Miss Toklas who has to winnow through it all. The paintings I have seen her move but never remove from the walls of the studio. Miss Toklas has an ostrich feather duster that she uses to sweep their nubby surfaces clean. Religiously is an apt way to describe the intensity and frequency with which she accomplishes this task. As for the molting saints and the souvenir fountains, Miss Toklas has found for them sconces along dark hallways, alcoves inside of closets, and other similarly intimate spaces within 27 rue de Fleurus. GertrudeStein never seems to notice the change in their locales. GertrudeStein, of course, never has to get up from her chintz-covered armchair to get any of these things for herself. Miss Toklas prefers to keep her that way.

Miss Toklas often will return to the studio with something entirely different from what she had been sent for, or, as in the case of La Argentina, she will return with nothing at all. Miss Toklas shrugs her shoulders and waves her empty hands, and soon the photographers depart, disappointed but apparently undeterred, as more of their profession continue to arrive at the rue de Fleurus. Without Miss Toklas around, I know that I would have much more to worry about. Left on her own, GertrudeStein would trot the photographers all through the apartment. Hell, GertrudeStein would drink tea with them while reclining on her bed, covers undone, sheets untucked, pillows unfluffed.

Left on her own, I am afraid that GertrudeStein would have that cupboard wide open as well, distributing Miss Toklas's typewritten copies and her own notebook originals to all those who cared to see. And these photographers, believe me, are far too inclined to see. That is precisely why Miss Toklas is always around, for it is she who reminds GertrudeStein never to give it away for free. I can always tell when other writers have come to tea. They always leave a stack of papers behind, gratis. Miss Toklas is the first to read through them, and often she is the only one. GertrudeStein is a writer, not a reader, Miss Toklas thinks as she aims for the wastebasket. She never misses. Writers, I suspect, are in this way like cooks. We practice a craft whose value increases tenfold once its yield is shared and consumed. A notebook inside a cupboard is a cake languishing inside an oven long grown cold, unappreciated and in danger of being forgotten. If one looks at it that way, I have done nothing that GertrudeStein has not desired to do for herself. I have generously increased her readership by one.

The garret door swings open with a slight nudge of my shoulder. It has lost its usual creak. Sweet Sunday Man must have had it oiled during the week or, maybe, it is just the change in the weather. Wood does have a tendency to expand and contract like a lung out of air when the temperature outside plunges and then soars. Never mind the door. I know by the smells. Fresh paint and fresh air can mean only one thing. Sweet Sunday Man once told me that of the five senses, the one that he most distrusts is our ability to see. It is the one most easily fooled. More often than not, he claimed, it is the heart that tells us what is and is not there.

I see a Buddha belly stove. I see a desk facing the sunlit windows. I see shelves lining the walls. I see a rug by the foot of the bed. I see a piece of paper folded in half, lying tented on the floor. I have a hair from his brush. I have a handkerchief from his coat pocket. I have the worn laces from his shoes. I have every note that he has left me. I have saved them all. Their subjects are usually about time. His anticipated lateness, his eventual return, represented by a number floating lonely on the page. Sometimes the notes contain a short list of ingredients that do not exist. Ripe figs when there is frost on the ground, lamb when all the trees have already lost their leaves, artichokes when the summer sun is fast asleep, these are the foods that he has wanted to see on his plate. But week after week, I have had to tell him, "Wait." The ground underneath us is frozen. It has been that way from the very beginning. December, January, and February are months, though, that reward a resourceful cook. So, for him, I have simmered strings of dried figs in bergamot tea. I have braised mutton with bouquets of herbs tied in ribbons of lemon rinds until their middle-aged sinews remember spring. As for the artichokes, I have discarded all the glass jars of graying hearts afloat in their vinegared baths that I found hiding inside his kitchen cabinets. Sometimes, Sweet Sunday Man, it is better to crave.

I kneel down to see what he hungers for today. A gust of air enters through the wide-open windows and sends the note tumbling across the floor. It lands on one of its sloped sides, near the bolted-down feet of the Buddha belly stove. The little tent, I see, has a blue inside. Like the cloudless sky outside, I think. All of Paris has been out under it. The change came so swiftly that it is not accurate to say that Tuesday's sun melted Monday's snow. It evaporated it, and the inhabitants of this city rejoiced. My Mesdames were no different. They canceled all their appointments. Miss Toklas telephoned the photographers one by one and told them to come back next week. So except for the two Spanish photographers who came on Monday for tea, the rest were all turned away. Miss Toklas and GertrudeStein then went and sunned themselves at all of their favorite outdoor cafés, which had been hastily reconfigured for the happy occasion. The sun, I know, saved me. It emptied 27 rue de Fleurus. Vacant rooms are notably discreet. They keep secrets and forget indiscretions. They echo praise and absorb curses. They are themselves prone to constancy and therefore prefer the company of the familiar. This is all to say that the contents of the rue de Fleurus sat mercifully undisturbed for the majority of the past week. So by yesterday when the last of the young men departed the Saturday tea for a premature spring night, I sighed. A gamble worth taking, I thought, as my eyes rolled back into sleep for the first time in five days. The sixth had just passed without incident and without photographers. Then when this morning arrived bringing with it a lemon tart sun, I sighed again. Threatening weather is the harbinger for most dismissals. A bonny blue day, I thought, rarely produces the same ill effects.

Blue is the color of a pristine sky, the color of a placid, sleeping sea. Blue is the iridescent gleam on the scales of a fish, a color that swims deep and fares best far from shore. Blue is the last bit of beauty that this animal has left to share, before a knife finds its soft underbelly and guts it. And here in this garret of city air and lingering paint fumes, blue is the color of all that remains. Blue, I know even before my fingers can confirm it, is the receipt from Lené Studio. The thin slip of paper is attached to the inside of a note card with a small dot of paste. The adhesive has bled through and left a greasy spot around the word "Lené." Even its elegant script could not save the receipt from looking soiled and sullied. Careless, I think. Sweet Sunday Man could not even wait for the paste to dry. He must have slapped the two pieces of paper together without a moment of hesitation, ran a crease through them both, and left them for me as one inverted V. The ink on the note is probably smeared, I think. For ink to dry, it also takes time.

From the look of this place, Sweet Sunday Man

had none of that to spare. The walls are awash in a fresh coat of paint. The floors are waxed and spotless. The wood-burning stove has been scrubbed a shade closer to clean. The door is fixed and muted. It must have taken the landlord days. Sweet Sunday Man must have had at most two or three to pack up his belongings. He did a meticulous, well-thought-out job until the very end. As he closed the door to the garret, he looked back at the city's chimney pots framed by the open windows, a landscape reserved for the very rich or the very poor, and he remembered me in a flash of white light. He knocked on a neighbor's door and smiled. She would have given him anything, but he asked her only for a pen, a piece of notepaper, and a pot of paste. Sweet Sunday Man wrote: "Bee, thank you for *The Book of Salt*. Stein captured you, perfectly." The note was written in French except for the four English words. The title of my Madame's notebook, I assume. In his haste, he could not even translate it for me. Why bother, he probably thought. In his haste, he also forgot to sign his name. He reached into his coat pocket and found there the receipt from Lené Studio. He pasted and he folded. He left his final note to me on the floor because there is nothing left inside his garret but the Buddha belly stove, which is still radiating heat in spite of the change in the weather.

CHAPTER 23

Bão was wrong. Useful foreign words and phrases have little to do with drink, money, or girls. The more impenetrable the language, the more unpronounceable it is, the easier life becomes for a man like me. Choices lose their numbers. Decisions are freed from consideration. Options become explicit and clear. If I do not see it, I cannot have it. If the man next to me is not drinking it, I am unlikely to order it for myself. A quick nod, a finger raised, an eyebrow arched, says: "I will have what he is having." Then I sit tense until the waiter returns, praying the entire time that the liquid in my neighbor's glass is not twenty-five-year-old Scotch or vintage champagne. I do tend to exaggerate. The kind of establishments that I frequent carry little that is over a year old. Youth in such places is cheap, just like the clientele, mostly boys but sometimes girls as well. One can never really tell until there is a thorough examination of the hands. Feet can be made to appear smaller with pointed-toe shoes. High heels can create the visual impression that there is nothing beneath that skirt but ten diminutive tippytoes. But hands, nails painted or bare, are red, waving flags. Gloves—black is best as pastels and bright colors only accentuate size—are therefore a standard giveaway. In fact, some "girls" wear them just in case the customers are too dumb or too drunk to identify their unique services. As for me, what they see is what they get.

Bão, for one, had no interest in what he saw. On the *Niobe*, he had a collection of already-paid-for memories, which he coaxed forward with hands warm like the South China Sea. While the ship, a hammock strung between two falling stars, swung us to sleep, I often heard him moan.

"Serena the Soloist," Bão whispered, "always had them on."

"Had what on?" I asked, bracing myself for yet another tale about female self-love.

"Gloves."

"Oh."

"Black and elbow-length," he added, "and nothing else."

"Nothing?"

"Nothing."

Bão's quickening breath told me that *that* was what he wanted to believe. Who am I to question this man's recollection? I thought, and then I heard myself doing it anyway. "Listen, I do not know how Serena, umm, managed the top half, but let me show you how the rest is done." I climbed down from my bunk and stood before his. I took his hands, warmer than the South China Sea, and

I showed him how to form a cleft in between my legs that disappeared into my inner thighs. In the dark, I again heard him moan. This time for me, I told myself.

I have learned my lessons well. Believe me, Blériot had many idiosyncrasies, and that was just one of them. "Let's play Monsieur and Madame," Blériot would say before turning off all the lights. What he meant was actually a variation on the theme: Monsieur and Madame's secretary. Blériot liked the additional layer of sin.

"Tell me the word for 'sweet,'" the *chef de cuisine* commanded in French.

"Sweet," the *garde-manger* obliged in Vietnamese.

"Sour?"

"Sour."

"Bitter?"

"Bitter."

Pleasure for Blériot depended on the careful combination of such words. They worked for him during the day. Why should they not during the night?

"Tell me the word for 'salt.'"

The voice demanding in the dark was this time mine. I had played the same game of words with Sweet Sunday—I mean Lattimore. I remembered him smiling. At first I thought he could not understand my laborer's French, but then he bent down and licked the traces of it from the corners of my mouth. He had already taught me the English word for "sweet." "Sour" and "bitter" were soon to come. The word for "salt" I eventually also learned but not from him. In any language, these four words repeated, emphasized with a shake or a nod, are invaluable to me in the kitchen. In the other rooms of the house, they have on occasion allowed me the semblance of poetry, spare not because of a limited vocabulary but because of the weight of the carefully chosen words. Unlike Blériot, I do not forget these words at the night's end only to demand them repeated again at the most inopportune times, when words of all things are unnecessary. Yes, Blériot had many idiosyncrasies, and *that* was just another one of them.

At moments like those, Bão preferred silence, at least on my part. He is a man, after all. He always enjoyed the sound of his own voice. The night before the *Niobe* docked in Marseilles, neither one of us, though, said a word. The lights of the nearby harbor traced the horizon with a thread of gold. Seagulls, the indigenous birds of busy ports, circled the ship swooping down onto our trash-strewn wake. Voices, caught in the curling waves, came out to greet us, a shipful of men almost safe from the grasping arms of the sea. The next morning, I, of all men, longed for water. I was not the only one. Within hours of docking in Marseilles, Bão had signed up with an ocean liner bound for America. He waved to me from a deck that he would personally swab clean. In his shirt pocket that morning was a slip of paper with the name of Minh the Sous Chef written on it for when Bão was next back in Saigon, and at the bottom of his bag, wrapped inside two of his shirts, underneath a pair of shoes, was my mother's red pouch. I gave him my brother's name. The other he took. Worse, if he had only asked, I would have given this man of my own free will my mother's gold, my father's skin, my brother's hands, and all the bones that float loose in this body of mine now that he has gone.

Má, please do not cry. I know I could have bought bread with it, a room for the night. I could have bought acts of love with it, but I could have never bought back the years of your life. Sorrow, even when tempered by sweat and toil into a whisper weight of gold, is still sorrow. Worthless to us both in the end, Má. Better that a stranger circles the globe with it than your youngest son.

An unsatisfying and unbearable ending, I know. That is why the saga of the red pouch, for me, never ends there on the docks of Marseilles:

Bão, the sailor whose name means "storm," traveled the seven seas in seven months, returning eventually to the familiar embrace of the Mekong. Still in his possession was my oldest brother's name and my mother's heart sealed inside an allegory of red and gold. Upon his arrival on land, Bão asked for directions to the Governor-General's house, and at its back gate he asked for Minh the Sous Chef. "Whew!" Bão whistled, when he saw the long white apron and the starched toque perched upon my brother's head. Half the height of the one worn by Chef Blériot, it had been presented to my brother along with a slew of new protocols, all for improving the hygienic standards within the Governor-General's kitchen. But everyone in the household staff knew that the white hat, the "poison mushroom" as they called it behind my brother's back, was in fact the only visible manifestation of Chef Blériot's guilt.

"This is for your mother," Bão said, placing the red pouch in Minh Still the Sous Chef's hands. "Bính wanted her to have it back."

"Who?"

"Bính. Your youngest brother—"

"That's not my youngest brother's name," Anh Minh replied.

"Oh," Bão said, opening his mouth in a long silent laugh, relieved in the end to hear that the kitchen boy was not the only fool on board the *Niobe*. "Doesn't matter," the sailor said to no one in particular, and he turned and walked back toward the sea.

I never meant to deceive, but real names are never exchanged. Or did my story about the man on the bridge not make that code of conduct already clear? I saw him again the other day. He looked younger than when we first met. The same lips, though fuller than I had remembered. The same eyes, alive and inquisitive. Eloquent even, if I am to believe that the eyes can tell the entire story

344

of a man. The same shock of hair parted on the left but a bit longer, more like that of a poet in a Left Bank café than a scholar-prince in a teak pavilion. I have looked for him on the avenues, on the quays, on the park benches of this city. I have even gone back to the restaurant on the rue Descartes and stood across from its red-lanterned entrance, but two months ago I went there and found the lantern gone. The chef, I imagined, had gone back to Vietnam to see his mother, or maybe he experienced a second bout of wanderlust and was again roaming the world. I have heard that at a certain age men either renew a longing for the bosom of the woman who nursed them or those of distant mountains. I have also gone back to the bridge where we met, hands on the railing, face turned to the river. There have been times when I have stood there until my legs felt as if they too were remembering the persistent motion of water. Usually that meant that it was very late, and I had had too much to drink.

The last place I expected to find the man on the bridge was at Lené Studio. Of course, I went back there, the same Sunday that I received Lattimore's note in fact. I wanted my photograph. I had earned it fair and square, as he would say. I could always cut it in half, I thought, and hide his face away for when a knife blade is no longer sharp enough and his smile will have to do. Also, I thought the photograph was already paid for. I was wrong. Lattimore had been required to leave only half of the cost as a deposit. Unfortunately, this simple matter of a deposit and partial payment took almost half an hour to extract from the clerk, who kept running back and forth between the front office and the back room, where the photographer Lené was presumably in the middle of a session. It did not help matters that the pointy-nosed clerk had little patience for my accent. The French prick kept looking at my receipt and asking, "But, where is Monsieur Lattimore?" Instead of telling the clerk that "Monsieur Lattimore is in the goddamn photograph!" I dropped into my most servile French and begged Monsieur Prick to ask Monsieur Photographer whether I might pick up the photograph now and continue to make the other half of the payment in weekly installments. It was understood, at least on my part, that the weeks were not necessarily going to be consecutive. To my surprise, Monsieur Prick agreed to broach the matter with his employer and disappeared into the back room, where I assumed he was having a series of complicated negotiations with the photographer Lené on my behalf, or where he was merely waiting until I gave up and left.

Meanwhile in the front office of Lené Studio, I had calmed down enough to remember that I had not eaten anything since dinner the night before. I sank down onto a fussy little chair that was only meant to be looked at or photographed. Nothing about it gave comfort, not the ornately carved back or the green velvet seat, which felt suspiciously as if it were stuffed with uncooked lentils. After a few uninviting minutes, I decided that it was better to stand on my own two feet. I got up and slowly walked my hunger around the room. The walls of the front office were covered with sample photographs. There was a wide range of sizes represented, beginning with those tiny enough for a locket. The profusion of faces, I thought, gave the empty room the appearance of being crowded. I studied the expressions of the people who stared out at me from their carefully chosen photographic tableaus—the photographer Lené is well known in the city for his ability to provide his sitters with a wide selection of fantasy locales, from the simple Grecian Garden in Springtime to the more exotic Midnight in the Harem of the Last Moor—and I wondered how they came to be placed on these walls. I tried to find the commonality that brought them all here. Uncanny beauty, soulful carriage, fearless engagement with the camera's lens? Or maybe these sitters also could not pay for the other half of their photographs and had to forfeit their faces and their bodies to the front office of the fabricator of their now forsaken dreams. I had had no dealings with the photographer Lené, as Lattimore had done all the talking the last time we were here, so it was difficult for me to say which method of culling his subjects was more true to the photographer's character. As I made my way from photograph to photograph, a journey from one fantasy to another, I began to notice that some of them were not black and white. Some showed subtle washes of color, purples and blues, roses and browns, as if they were taken in the subdued light of dusk or dawn. I scanned the walls, spotting the variations in tone. That was when I saw him. I climbed atop the fussy chair for a better look at the man on the bridge, or rather his youthful face, in a photograph no larger than the size of my open hand.

"Do you know him?"

I turned around to see the very top of the photographer Lené's balding pate addressing me. But before I answered him, I thought it best to have the good graces to climb down from his chair.

Lené repeated his question.

"Yes . . . I mean no. I am not sure." I replied in a fine example of how this language delights in catching me off-guard and ill-prepared.

"That describes him perfectly." Lené laughed. "The best photograph retoucher I have ever had. Better than that idiot whom I've working for me now."

"What is his name?"

"Pierre Bazin."

"No, no, the man in the photograph."

Lené's assured but atonal response told me that I needed to take a different approach. I handed Lattimore's receipt to the photographer. I asked him to please write down the name of the man in the photograph. When Lené gave the blue slip of paper back to me, there was an

348

unmistakably Vietnamese name written on the back of it: "Nguyễn Ái Quốc." Clever, I thought, a bit heavy-handed but clever all the same.

"So what's this I hear about weekly payments, Monsieur?"

I looked up from the receipt and without hesitation replied, "Give me that one." I pointed to the photograph of the man on the bridge.

"Ah, you do know him then," Lené said. "Let me tell you, no one can paint eyelashes like that one. No one. More delicate than the real thing. Remarkable, remarkable."

"Please, I will pay for the other half of this," I said, again handing him Lattimore's receipt, "but you can keep the photograph for . . . for your walls. I will take that one instead." I pointed to the photograph of the man on the bridge.

"I can't, Monsieur. That print is dear to me. It is, you see, an old method from the last century. I charge four times the usual price for a salt print like that one, Monsieur. It takes a full day of sunlight to develop. A full day of sunlight in Paris! Monsieur, can you imagine?"

No, I shook my head.

"You can come and visit him," Lené raised his chin toward the man on the bridge, "anytime."

Yes, I nodded. There was nothing left to say. With me the subject of money always ends the conversation. Lené stood there staring at me as if he knew.

"Here, take this," I heard him saying.

The photographer Lené was by then standing behind the desk where Monsieur Prick had sat and ignored me until I shoved a scrap of blue underneath his face. I looked down at the envelope that the photographer offered in his hand, and again I said, "For your walls." Nobility, pride, a heretofore dormant sense of self-worth had nothing to do with it. I saw the price written on the corner of the envelope, and even though Lattimore had paid for half of it I knew that I would need many weeks, consecutive or not, before I could pay the rest. I would rather save my money, the sweat of my labor, for the man on the bridge awash in storm water blue, I thought. It was the color of the sea that first caught my eye, that made my body draw near but that, believe me, was just the beginning. The photograph was printed on paper that had the appearance of something that breathed, with a porous surface that opened with each intake of air, into which the features of the man on the bridge seeped. Less of a photograph, more of a tattoo underneath the skin.

Clever, I again thought. "Nguyễn Ái Quốc" was obviously not the name with which the man on the bridge was brought into this world. I and almost everyone else in Vietnam have the surname "Nguyễn." So it was certainly possible that it may be his as well. The giveaway, however, was the combination "Ái Quốc." By itself, the words mean "love" and "country" in that order, but when conjoined they mean "patriot." Certainly a fine name for a traveler to adopt, I thought, a traveler whose heart has wisely never left home.

When Bão first introduced himself with a hand thrust in front of my face, followed by the grunt of his unseaworthy given name, I was speechless. I, who had never even crossed a river, a creek, a rain-swollen street, was standing barely upright in the middle of an ocean and sharing a berth with a man with whom I had nothing in common except a highly inauspicious, fate-defying given name. Two "storms" aboard one ship, I thought, was certainly a sign from somebody's god, a sign to jump overboard and swim back to shore. My inability to tread water, however, had made that course of action impossible from the very beginning. By the time my close-lipped but physically expressive bunkmate bothered to ask me what I was called, I had had a lot of time to consider the matter. In the course of which I experienced what I thought was crippling seasickness, but later when I suffered the same symptoms on land—the spirals inside my eyelids, the taste of my own liver inside my mouth, the sensation of my stomach dropping into a bottomless sea—I understood that water travel was not at fault. Regret was. Not over Blériot. His betrayal, though that would imply a bond of trust, was only a matter of time. I was hoping for several decades during which Blériot would grow old and I would grow strong. No, what happened between myself and this man, who insisted that I call him "Chef" or, worse, "Monsieur," even when our clothes were on the floor, was unfortunate but hardly worth the physical distress that accompanies regret.

I stand there still.

Will you wake up tomorrow, Old Man, and look at yourself in the mirror and declare to your right foot, "No, *you* do not belong to me"? The day after that, will you deliver the same judgement to your two hands? Will the ritual continue with your vicious mouth doing the bidding of your vicious heart until you, Old Man, are nothing more than a torso and a head? Then Father Vincente, I imagine, will devote the rest of his natural life, tirelessly campaigning for your beatification. A martyr able to self-inflict such wounds is a sure-fire candidate for sainthood, Father Vincente will think, as he envisions himself kneeling with your remains before the Holy See.

I stand there still.

In my then twenty years of life, I had been exceedingly careful about all matters of faith. I had been meticulous, vigilant, clear-eyed, even cold-hearted. The Catholic Church had, for me, never been a threat. From the time that I was old enough to walk, I followed my brothers to Father Vincente's church and into the second-to-last pew. When the Old Man led his new converts to morning Mass, their mumbled prayers perfumed the streets with so much alcohol that the children and stray dogs who followed them along the way often fell down drunk, pissing all over themselves.

My forced participation in these processions left me in all respects profoundly unmoved. I was not one to lay offerings before the ancestral altar, either. I would never feed the souls of a man and a woman who were so eager for the afterlife that they had left their only daughter behind to him. Even Anh Minh's beliefs in Monsieur and Madame had no effect on me. I am afraid that the only way that my dear brother's prayers will be answered is for him to lay down one night and die. Then, he must hope that when the next morning arrives, his bruised but uncrushed spirit is reborn inside the body of a Frenchman.

I stand there still.

I hear your voice, Old Man, and I know that despite my vigilance, my clear eyes, my cold heart, I have failed. I have guarded myself against all the false idols except you. Faith, after all, is a theory of love and redemption. In my life, there was no vessel more empty of that than you, Old Man.

Má, please do not cry. From the morning of my birth to the night of my death, I will never have to want, to question, to solicit your affection. *That* is the gift that you have given me. But I, like the basket weaver, looked at the abundance around me and believed that there was something more. Fire ants and tiny orange marigolds make me shudder as they spin the globe the other way, bringing me back to the dirt path where I stood looking at your straw hat, hanging in its usual place at the entrance to the kitchen, and I, blind, saw there nothing but a fraying chin strap, moving listlessly in the sun.

"Bình," I replied without blinking an eye. Bão's raised voice told me that he had had to ask his question one too many times. I apologized, blaming my inability to hear him on the waves, foaming their mouths outside.

"Bình, huh? That's good. We cancel each other out," Bão said, punching my arm to let me know that I was forgiven and also to highlight his own effort and rare success at wordplay. What he meant was that since the name "Bình" means "peace," it was a lucky, not to mention an elegant counterbalance to his "storm." Thank you, I thought the same myself.

But when Bão again encouraged me to choose a new name in preparation for the following morning's arrival on shore, I was surprised. I asked him, "But how many days have we been at sea?" His reply was a revelation. When I signed up with the *Niobe*, I needed a ship that was leaving that same day, as I again had no place to sleep for the night. My dismissal from the Governor-General's was abrupt but inevitable. My dismissal from the Old Man's house, that I did not expect. I gave no thought to the *Niobe*'s final port of call and even less consideration to the duration of its run. Though sea travel, I had assumed, was something that generally took many years to complete. The world was enormous before I left my corner of it. But once I did, it grew even more immense. As for that corner, it continued to shrink until it was a speck of dust on a globe. Believe me, I never had a desire to see what was on the other side of the earth. I needed a ship that would go out to sea because there the water is deep, deeper than the hemmed-in rivers that I could easily reach by foot. I wanted the deepest water because I wanted to slip into it and allow the moon's reflection to swallow me whole. "I never meant to go this far," I said to Bão. What I meant was that when I boarded the *Niobe* I had no intention of reaching shore. In the black-and-white photograph that is the world at night, Bão looked over at me as if he knew.

CHAPTER 24

"Oysters, Lovey, there will always be oysters," Miss Toklas insists.

GertrudeStein shoots a rueful look at Miss Toklas by way of expressing her growing apprehension that oysters alone may not be enough.

This exchange, repeated every few minutes or so with Miss Toklas's words getting lost now and then in the whistle of the train, has taken us from Paris right through to Rouen. Miss Toklas began her mollusk mantra right after the last of the photographers were escorted off the already moving train by a conductor who, like the concierge at 27 rue de Fleurus, kept on shaking his head, unable to comprehend the source of the attraction. The looks of dismay from GertrudeStein followed soon after.

"And honeydews," Miss Toklas offers, "they assured us that there will be honeydews."

This addition to my Madame's repertoire confirms, as I suspected, that we have just passed a significant juncture in our journey. If I push down the window and hang my head out, I know that soon I will smell the sea. The church bells in Le

Havre, like those in all port cities, transmit the city's proximity to the water with every swing that they take, wafting its salt breezes, its mineral odors, far beyond the usual boundaries of such things. Miss Toklas must know about this as well because for the first time since our journey began she leans over and cracks open the window closest to her. I take in a long, slow breath. Oysters, I think. Really, what else could I think about with Miss Toklas's incessant intoning? To ride the train with my Mesdames has long been my wish. To share a first-class compartment with them a secret desire. Wishes, as I have always known, can be cruel in the terms and conditions of their fulfillment. Yes, since our journey began I have thought of nothing but oysters. Even before I knew their word for them, I knew that Americans, at least those who were invited to the rue de Fleurus for dinner, were all very partial to oysters. GertrudeStein, however, was an exception. She has rarely exhibited in the years that we have been together a great love or appetite for them, especially in their raw, gelatinous state.

"And honeydews," Miss Toklas again reminds GertrudeStein, "they assured us that there will be honeydews."

Now *that* surprised me even more. Even when we were in Bilignin, where fruits of all sorts grow lush in the gardens of my Mesdames' summer house, I have seen GertrudeStein wave away a vine-ripened Charentais melon, split in half, baring its orange belly and its button full of seeds for all the world and especially for GertrudeStein to see. Miss Toklas, I knew, trembled with a mild form of heartbreak each time. She was the gardener, the only one, who tended to that beauty from the time it blossomed to when it globed in the heat of the summer sun.

As the train pulls us closer and closer toward the sea, I understand more and more about my Mesdames' unusual pairing of oysters and honeydews. I want to tell Lattimore that his color-based explanation is not complete, but as usual my conclusion is too slow in coming. Lattimore had left me and presumably Paris at the end of February. The train that my Mesdames and I are on is smoking its way through a French countryside lit by October's harvest light. There is no doubt in my mind that he is right. Oysters and honeydews are soothing to GertrudeStein. Miss Toklas has been acting on that very assumption from the moment our train left the Gare du Nord, and even now as it is coming to a stop in the Le Havre station. Miss Toklas believes that just hearing the words is enough to sedate her Lovey. As for the effect on her cook, Miss Toklas for once has made me very full. Raw oysters, I think, can slide down my throat, and honeydews, as with very ripe melons of any kind, can become a pool of juices once in the heat of my mouth. It is precisely these fluidlike qualities, I conclude, that recommend these two foods to a nervous GertrudeStein. One thing I know about my Madame is that she is unable to do more than one thing at any one time. That is what Miss Toklas is here for. If GertrudeStein is anxious before she lectures, then she cannot be expected to worry *and* to chew her food at the same time. If Miss Toklas could, she would perform both of these acts for her Lovey. As she cannot, she has devised a menu composed of foods that are solid in form—thereby never acknowledging GertrudeStein's condition or injuring her pride—and yet both courses can be consumed without the pesky need to chew. Miss Toklas is a genius after all.

"Oysters, Lovey, there will always be oysters. And honeydews, they assured us that there will be honeydews," Miss Toklas whispers to GertrudeStein as we step from the train onto the platform at Le Havre.

"Oysters" and "honeydews" are two words in the English language with which I am by now overly familiar. As for the rest of Miss Toklas's words, well, the rest I can imagine. But even if I was not equipped with such skills, my Mesdames' behavior alone is telling. I have, believe me, heard them say things over and over again to each other before. Lovers who have lived a lifetime together have the luxury of never having to say anything new. Also, my Mesdames are both reaching that age in life when repetition is the mind's way of retaining all the tiny details that it would otherwise lose. Miss Toklas's voice, though, is softer than I have ever heard it, and GertrudeStein's expression, made worse by the red spiders in the whites of her eyes, gives her the appearance of a child abandoned on a train.

At first I thought my Mesdames were distraught because they were missing Basket and Pépé. Dressed in their finest, those two were beyond consolation when their leashes were handed over to the concierge. Miss Toklas and GertrudeStein had given the concierge enough money to keep His Highness and the Pretender well stuffed with livers for at least a year. In addition to the wardrobe that they brought with them, there was also an emergency fund for extra leashes and new coats for the winter. As Basket and Pépé both have a tendency to gain excessive weight during the colder months of the year, there was no way for my Mesdames to anticipate their eventual sizes in the months to come. That detail was therefore reluctantly entrusted to the concierge. Basket pressed his body into GertrudeStein's tweed skirt, leaving behind curls from his molting fur. Pépé dug his front paws into the pile of Miss Toklas's new mink coat, his howl so desperate and high that it was beyond the range of the human ear. The other dogs in the neighborhood heard him, though, and a chorus full of pity and how-could-you's began. Pépé always had a flair for drama. Basket's approach was more straightforward. He used his body weight, the only thing that he had available to him besides his delirious barking, to keep his Madame by his side.

"Bye-bye, bye-bye, my babies, bye-bye," said Miss Toklas and GertrudeStein, their voices unified in grief, as our taxi drove away. Miss Toklas dabbed the corners of her eyes. GertrudeStein was able to blink hers away. Why the tears, my Mesdames? Are there no dogs in America? I thought.

First-class accommodations, an express train, and now this floating city passing itself off as an ocean liner all the way home, my Mesdames. And if the photographers here on the deck are any indication, there will be so many flashes going off in America that for you there will never be darkness on the shores of the country where you were born.

Standing on the glass-enclosed deck of the SS *Champlain*, Miss Toklas looks regal as always, lips pursed, moments away from saying "Shoo!" GertrudeStein looks remarkably relaxed. She looks as though she has a present to give, one that she knows will be a delight to receive. Both my Mesdames, but especially GertrudeStein, always perk right up when photographers are around. A new group of them along with the captain of the SS *Champlain* were on deck waiting for us, and this time GertrudeStein and Miss Toklas seem genuinely surprised by the commotion that is intent on following them back to America. I have just returned to the deck after accompanying a line of porters as they carried my Mesdames' many trunks and cases into the sitting room of their

361

suite. I make my way past the photographers and stand next to Miss Toklas. I am thinking about the bouquets of yellow roses waiting for them in their suite and how they are larger than anything that I have ever seen at the flower market on the Île de la Cité. Miss Toklas looks over at me and mouths, "Here, take this." She slips a small sewing kit into the pocket of my coat. My Madame points with her nose to GertrudeStein's brown velvet-trimmed shoes. Lying in between them is a single pearl button leaning on its metal loop, like a toy top at rest. The strap to GertrudeStein's right shoe flaps up and down, elated to be free. The strap flies especially high every time my Madame shifts her weight from foot to foot. GertrudeStein is dancing a jig because her feet are unused to the new leather and to the extra padding of the velvet trim. Miss Toklas slides her hand out of my pocket, and she grabs onto my hand, the one closest to hers. She squeezes it twice in quick succession. "Please, Bin, sew on GertrudeStein's button. We cannot have photographs of her looking so disheveled in this way!" is what Miss Toklas intends the first palpitation to say. The second, which is thankfully not as blood-stopping as the first, is less of a command and more of a plea: "Please, Bin, sew on GertrudeStein's button. I cannot have photographs of *me* prostrated before her in that way."

Of course, Madame, of course.

I pull the sewing kit from my pocket, and I do my part to make sure that GertrudeStein will continue to travel in style. The SS *Champlain* for my Madame and Madame, I know, is just the beginning. When we boarded this ocean liner, I saw no similarities between it and the *Niobe*. Believe me, there is nothing about my Mesdames' suite of rooms or the boulevard-wide decks of the SS *Champlain* that remind me of my previous voyages at sea.

Years ago when the *Niobe* docked in Marseilles, I stayed in that port city for a handful of weeks until I remembered what Bão had told me: It is easier to be broke at sea than on land. I signed up for another freighter of the same class as the *Niobe*, and I went back to living with water beneath my feet. I jumped from freighter to freighter for the next three years. During that time, I slept on land for a total of forty some days, nonconsecutive. Looking back, I cannot say what kept me on water or what kept me from land. I do remember that the moon's reflection was hypnotic when it shimmered on a saltwater canvas and that when I looked down into that circle of light I always believed that on the next ship, at the next port of call, I would find Bão. I found men like him, but I never did see that GoodLookingBrother again. Then one night as I scrubbed the cooking pots with another kitchen boy, who was from the Chinese island of Hainan but who spoke a bit of barter-and-trade Vietnamese, I mentioned that the moon had changed its shape, that it had grown more oval and long, like an unripe mango. Without even looking over at me, the kitchen boy said, "You need to shit on land again." While I had certainly received more elegantly worded pieces of advice, I thought that there must be some truth in what this kitchen boy said. His tone was confident, almost automatic. To this day, I am still impressed by decisiveness in precisely that form. So when our freighter finished its run in Marseilles, I said so long to the Hainanese kitchen boy, who was actually a man of thirty-five and a father of three, and I went to find a job on land. Besides Marseilles and Avignon, Paris was the only other French city that I had ever thought about. Through various means that even I do not want to remember, I found my way to the city that the Governor-General's chauffeur had made vivid with his stories, his cigarette waving about in the excitement of the retelling, its smoldering tip standing in for the streetlights along the Champs-Élysées, for the great rose window of Notre-Dame, for the beacon atop the Tour Eiffel. When I arrived in Paris, I was twenty-three years old, and cooking was still my only legitimate skill. I began searching for a position as a live-in cook because I knew that it would provide me with the two things that I needed whether on land or on water: a job and a place to sleep for the night. But as with the freighters before them, I am afraid that I was not able to stay at any of these berths for any real length of time. Messieurs and Mesdames were universally difficult but each in their own inscrutable way. Lessons learned in one home were useless in another. I gained experience all right, but never, never the right kind.

After a year of disastrous placements, one after another, I was contemplating water again. Every day and every night, I stood silent on a bridge as Paris hummed. I looked down and saw how the reflection of the moon was smaller in the Seine than it had been out at sea but how it was still generous enough. I measured the distance down to the water, felt my body numbed by the cold, thought about how all the rivers of the world desire to flow to the seas. I gripped the railing. Its iron cooled my fingers, each cut by a flameless fire. Blue sparks and silver threads clung to their tips, marring their surface, forcing them not to heal. I kept my gloves on when I interviewed with a new Madame or Monsieur. That was all right for now as it was still cold outside, but what was I going to do with my gloved hands when the temperature began to rise? Eyebrows and suspicions would certainly be raised, I thought. Then one day before the season had had a chance to change, I stood on that bridge, and I met a man. I do not mean to mislead. Not all of my friendships were so easily formed. A fellow countryman, though, a fellow countryman in Paris was not particularly rare then or now, but he was somewhat of a surprise. Think of it as biting into the cheek of a persimmon when the city's markets are offering only pears. In the course of a day, in the course of a meal, in the course of saying our fond farewells, lit from above by the multiple moons of lampposts in a park made private by a mist that had thickened into a fog, I decided to stay. The man on the bridge was leaving that night and I, of all men, decided to stay. I wanted to see him again. But the man on the bridge did not tell me where he was traveling to, and the world was too vast for me to search for him, I thought. The only place we shared was this city. Vietnam, the country that we called home, was to me already a memory. I preferred it that way. A "memory" was for me another way of saying a "story." A "story" was another way of saying a "gift." The man on the bridge was a memory, he was a story, he was a gift. Paris gave him to me. And in Paris I will stay, I decided. Only in this city, I thought, will I see him again. For a traveler, it is sometimes necessary to make the world small on purpose. It is the only way to stop migrating and find a new home. After the man on the bridge departed, Paris held in it a promise. It was a city where something akin to love had happened, and it was a city where it could happen again. Three years later in a park on a bench beneath some chestnut trees, I saw the classified ad that Miss Toklas had placed, which began: "Two American ladies wish . . ."

In the end as in the beginning, there are specific instructions to see the concierge. As the blaring horns of the floating city announce to the inhabitants of Le Havre that a journey is about to begin, Miss Toklas tells me to leave my name and forwarding address with the concierge so that when she and GertrudeStein return to 27 rue de Fleurus to collect Basket and Pépé, they can send for me if the need should arise.

Of course, Madame, of course.

Within minutes, I am back on the docks standing in a crowd of waving well-wishers, bidding "safe journey" to those aboard the SS *Champlain*. For GertrudeStein and Miss Toklas, I expand upon the general sentiment and add the word "home."

Believe me, I was never so naive as Basket and Pépé. I realized early on that I, like those two dogs, was never going to see America. Not with GertrudeStein and Miss Toklas, that is. I held no resentment toward my Mesdames. By the sound of those hotel menus, their culinary needs would be well taken care of in the months to come. So when my Madame and Madame requested that I accompany them to Le Havre, I did not hesitate to say yes. From the number of trunks that were lining up against the walls of the studio, I knew that GertrudeStein and Miss Toklas would require an extra pair of eyes to ensure that the first leg of their journey went smoothly, that nothing of importance would be left behind. In exchange, Miss Toklas asked me whether I wanted a round-trip train ticket back to Paris or the amount in cash so that I could purchase a one-way ticket to some other destination. With this question, I again did not hesitate. "The money, please," I replied. I did not know where I wanted to go after Le Havre. So asking for cash as opposed to a prepaid ticket was my way of making no decision at all.

In the weeks prior to my Mesdames' departure, I must admit that I had slipped out of 27 rue de Fleurus for a number of post-midnight, mid-workweek drinks. When I am in Paris, I suffer from the delusion that drinking will help me think. It does not. I, unfortunately, did not remember this until I was broke. Another summer in Bilignin had built up my tolerance for alcohol, one that my limited budget could not sustain back in Paris, the City of Lights and, I would add, Very Expensive Drinks. This past summer, my Mesdames' sixth and my fifth in Bilignin, the farmers had been more generous than ever. When I got off the train, I was dressed all in white and without the customary hat, and they, in their own way, understood that that meant that I was in mourning. I did not have to tell them in words that my mother had passed away during the first full moon of the year. When it became clear to the farmers of Bilignin, after the first couple of weeks, that my traveling outfit was going to be my attire for the rest of the summer, they wondered aloud whether I was also mourning a lost lover. When I asked them why they would say such a thing, they claimed that they have seen lost love turn a man's hair white so why would it not do the same to his clothes? I did not have to tell them in words that Lattimore had gone, that an unseasonably warm February day had come to

Paris and taken him away, leaving nothing behind in his garret except wide-open windows, still wet walls, and a warm Buddha belly stove that I, in a moment of longing, stooped down and embraced. But, of course, let me not forget the pithy note of thanks. A man of good breeding through and through, Lattimore wanted me to know that he was grateful for all that I had given him in exchange for what turned out to be a half-paid-for photograph of a satisfied customer and me.

You are more than welcome, Lattimore, or shall I call you "Monsieur"? If you care to know, if you are ever denied a minute of sleep when you close your eyes and you see the silver glint of guilt at your throat, please rest assured that my Mesdames have yet to discover their loss. In my long experience with broken dishes, misplaced silverware, and similar unforeseen removal of personal effects, if Monsieur and Madame do not take note of the item's disappearance within the first week, then they are unlikely to ever. Or if they do notice, I am usually no longer in their employ and am no longer the paid recipient of the fine spittle of their rage. Words are words, I tell myself. Handwritten, typewritten, all were written by GertrudeStein, and as you would say, anything written by GertrudeStein is an original. Miss Toklas, I assure myself, must also have her usual three typewritten copies of *The Book of Salt*. I know what those words mean now, Lattimore. I copied them from your thank-you-but-no-thank-you note onto a clean sheet of paper and gave it to the concierge. While the concierge had no sentimental attachments toward my Mesdames, he did have dreams of America and was learning English in preparation for the day when his dreams would come true. Until then, he intended to practice his English with Basket and Pépé. He translated the words into French for me, and then he asked whether it was the title of a cookbook. "No," I answered, "a book about a cook." The concierge seemed impressed anyway.

Salt, I thought. GertrudeStein, what kind? Kitchen, sweat, tears, or the sea. Madame, they are not all the same. Their stings, their smarts, their strengths, the distinctions among them are fine. Do you know, GertrudeStein, which ones I have tasted on my tongue? A story is a gift, Madame, and you are welcome.

GertrudeStein, unflappable, unrepentant, unbowed, stares back at me and smiles. This photograph of her and Miss Toklas, the second of two that I have of that day, was taken on the deck of the SS *Champlain*. It captures my Mesdames perfectly. I am over there, the one with my back turned to the camera. I am not bowing at GertrudeStein's feet. I am sewing the button back onto her right shoe. The button had come loose in the excitement of coming aboard ship. When I saw this one printed in the newspaper alongside the photograph taken at the Gare du Nord, I cut them both out, and I have kept them with me ever since. My Mesdames, I know, have them as well, carefully pressed in their green leather album, bulging by now with family photographs of only the public kind. I am partial to the one of them at the train station. GertrudeStein and Miss Toklas are perched on the bench ahead of me. My Madame and Madame are posing for a small group of photographers who have gathered for the occasion. GertrudeStein looks almost girlish. The folds of a smile are tucked into her ample cheeks. Miss Toklas looks pleased but as always somewhat irritated, an oyster with sand in its lips, a woman whose corset bites into her hips. We are waiting in the Gare du Nord surrounded by the sounds of trains—their arrivals a jubilant clanging, their departures dirgelike, spent sorrows and last-minute sentiments caught underneath their accelerating wheels. My eyes are closed because thinking, for me, is sometimes aided by the dark. I see there the waters off Le Havre. I see there how that body is so receptive to the light of a full October moon. I feel there my body growing limp in that soft light. "What keeps you here?" I hear a voice asking. Your question, just your desire to know my answer, keeps me, is my response. In the dark, I see you smile. I look up instinctually, as if someone has called out my name.